STAY MAD,

Sweetheart

HELEEN KIST

D1434235

RED DOG

CRITICAL ACCLAIM FOR

STAY MAD,
Sweetheart

"With *Stay Mad, Sweetheart*, Heleen Kist takes the psychological thriller out of the domestic setting and into the workplace. With its on-the-money themes of technology, the darker side of the social media and the #MeToo movement, Kist has crafted a **superb and thought-provoking** page-turner."

—Alison Belsham, internationally bestselling author of
The Tattoo Thief and *Her Last Breath*

"This is one book that engaged and enraged me. A **contemporary feminist novel** that packs an **almighty punch**."

—Chapter In My Life crime fiction blog

"This **incredibly important book** will make you think about **everyday sexism**, what consent looks like and cancelling your social media!"

—Madeleine Black, author of *Unbroken*.

Published by RED DOG PRESS 2019

Edited by Sara Cox

ISBN 978-1-913331-19-1

www.reddogpress.co.uk

*to Lyda,
lifelong crusader for the rights
of women and the girl child.*

I am her girl child.

1.
JUST ME, LAURA

A tear fell onto the page of my book in a star-shaped splotch. I wiped it with my thumb. The stationery cupboard's dry, inky air tickled my throat as I sighed.

Those poor people.

The photocopier vibrated against my back, mirroring the movement of the novel's train carriage, its heat evocative of the bodies pressed together, its persistent humming an echo of the stoic prayers uttered by the captives being transported to their final destination.

I hated to leave them, but my time was up. I waved the still damp page side to side and blew the coldest air that I could onto it. The translucent spot rippled the paper. I closed the book and held it to my chest, stroking its edges. It wasn't the first one I'd ruined this way.

I heard giggling. The door clicked open. I froze. Restless rustling of fabric, the smacking wetness of lips, and baritone groans filled the tiny space.

Crap.

'Hurry up,' said a woman.

The man whispered, 'Let me help.'

It may only have been seconds, but the intensifying moans suggested they were being well spent. I shrunk into my slot between the photocopier and the side wall, forced to listen to the unmistakable *swoosh* of skirt-lining against tights, the metal tear of a zipper, and the thud and tinkle of a belt buckle hitting the floor.

The room's flimsy rear partition shook against my shoulder. Through a small gap I saw snippets of skin: her braceleted arms outstretched above their heads, the tips of his fingers digging into her wrist.

I looked away. Beside me, rattled pens rolled towards the edge of a metal shelf. I willed them to stay put.

Her voice again, breathless: 'I have a better idea.' She cooed, 'Help me up.'

I stiffened. Up?

The man grunted. The photocopier creaked and a cascade of red curls fell over the side of the machine onto my head. Definitely Sally. But who was he?

I winced. I preferred not to know. But what if they saw me? They'd think I was some kind of pervert. Steeling myself for intense awkwardness, I cleared my throat. Twice.

'What the...?' said the guy.

The mass of hair bounced out of view.

My knees complained as I rose. 'Sorry. I was reading.'

'Oh my God, Laura, if I'd known...' Sally hopped off the machine, clutching the panels of her blouse. She swooped down to pick up her skirt, not realising that swift move exposed me to a full-frontal of the newest data science recruit, his stunned face up top and trousers bunched around his ankles below.

My blush felt incandescent. I covered my eyes to let the interrupted love birds regain their modesty, the three of us developing an unspoken understanding that *this* never happened.

As the door closed behind them, I caught his worried murmur, 'Do you think she saw it?' and her replying with a chuckle, 'If she did, it will have been her first.'

Though it was true, it was unnecessary. I crouched to retrieve the book from my rudely invaded personal haven. The guy's head popped back in. I jumped, hitting my shoulder against the shelf.

'Forgot to tell you.' He smiled meekly. 'Justin is looking for you.'

THE FILTERED-WATER dispenser in the corridor provided me with much-needed cooling down. The heat receded from my cheeks but immediately fired up again as I saw the clock overhead and stress took hold: I was late.

How did I let time slip away? I grabbed my phone for my regular check-in with Emily, my best friend. The line rang out. I let out a high-pitched whine, torn between wanting to wait to try again and rushing to Justin's supposedly mission critical meeting.

I walked on.

Five colleagues huddled ahead of me, deep in discussion, drawing flow charts with black marker pens on a long length of wall coated with a special, wipeable paint. One of them spotted me approaching; he nudged another. Their semicircle fell silent and broke open, revealing their work. Hopeful faces sought my contribution, my approval. I passed them with a brisk pace and my most courteous smile.

I dialled Emily again as I strode past rows of desks, their occupants tip-tapping away at their keyboards, their screens faded by the rays of a rare Scottish sun. This time, her line was engaged.

Please God, let them not have found her mobile number, too.

In the lobby, the multicoloured logo of Empisoft stretched across the surface behind the reception desk. Underneath, a shelf showcased our many technology awards, oversized engraved dust-gatherers bearing testament to our team's hard work. Next to them, an embarrassingly large photo of Justin and me holding yet another trophy, my thin smile doing its best, my eyes missing the lens by a mile.

Liv stood watering the plant next to the visitors' TV tuned to the non-stop horrors of the outside world. She dried her hands on her cardigan and flashed a motherly smile. 'There you are. A dose of book time again?'

I nodded, ready to speed on, but my eyeline flicked to the sixty-inch screen. Adam Mooney, the Hollywood star, was exiting Edinburgh's Festival Theatre and making his way down its stone steps. Saliva flooded my mouth in revulsion.

A sea of outstretched arms shoved microphones towards his angular jaw as reporters pelted him with questions. *'How do you respond to calls for your arrest for sexual assault?'* I spotted errors in the closed caption transcription. Too many voices. But it perfectly captured his response: *'No Comment.'*

Liv stood at my side. 'That's a real tearjerker, isn't it?'

'What? You feel sorry for him?' I asked.

'No, your book. The concentration camps.'

'Oh.' I looked down at the blue-and-white-striped cover. 'Yes.'

'I do feel a bit sorry for him, though.' Liv gazed back at the screen. 'It's so easy for this kind of thing to destroy a career. I'm not convinced he deserves to suffer like that.'

I spun towards the boardroom. 'I don't think he can suffer enough.'

2.
MY EMILY

The kettle beeped three times, the red numeric display showing the water had reached the programmed temperature of seventy-three degrees. Perfect for herbal tea, according to the manual.

Emily drew a green tea bag from the overhead cupboard of her galley kitchen and plopped it into a brown-rimmed mug. She loved her gadgets, but had she known it was a required safety feature for the voice-controlled kettle to beep when ready, she would have sent the freebie back to her client. It was getting on her nerves. And her nerves were frayed enough.

Swirls of yellow liquid formed underneath the steam in her cup. Unable to find a clean teaspoon in the drawer, Emily fished the tea bag out of her brew with a chopstick pulled from last night's microwaved egg fried rice. She threw the bag into the sink, onto a pile of its discarded kin, white-rimmed squares of thin, drying paper shrunk around increasingly mouldy lumps of leaves.

With the other end of the chopstick, she scratched behind her ear, stirring thick strands of unwashed hair. She returned the stick to the plastic container as though that small semblance of tidying made up for the surrounding week-worth of filth.

Emily shuffled to her armchair. Her fuzzy slippers stirred dust bunnies into the sunshine streaming through the living room's large, Victorian window. She blew on her drink out of habit —

from when kettles just boiled water to a throat-scorching one hundred degrees centigrade. A dribble of drool escaped her mouth.

The remote control for the TV was out of reach, where she'd hurled it last. That was okay. She'd seen enough. Too much.

But perhaps this time...

Her mobile rang, diverting her attention. But it, too, lay far away and her limbs were heavy. By the time she managed to propel herself forward, the ringing had stopped. She shrugged. Laura would retry later. She always did.

Emily took a tentative sip of her drink. The phone rang again. She groaned. The side table was covered with dirty crockery and technology magazines sticky with donutty finger marks, so she put her mug on the floor. It would mark the floorboards with a ring but sod the landlord.

She read the caller ID and her shoulders slumped. She slid the green strip aside.

'Hello, Claire.'

'How are you, Em?' Claire's voice wavered. 'We haven't heard from you at work.'

'I'm ... I don't know.'

'Listen, Darren was having a hissy-fit yesterday, stomping about the place, shouting about deadlines. I'm not sure how much longer I can cover for you... I mean, everybody knows you're not really sick-sick.'

Emily flinched. No, she wasn't sick-sick. But *this* didn't have a name.

'Anyway,' Claire continued. 'I'm calling because of the Empisoft conference. It's only weeks away and I need your help. I'm not up to speed and I've got my hands full with my charity gig's PR and coordination as it is.'

Emily suppressed a sigh. Her mind was a million miles from the office, but this was Laura's company and the most important event of the year for them. 'What do you need?'

'I've sent you a long email with questions. Would you have a look, please?' Claire asked.

Emily scanned the room. Where was her laptop? A black triangle poked out from below a blanket of newspapers and magazines on the dining table. 'Will do.'

'Honestly, Em, we need you back … and we're all worried about you.'

Emily massaged her forehead. 'I guess I could come in tomorrow.'

'That's great. But don't rush-rush. Darren's gym sessions don't start until 8.30 now. I'm glad you're feeling a bit better. See you tomorrow.'

'Uh-huh.'

Emily rifled through her papers on the dining table, shoving aside print-outs of emails and letters from the council. She found her charger cable and the red sock she'd lost the week before. The TV remote by her feet lured her to have one more peek. She knew she shouldn't, but she picked it up and took aim.

It was that dreadful women's talk show. The one where the presenters fanned themselves when the resident Italian chef spoon-fed them *tiramisu*, the one that ensured guests stormed off to keep the viewers coming back.

Why was the dippy blonde on the right pointing and shouting this time? Emily upped the volume. She leaned closer, her body tensed.

'*How can you say non-verbal cues should be enough?*' the blonde demanded. '*What is a non-verbal cue, anyway? A squirm? Does that count? Why not say "no" like a normal person?*'

The one with the over-white teeth replied, '*We're British. We're polite. A firm "no" is too... punitive, like a slap in the face. When all we want to signal is to slow down.*'

'*We can't expect men to read minds, though,*' interjected the third woman, older, her lips puffed out with fillers

Emily stood transfixed. She knew it was wrong for her to be so unreasonably — unnaturally — drawn to the incessant coverage; but she couldn't help it. It was about her. It was *her* harrowing encounter they probed, as selfishly as he'd touched her. They were lifting the lid off *her* life, as insensitively as he'd lifted her dress.

She bit her lip to channel the hurt; she needed to watch. Which way would it swing today? Would they see it her way? Would they see *her*? A person. A real, pulsing, sentient human being. Not some slab of meat offered for dismemberment, for them to pry apart her motives, her honesty, her morals — to judge.

Occasionally, throughout this whole ordeal, she'd catch a glimmer of hope through all the contempt, a sliver of validation. So the fascination persisted. She longed to understand what it was that hurled some to her defence and others to the edge of crazy.

'*Exactly.*' shrieked the first panel member on the TV. '*I'm sorry, but in my day, you knew not to go to someone's flat — or in this case a hotel room, which is even worse — unless you were up for it. This girl throws herself at a famous actor she's only met that night and what? She expects him to read her mind? She can speak. She should've spoken up if she didn't like his kisses or him performing oral sex on her. Quite frankly she should have left the minute she became uncomfortable.*'

'*Don't you think there was a power dynamic at play that made it harder? I mean he's Adam Mooney, for Christ's sake.*'

'*She doesn't work for him—*'

Emily zapped the screen into darkness. Enough. There was nothing new. Nothing that would make the haters hate less. Nothing that would make this '*she*' they spoke of so callously feel uncorrupted again. Emily covered her mouth; felt a tear hit her hand. They knew her name. Why did they never use her name?

Questions she'd asked herself over and over swirled round in her head. Why hadn't she just said 'no' that night? Why had she thought it a good idea to write her story and have it posted online? Why had she believed that blog when they said she'd remain anonymous? What an idiot. What a fool to think she would be a force for good, for girls' empowerment, for healthy debate. It had been the worst decision of her life. And now nothing could turn back the clock.

She rubbed her face to loosen the tension and filled her lungs slowly. Must try to move on. Maybe work would help after all?

The itch behind her ear didn't let up. She scratched it once more and scooped her hair into a messy bun, wincing as the rank-smelling bobble she'd been carrying around her wrist all week passed her nose. Once the bun was secured into place, she knotted the belt of her bathrobe and strode to the table.

The computer broke free from its surrounding papers and magazines with a single yank. She watched the disturbed pile wobble and slip to the ground in a colourful spread. Emily cleared more space on the table, flicking crumbs of who-knows-what into the void with the back of her hand.

There.

She sat down. The laptop whirred into action, the screen's static attracting a plague of dust. She clutched her sleeve and rubbed it away.

A thump by her door.

She listened for more, the back of her neck tingling. She hoped, of the two things it might be, that it was her neighbour coming to check on her again. But no knock came. Her stomach dropped.

Shit.

She shook her head. Ignore it.

The waterfall background on her screen was meant to be a serene, calming image but all Emily sensed when she looked at it was the thunderous pressure of the water on her head, its silvery foam enveloping her, the absence of air — drowning.

With a slight tremble in her finger, she inched the mouse towards her email. At the top of her inbox was Claire's red-flagged message: *Help! Questions for Empisoft conference.*

Emily breathed a wisp of relief when she saw that the fifty-odd other messages were business-related and all from people she knew, including one from HR she'd check out later. She mentally blew a kiss to the IT chap who'd assured her he would filter out all the hate mail, so she wouldn't be confronted with it.

Her brain wouldn't focus. She re-read the same piece of text five times. The planning around the annual conference of the city's most celebrated high-growth start-up was a challenge, sure, but she knew that wasn't the real problem. It was the thought of returning to work, to the stares, the whispers. They'd had to get extra security at the office when she'd been identified as the anonymous woman behind the incendiary blog post; a daily hassle no one appreciated.

For the best part of two hours, she resolved logistical issues with the catering and stupidly constrained parking around the large conference venue. No reason Claire couldn't have handled those herself.

Emily's cramped thighs begged for movement. She got up for another cup of tea, leaving the previous one cold, iridescent plaques lining the surface like an oil slick.

As she passed the front door, she remembered the earlier sound. Despite alarm ringing in her ears, she pulled at the knob.

On the landing lay a medium-sized box, addressed simply to *The Bitch*. Emily peered over into the stairwell of her tenement, knowing it was pointless. Whoever had finagled access to her building would be long gone.

The box didn't weigh much, but its content sounded solid when shifted. She carried it inside, her pulse throbbing in her temples, her teeth clenched.

She walked straight to the kitchen, flipped open the stainless-steel lid of her bin, and shook the 'gift' out of the box. The large purple dildo fell atop layers of gloopy plastic film pried from ready meals. Underneath, she could still see the fat, curved tip of the other veiny, flesh-coloured sex toy.

Emily smacked the metal lid down and crumpled onto the tiled floor. Tears rolled down her cheeks, her body convulsing with each staggered sob.

She couldn't do this anymore.

3.
ME

'Ah, there you are, Laura,' Justin said as soon as I pushed through the unnecessarily heavy floor-to-ceiling door. 'Now we can begin.'

He pressed a button by the light switch. The glass partition that separated the boardroom from the adjacent corridor frosted over for privacy — one of many high-tech features in the room.

The transition seemed to impress the older man in the suit. We didn't get many suits as visitors, and this one looked expensive. Who was he? The young woman sitting opposite smiled at me broadly, although her white-bloused outfit suggested she meant business, too.

A tray with a pot of coffee stood untouched on the sideboard. Justin signalled for me to sit while he stayed standing. 'Laura, this is Angus McLeod, managing partner of Madainn Finance, and his senior associate, Suki... erm, sorry...'

'Ak-sorn-pan,' she offered, enunciating the syllables as if for a child.

'Yes, right.' A barely perceptible frown crossed Justin's brow. I'd known him long enough to recognise his '*I'm insulted*' face. He continued, 'This is the incredible Laura Flett I've told you so much about. Laura, Suki and Angus here are the corporate financiers who've been working with me and the board these past few months on the sale of the business.'

'Ah.' The suits made sense.

'Now we're getting close to a deal with PeopleForce, it's critical to involve you as co-founder and head of Research & Development.' Justin bowed to the guests and sat. 'Over to you.'

Angus smoothed what little grey hair he still had on the side of his skull and cleared his throat. Suki slid grey-covered presentation decks across the table with manicured fingernails.

I peeked inside my copy and found a fat stack of PowerPoint slides, beautifully styled in corporate blues. The thick paper between my fingers screamed money.

Angus spoke first. 'If everything goes according to plan, we're looking at one of the most exciting things to happen to the Scottish technology scene since Skyscanner was acquired by the Chinese.'

I glanced at Suki, wondering if that's where she was from.

Angus prattled on, 'That woke Silicon Valley up to the potential of Scotland — and Edinburgh in particular — as a breeding ground for tomorrow's unicorns.'

That word sent a ripple across the room. Unicorn: a company valued at one billion dollars. Every technology entrepreneur's dream. Justin's dream.

'Of course, Empisoft isn't there yet,' continued Angus. 'However, I'm sure you'll agree the offers we received are worth celebrating, particularly for a start-up only three years old.'

Suki opened her folder on cue. I looked over at Justin, who could hardly contain his glee as he flipped over the title page.

'On page one,' Suki said with a mild, local accent, 'we've set out a reminder of the bids that came in. Of the eight different parties we approached to buy the company, five made an offer — which is exceptional. PeopleForce was by far and away the most interested in acquiring you, which is reflected in their offer.'

The digits on the page confounded me for the first time in my life. I'd heard the numbers from Justin before, but seeing that many zeroes brought it home: I was going to be rich. Me, the distinctly average girl from Peebles. What the hell would I do with all that cash?

Angus leaned forward. 'I'd even go so far as to say they've been pestering us to move as quickly as we can throughout this whole process.'

'I don't want to lose this,' said Justin. 'We should hurry. I need us to pull out all the stops to be able to announce the deal at our conference. That's the biggest opportunity to make a splash.'

'It's all in hand, Justin,' said Suki. 'It will be tight timing-wise, but that's why we're here to discuss next steps. I'm confident the deal will go ahead. PeopleForce are unlikely to back away. By acquiring you, they stay ahead of competition and quash the rumours they've run out of ideas. Your technology is extremely valuable to them, a perfect complement to the market-leading suite of Human Resource applications they sell to big companies worldwide. With your innovation, their clients will be able to monitor their internal communications to determine employee satisfaction automatically, without the need for questionnaires or appraisals. It's gold dust. And your latest sick-leave upgrade is transformational.'

Angus nodded along blankly, and I wasn't sure he understood Suki's description of our technology. A few seconds later, my instinct was confirmed when he asked, 'What's the sick-leave upgrade again?'

I took pity and kept it simple. 'Our software scans the words and phrases people use in their emails and other written interactions at work. Our models determine if employees are happy or harassed, feeling motivated or frustrated, empowered, loyal, and so on. Recently we've taken it one step further. Building on the latest medical research, we're able to give warning indicators when an employee might be at the early stages of depression, which can lead to long-term absences. Basically, employers can now offer people help before they even know they need it.'

'That one still blows my mind.' Suki gestured an explosion escaping from her head that made us laugh. She nodded at me. I wondered if it was to acknowledge I'd built this or as a thank you for keeping Angus enlightened.

Justin rubbed his hands. 'So now what?'

Angus leaned back in the leather chair, 'Suki will pull together a data room for PeopleForce to do their due diligence. That means we need to put a mountain of documents in a central location for them to review so that their acquisition team can verify what we've told them about your company is all true. This process can take weeks or months, depending on how well we put the information together and how many questions they have. Therefore, it's important we put our best foot forward.'

'Could their offer still change?' Justin asked.

'Aye, it's possible,' he said gravely. 'If they find inconsistencies, they might reduce the valuation. However, we've been fully transparent from the start, and Suki thinks we may even have underestimated the value of your new projects in R&D.'

Suki flashed her wide smile again. 'That's because we didn't have much information on what else you've been developing, Laura. Hence, why we need you.'

'Ah yes, our secretive Laura,' teased Justin.

I squirmed.

Angus looked at his watch. 'Smashing. PeopleForce's man in San Francisco has a team in place ready for when we are. You two girls make friends and huddle together until it's all set up.'

Suki rolled her eyes to me.

Justin patted the table. 'They're women, Angus. Not girls. They are tremendously competent women, in fact.' A stunned silence filled the room. He winked at Suki. 'If anything, I'm the one who's just the pretty face around here.'

Angus laughed a little too loudly and pushed his chair back.

We all stood. Angus approached Justin with his hand outstretched. 'My man, I'll bid you farewell for now. Get ready. Soon you'll be joining the millionaire's club.' Justin's grin stretched from ear to ear as he returned the handshake. Angus gave a little wave all round and left.

Justin asked. 'Suki, may I have a moment with Laura please?'

She collected Angus's papers and stuck them under her arm. 'Sure thing. I'll wait outside.'

'SO. HERE WE are, partner,' said Justin after Suki disappeared.

'Here we are.' I shook my head. 'It's incredible.'

'It's what we've worked for.' He ran his fingers through his wavy, auburn hair. 'How are you feeling?'

I wasn't sure how I felt. To me, it had never been about the money. I created the software because I loved words; had loved words ever since the hungry caterpillar chomped its way through a week's worth of food and burst out transformed; since the adventurous family had braved the dark woods and the squelchy mud to hunt a bear. I loved how authors used words — the perfect words — to convey a thousand emotions and take me on a journey from which I could emerge simultaneously drained and invigorated to face reality again.

I'd devoured books as a child, being the first to exhaust my small town's primary school library. I continued reading mornings, evenings and during meals throughout my teenage years, deaf to Mum's pleas for me to go out and have some fun for a change. When my computing teacher suggested I could marry my talent for maths and my love of words by studying Natural Language

Programming, I thought all my Christmases came at once. Who knew it would lead to all this?

Justin's voice shook me from my thoughts. 'Listen, Laura. I'm aware this whole business side isn't what you're used to. And probably the last thing you want is Suki tagging along with you all day. But this is important. Not only for you and me, but also for the employees we could only pay in shares when we first started. It's life changing. I'm relying on you to get this data room sorted with Suki ASAP. Show her everything she needs to see — and I mean everything. All access, okay?'

I frowned. 'Why does it have to be me?' I'd planned to check in on Emily again.

'I could ask Sally or one of the other data scientists, but you're excellent at explaining things in layman's terms. And you're the only one who can talk intelligently about what we're up to with our R&D. Remember, I'm just a pretty face.'

'Oh, ha ha. Fine. Of course, I'll do it.'

'Good *girl*.' Justin stuck out his tongue.

I snickered and replied with my own tongue as I left the room.

SUKI HOVERED around the corner, inspecting the calculations on the wall.

'Sorry to keep you waiting, Suki.'

She put her phone in the outside pocket of her bag. 'That's okay. I'm all yours.'

Justin wandered up, readjusting the brown leather belt around his waist. He whispered something to Suki through her sleek, dark hair, nodded to me and strode down the corridor to the open plan office that housed our staff. He thought the lay-out was great for team building; it was my idea of hell.

Suki watched Justin swagger away. 'He's quite the charmer, isn't he?' she said.

'Yeah. But don't worry, he's harmless.'

She checked her watch. 'Do we go back to the boardroom? We should block it off for at least four days while you and I team up to get our ducks in a row.'

I pressed my book against my stomach. Suki must have read the horror on my face because she changed tack. 'What's that you're reading?'

'It's about prison camps.'

'That sounds heartbreaking.'

'Yes.' I wasn't interested in her small talk.

Suki briefly pressed her lips together. 'Listen. Why don't we exchange numbers, and I'll call you later to arrange a time to meet tomorrow? You'll have stuff to finish.'

'Thanks.' I pulled my phone from my rear pocket.

She came close, smelling of jasmine and sage. 'Wow, a Nokia brick. I haven't seen one of those since I was a kid. And you're a techie. Aren't you all supposed to be Apple fanboys? How do you keep up with work emails?'

'I don't. Not outside of the office.'

'Lucky you. I wish I could get away with that. The world of finance never sleeps.' She eyed the phone again. 'What about your friends though?'

'My friend knows where to find me.'

Suki blinked. 'No social media either?'

'No.'

'Well, you're right to avoid it; it's—'

'Evil.'

Suki looked perturbed but returned to the task at hand. 'It's S-u-k-i Ak-sorn-pan.' She recited her number. I punched it into my address book, to join my two other contacts.

'Can't you just send me a list of what you need?' I proposed. 'Might save you sitting around while I search for things?'

'We can do that for some bits, but I need you to walk me through your technology. How it works, where it came from, the recent upgrades and, most importantly, the future R&D roadmap — the projects only you know about.'

'Fine.'

Suki tipped her head sideways, examining me like a specimen. 'You don't say much, do you?'

Her directness took me by surprise. All I could think to say was, 'No.' We both laughed at the irony.

Suki smiled. 'I can tell this isn't your bag, and Justin had given me the heads up you might be resistant. So, here's my offer: if you work with me — and if you trust me — we can change our lives together. But I need you to step out of your little cocoon. What do you say?'

I squirmed. I treasured my cocoon. Nothing wrong with my cocoon. Why would I ever willingly choose to step out of it?

My shoulders slumped. I had no choice but to collaborate. Only for a short period, mind. Then I would get back to my software models.

I looked at her expectant face, at the curiously over-confident creature that was disrupting my routine and extended the tug of war. Just for kicks. 'I like my life just fine, thanks.'

'Okay, then we do it to change *my* life. I'm getting paid a success fee on this deal, and I have many shoes to buy.' Suki raised one leg to show off an undoubtedly pricey black patent pump with red sole I'd failed to notice before. Why would I, when my own wardrobe consisted of identical black long-sleeved tops and jeans?

'In that case, we'll meet here tomorrow. 10AM,' I said.

This triggered a little high-heeled skip.

4.
ME

At six o'clock, I put my computer to sleep. I looked around the open plan space. Only a few heads remained partially visible behind rows of computer monitors.

Outside, office workers walked past to grab a drink in the various cafés and restaurants at the centre of the trendy Quartermile district on their way home. A few peeked into Empisoft's colourful, fully glazed enclosure, no doubt expecting a glimpse of the magic being created by this celebrated start-up.

The Royal Infirmary Hospital formerly stood on the Empisoft site, but the cost of maintaining such a giant Victorian structure had become prohibitive. Despite residents' objections, the council gave permission to eager developers eyeing prime city-centre real estate, which spawned six shiny black metal-framed, multi-storey office buildings. Those indoors were afforded views of the renaissance architecture of the George Heriot school on one side and the Pentland hills lying in the distance on the other.

On the ground floor, however, the views were of passers-by, Lothian buses, and, when school broke out in the afternoon, queues of taxi-rank-hogging black SUVs picking up their owners' blue-blazered young.

When I stepped outside, I threw my blue backpack over my shoulder, careful not to snag my ponytail, and turned right toward the Meadows. I greeted the woman closing up her little food truck on the main path to the park with a nod, as I did every day. I no longer experienced a pang of guilt for never buying anything. She waved in return, as usual.

Further along, sun-seekers hung out in groups on the large open grassland that divided the city in two, their portable barbecues infusing the air with the scent of fried fat usually associated with Friday night.

Five American-looking tourists wearing baseball caps sat on the grass up ahead, mesmerised by two jugglers with colourful ribbons threaded through their dreadlocks throwing unlit fire torches through the air. I passed a group of teenagers leafing through the giant programme of the Fringe Festival, an annual smorgasbord of arts and culture that stole Edinburgh from its residents every August.

The elm-lined path along the middle brought me straight home to Marchmont. My tenement's front door groaned. A gust of wind threw papers from the console table onto the floor. I crouched down and gathered it all up to sort again into piles for each of my fellow apartment-dwellers. In my three years here, nobody stayed long enough to want to invest in post boxes. Through a few bribes, I'd at least convinced the postman to put a rubber band around the stuff for me.

Someone had discarded the free newspaper you get on the bus. Half the front page consisted of Adam Mooney's face. *Movie star's play under threat*, read the headline.

A quick, reluctant, scan of the article revealed that female demonstrators were blocking ticketholders from entering the theatre at showtime, verbally shaming them for supporting a man accused of sexual assault. What was the point? The scandal wouldn't impact box office takings — it had been sold out for months. I supposed they were hoping to cause enough disruption for the actor to cancel and go home. I climbed the stairs and wondered if he would. Probably for the best. Get the whole sodding thing over with. Forget he hurt Emily.

I swung the door into my flat. Atticus meowed.

'Hello, there.' I scooped him up. With my thumb, I stroked the ginger fur above his nose. He purred. 'Let's see what we've got today, shall we, greedy chops?'

The cupboard over the sink held a carton full of sachets of *clucktastic* chicken and *purrfect* pork I swore smelled the same. Atticus wound his striped tail across my legs, circling. 'You're not helping.'

I sat on the tiles next to my glutton hoovering up his food. 'Slow down, buddy. You'll choke.' I knew better than to stroke him when he was eating. My gaze wandered across the apartment while I waited.

Four overflowing bookcases took up most of the walls, novels placed two-deep on the many shelves. The occasional picture frame interrupted the line of colourful spines: a youthful portrait of Mum holding me as a baby, the obligatory capped-and-gowned graduation shots for both my undergraduate and graduate degrees, two silhouettes of little girls reading with flashlights inside a tent. Another one of Emily and me, posing ruddy-cheeked, pig-tailed and wellie-clad outside Peebles library. So alike, then, only me brunette, her blonde.

I sighed, tears prickling behind my eyes. If only I could make the last few weeks disappear. As if summoned, Atticus abandoned his bowl, stepped over my leg and landed his heavy body on my lap, offering comfort. He rolled onto his back, shamelessly exposing his full, white floof. After a while, I pulled the mobile from my jacket pocket and pressed the speed dial.

Emily didn't pick up. For a moment, I contemplated popping round and checking up on her, but I hoped it meant she'd finally gone out. I shut my eyes and drank in the quiet. There had been enough people to deal with for one day already. And it was my turn for something to eat. Conflicted, I vowed to try again later.

I set the Nokia aside where I could still hear it. It fulfilled an important function of late: I'd programmed things such that my mobile would receive a text message when Emily posted on Twitter. The device would alert me at its loudest setting. My role was to phone Emily and berate her for disobeying my orders to stay away from the cesspool that was causing her such harm. Just because I didn't use social media myself didn't mean I couldn't work it.

The texts had slowed in the last five days, Emily seemingly accepting her mental health was too high a price to pay for curiosity.

It still puzzled me: why Emily thought she wouldn't be identified when giving the interview about her night with Adam Mooney to that blog. Edinburgh is a small town. You're never far from prying eyes.

But nobody could have predicted the scale of the backlash, or its duration.

I got up and walked to the fridge, Atticus close behind, hopeful of a double dip.

A cheese sandwich in my hand, I crossed the living room to the sofa, resigned to dealing with life's administrivia before I could bury myself inside my book again. I removed the elastic from the post and discarded all the un-addressed leaflets that cluttered the planet.

What remained were a bank statement and a postcard with an image of a volcanic terrain, ragged red-tinted rocks at the base of a grey, sun-lit peak; the word *Lanzarote* hovering in the sky. My mother was on holiday with Oliver, her boyfriend. Or should I call him her partner after all this time?

Wish you were here.

Always the same; unlikely to be true. Yet it brought a smile to my face.

I didn't understand what Mum saw in Oliver, although he was a nice enough chap and he seemed to treat her well. She still reassured me he wasn't there to take Dad's place. Such a silly thing to worry about: Oliver was a lanky, bearded florist and Dad ... I thought about my father's masculine, muscular arms hoisting me onto his square shoulders. No contest.

Plus, I was a twenty-five-year-old woman.

5.
EMILY

It felt good to be clean again. A white cotton turban held Emily's hair in place while she executed the cosmetic routine she hadn't seen the point of for a while. Foundation, blusher, concealer — oh but to conceal oneself entirely — eyeliner, eye shadow, lip liner, lipstick. Not the glossy type; matte. A quick brush of her neat, plucked brows completed the picture of groomed professionalism.

She waded through the sea of discarded clothes to pull a fresh gym kit from the wardrobe. She inhaled the lavender scent of the sports bra and wrapped it around her breasts. It was lucky she liked yoga, otherwise she'd never have the flexibility to reach that high up her back to fasten the tricky second hook. Athletic leggings and a short-sleeved top later, she blow-dried her hair, wondering if the scarf she'd settled on the night before was still the best choice.

A seamstress's mannequin stood in the corner of her bedroom, covered with long fabrics that danced in the rays of the morning sun. She'd wanted to wear the Hermes scarf, with its fierce jaguar roaring from an Aztec-inspired throne of bright-coloured feathers. Her prized possession. What a message that would send. Sadly, it was just too short.

No, she'd measured with precision and would have to make do with the dark-blue one with silver stars she got from her mum last birthday. She hoped people wouldn't read too much into that.

Emily knotted the scarf around her neck air-hostess fashion. The resulting triple-layered waterfall fell under her chin, the small ends of the knot sprouting from the side. It was one of many knots she'd mastered; most recently thanks to a magazine tutorial, but earlier during her era as enthusiastic cub scout. They would come in handy today.

She scrunched her nose at her reflection in the mirror. Not a great combo. Never mind. It wouldn't be for long, anyway. She gave the vivid jaguar a last, longing look and headed for breakfast.

There was little in the fridge beyond a collection of glass jars that stood on sticky circles, hints of green on the top layer of the liquid inside. They'd be someone else's problem.

The first bite of her cereal confirmed the milk was off. She poured the rest of the two pints onto the rot in the sink. With her spoon, she picked at the flakes in her plate and forced herself to finish. She needed her strength.

The pear in the fruit bowl was squishy to the touch. She bit into it, making sure to avoid the brown bruise, and held her hand out to catch the juice. She placed the core in the grey compost bucket and threw the plastic milk bottle in the blue recycling tub, where it balanced on a heap of cardboard and paper.

She found her trainers underneath a fleece throw by the TV. Her work bag rested by the door, a gorgeous red leather briefcase she'd treated herself to when she'd first started at Pure Brilliant PR & Events. Its large rectangular shape could be cumbersome when running from client to client or visiting different venues where she staged events, but it made her feel smart. Serious. And yes, glamorous. Her clients might be technology companies dominated by people who wouldn't know fashion if it hit them in the face, but that didn't mean she couldn't bring style to the mix.

She riffled through the vast pile of papers she'd plonked back on her dining table, unable to find the Empisoft folder. She shrugged and placed her laptop into the padded middle section of her bag, safe. It was right to return it.

A coat wasn't needed: it was a nice morning. She even looked forward to the walk to work. Fresh air.

Where were her keys?

Screw the keys.

She turned toward the door. As she grabbed the knob, she remembered one more thing. She sprinted to the kitchen, filled her green watering can to the brim and darted across her apartment soaking her houseplants with so much water she had to go for a refill.

She knew orchids shouldn't get that much but it seemed the kind thing to do. 'Sorry,' she said, drowning her flowering, pink dendrobium. She put the can down and repositioned her red bag on her shoulder. She took a deep breath as she looked around her chaotic flat one last time and stepped onto the landing, closing the door shut firmly behind her.

6.
ME

I wasn't an early riser. Never had been. Getting in a little later to work than the others was a welcome perk of being the founder. Many of my colleagues were night owls, anyway. That tended to be the techie way. Justin and I agreed that people should be able to set their own schedules, in line with their personal biorhythms. Productivity was what it was about, and I had it down to a T. This freed up mornings for a slow start, and evenings for reading.

I turned my head and patted my pillow down to check the time: almost half past eight. Still dark, but only because of my heavyset, blackout-lined curtains. They kept the warmth in during winter nights and prevented the summer's dawn from waking me at silly o'clock. The bird song was harder to silence, and it had roused me briefly a few hours earlier. I stretched my arms and legs into a star shape and let out a satisfied yawn. It popped my ears just as my mobile gave an almighty shriek.

I leapt out of bed and sprinted to where my phone lay in the living room, stubbing my toe on the door frame.

Atticus appeared by my side, his whiskers standing to attention. I peered at the small screen of my Nokia.

'No!' Nerves sprang to my neck with a vice-like grip. 'No no no no no...'

My shallow breaths made my hands shake. I missed the numbers on the keypad. Tried again. 'Pick up, pick up, pick up.'

Each echoey ring compounded my panic. 'Where are you?' I yelled. Atticus spread his paws, his eyes wide. 'No. Atticus. Sorry.' He scuttled toward the door. 'Damn.' I dialled again. Nothing. 'Where the hell *is* she?'

I paced back and forth. The door. My keys. Do I go to hers? What if she's not there? Why isn't she picking up?

I cast my eyes to the ceiling, stood still, filled my lungs with air. Who else could I call?

Emily's office?

Emily had been with a colleague when I'd first hired them for Empisoft's public relations. Nondescript, early twenties. Highlights. What was her name? That Claire woman. Could I remember her last name?

Yes.

I dialled Emily's work number and asked to be put through.

7.
THAT CLAIRE WOMAN

The phone on Claire's desk rang.

Claire glared at the phone from across the room. For goodness sake; she was only just through the door and hadn't even had her morning coffee yet. She considered ignoring the caller, but she looked around and there was nobody else. She dashed to her desk, placed her bag and umbrella on the floor, and picked up.

'Hello, Claire speaking.'

'It's Laura Flett. Where's Emily?' Claire recognised the name as the mousy girl behind Empisoft she'd once met. Why was she calling her? Claire's point of contact for the conference was the marketing guy. And that tone! She'd been sorely tempted to say, 'Good morning to you too,' but she was too professional to let her sarcasm loose.

'I'm Empisoft's liaison at the moment. Emily is off sick. May I help?'

'You don't understand,' Laura pressed, somewhat out of breath and unnecessarily shrill. 'Emily's not home. She's not picking up her phone. I need to find her.'

Claire remembered her first day at work, meeting all her colleagues and hearing about their clients. She'd been slightly in awe of Emily, who'd been there a year already. Emily had positively glowed when she spoke about her favourite: Empisoft, the company founded by her best friend. She'd recommended Claire also try to find tiny, ambitious companies to represent, because you never know how fast they'll grow. Emily convinced their boss Darren to take a chance on Empisoft with a discounted PR package — and crikey, had that paid off.

Claire softened her voice. 'She might be on her way to work still, Laura. I spoke to her yesterday. She said she'd be back today.'

'Could you check if she's there? Please. Her phone is ringing out. It's important.'

Emily's spot was two rows down from Claire's, near the window. She craned her neck to see whether the work surface showed any signs of recent life among the many gizmos that cluttered it. 'Hold on.' She put the receiver down and navigated across. Emily's red leather bag stood on her chair. So she *was* in. Claire looked around. No one. She dipped in and out of the surrounding conference rooms. Empty. The coffee area? Nope.

She gave her report. 'Sorry to keep you waiting, Laura. She's here. Her stuff is here. It's just... I can't find her. Can I give her a message?'

'No! We have to find her. Quick. Have you checked the toilets?'

The toilets were a step too far. Laura's insistence annoyed her, but it was also unnerving. Laura didn't strike Claire as the dramatic type. Something had to be seriously wrong.

'Laura, what's this all about?'

'I think Emily's doing something stupid. She sent a tweet. A few minutes ago. And I'm worried sick.'

'Why? What did it say?'

Laura sobbed.

'Goodbye cruel world.'

8.
EMILY

The basement gym was insulated from any office commotion upstairs. A small, windowless room with abysmal air circulation meaning that anyone entering was greeted by a wall of stale sweat, day or night. Emily knew from previous visits to take deep breaths before stepping in. Once you got going — properly going — your own perspiration would mask the odours of others.

If you wanted, you could turn on the smart speakers to play five pre-programmed soundtracks for the different recommended workouts. Today, she preferred silence.

A strange calm had descended on her the night before. And she'd made a plan. A plan that made complete sense then as it did again after an uninterrupted eight hours' sleep — the first in ages.

The clock on the wall showed 8:20. Bang on time.

She'd turned her mobile off as soon as her message had gone. She couldn't risk having her resolve weakened by reminders of what — or whom — she was leaving behind. It would be only natural for Laura to call. Dear Laura had been on her like a hawk since the abuse exploded; since the threats and condemnations directed at a previously anonymous woman by anonymous keyboard warriors veered to her and became personal. The online bile oozing into real life, engulfing her, suffocating her. Heat rose from her chest, spreading across her neck.

Emily Nairn. Emily Nairn. Emily Nairn. Everywhere.

That bitch who falsely accused a Hollywood hero of sexual assault. The ugly skank who should have been grateful to have Adam Mooney's tongue up her pussy — this from both men and women. The feminazi that represented all that was wrong with women these days. Her, a single target for the unleashed anger and frustration of a thousand men.

Yet somehow, she was also the *anti*-feminist who should be ashamed at devaluing the whole #MeToo movement with such a minor gripe. '*Boo-hoo,*' they'd taunted online as if her pain was unfounded; her anguish so easily dismissed, her consent not valid.

They'd soon figured out her name. Their brother's cousin or sister's colleague told them it was her. Emily Nairn, the prick-tease that wouldn't follow through. The cunt that needed to be taught a lesson.

Then: Emily Nairn lives at Flat 1/2, 78 Bruntsfield Drive.

Emily shook the haunting thoughts from her head and walked toward the cable function machine. It was as she'd recalled: a six-foot metallic frame housing a pulley system and stacks of weights on both sides. A suitably solid piece of equipment.

The metal was freezing cold.

Two bars for chin-ups protruded from the top, one for each hand. It would be easier to use those, but she needed the weights. Just gravity wouldn't be enough.

She hunched down and slotted the yellow separator between the fourth and fifth weighted plate. A hefty tug on the handle. Did that feel right?

Don't fuck this up.

She unwrapped the scarf from her neck and pulled at it twice, arms outstretched. She stranded one end through the right handle of the pulley mechanism and knotted it into place with a trucker's hitch.

Facing away from the machine, she dropped to her knees, bringing the handle down with her. She stuck the cable under her arm and leaned sideways to prevent it from slipping. She gave the scarf another swift jerk where it coiled around the handle. Good.

The silvery stars on the blue fabric twinkled, reflected the spotlights overhead. Maybe this pattern had been the best choice after all.

Her knees throbbed against the mat. She looked sideways to gauge the height of the machine's frame and gathered the loose end of the scarf. She made an 'S' shape and then a 'C'. Funny how you never forget. She wrapped the shorter length of fabric around the longer five times and threaded the end bit through the resulting loop.

There.

She was quite proud of that one.

She released the handle from underneath her aching armpit, holding the cable taut with her left hand.

Emily lowered herself onto her bum. The cable dug a groove inside her now extended fist.

She placed the soft, silk noose around her neck. Then tightened.

The weights were at their highest position.

She closed her eyes, counted to three and let go.

9.
ME

Atticus rubbed his head against the arch of my bare foot; his fluffy, fat body caressed my skin as it followed. After the tip of his tail tickled each single toe in sequence, he turned and repeated this action in the opposite direction for the umpteenth time. He still wasn't getting my attention.

Six hours since Emily's death. Six agonising hours in which it seemed like every last drop of liquid from my body had left through my eyes. Six numbing hours that kept me welded to the floor of my living room, my back to the wall, legs spread, staring into space.

After agreeing with Claire that I should come to Pure Brilliant myself to look for Emily, she returned my call within minutes. When the phone rang, I had one leg in my jeans and stumbled as I lunged for the device.

I'd strained to hear Claire's voice through the cacophony in the background. Pure Brilliant was being evacuated with a fire alarm. Rumours were flying about a blaze, but she said she didn't buy it: there were no fire engines, even after eight minutes. She'd gone to investigate and found Darren being led by Security to the side of the building. When she reached him, he was kneeled on the grass, head in his hands.

He'd found Emily.

Everything else Claire told me was a blur — and not only because of our combined sobs.

My stomach rumbled. Atticus climbed on me and massaged my thighs with his claws, preparing to cuddle up. I grabbed him and buried my face in his tummy, my hot breath fanning the ginger fluff across my cheek like a caress. If only I could stay here forever.

The phone rang. I peeked. Suki again.

Piss off.

I didn't want people around. *People* made Emily do this. I wished they would all die. I hugged my cat harder. The damp patch on his down grew with every tear. He wriggled free and took his warmth with him. A shiver ran up my spine.

Cold and alone. A memory flashed by. Seven years old. Stuck in a tree during a camping trip. Cold and alone, scared and longing for Dad to come rescue me. He did, then, but he couldn't anymore. I remembered Mum fussing over me, insisting on packing up and driving straight home. I remembered the hot bath.

I wrapped my arms around my chest. I yearned for that bath; for Mum — for the first in a long time; for Dad. I still missed him, fifteen years on.

The foreign dial tone signalled Mum was still in Spain. When she picked up, it sounded as though she was in a bar, glasses clinking, laughter.

'Hello darling, this is a nice surprise,' she said.

'I'm sorry to call. I... I don't know how to tell you this. Emily is dead.'

'What?'

'She killed herself, Mum. They found her this morning.'

'Oh honey, are you okay?'

'No. No, I'm not.' My whole body shook as my mother made shushing sounds from too far away.

''I'm coming home, darling. I'll get the next flight out. Oh my God, her poor parents. I can't believe it. I'll be there as quick as —'

My vision blurred. I dropped sideways. The phone smashed against the ground.

10.
ME

A glass-walled holding pen across the drive from the main chapel of Mortonhall crematorium served as a waiting room between tightly scheduled ceremonies. Mum and I arrived early and nodded to the other mourners out of courtesy. I overheard *'Poor Susan.'* Sweat sprang to my temples. This wasn't the group for Emily yet. I tugged at Mum's sleeve and motioned with my eyes to leave but she didn't get it.

Thankfully, black-clad people began to exit the crematorium and flowed down the hill. Staff moved floral arrangements out the back door and refreshed them with new wreaths that stood ready on folding tables in the side alley. I admired their efficiency.

The group we'd invaded left and proceeded in near single file to the concrete, accordion-like building. Mum and I sat on the chairs freed by the elderly. She placed her hand on my knee. I had nothing to say. She knew.

We waited.

Eventually, I heard the murmur of Emily's mourners arriving. First a trickle, then a steady stream walking up the tree-lined path from the parking lot.

I smiled awkwardly as they entered the pen. Emily and I had only a handful of other friends growing up, who'd all moved away. Who were these people? A dull ache spread across my chest. I remembered her inviting me to parties when we'd first moved to university. Awkward, smoky, clammy places with loud music preventing you from thinking, let alone allowing you to discourage the drunken advances of pale, randy students. I'd given up after a handful of attempts and she stopped asking. Her other friends would have been relieved the boring sidekick was out of the picture and I couldn't begrudge her enjoying her newfound popularity.

I studied the various clumsy greetings around us. Too young to have experienced anything more than the loss of a grandparent, they struggled for words and made do with mumbles, nods and pats on the back. What should one say about the utterly preventable death of someone in pain?

I looked at the tiles on the floor and ran my foot over the pretty swirly pattern. It made sense for Emily's parents to book the funeral here: Edinburgh was as far for them and those coming from Peebles as its alternative, Melrose crematorium — where Dad's funeral had been held. This place looked bigger, too. Just as well. We already didn't fit here. Many stood outside. Boxed in, surrounded by a noxious mix of cosmetic smells, I wished I'd done the same.

When the cortege of black cars headed by an elegant hearse came around the bend, the room fell silent. The others looked around, seemingly searching for a leader who would know whether this was the time to cross the road. A subtle wave from a man in a top hat and tails by the chapel suggested it was, and they spilled out.

'Come on, baby,' said Mum. 'It's time.'

My mother held my hand during the whole ceremony and squeezed whenever my grief hiccoughed from my body. I tried to concentrate on the readings, but it was as if the words floated in the air out of sync. I picked at my skirt.

When the curtain closed behind the coffin, and we sang the final hymn, Emily's family — her parents and her younger brother — shuffled past the congregation to stand in a line by the exit.

I didn't want to go to them. I didn't think I'd cope. Mum prodded me along, whispering what to say and do. I figured it wouldn't matter what I said: Emily's parents looked sedated through the parade of handshakes, hugs and condolences. When it was my turn, her mother grabbed me in a full embrace, my nose pressed to her black lapel.

'Oh Laura, you were such a good friend,' she said.

My cheeks flushed. Given what had happened, I'd been anything but.

THE FAMILY invited those closest to Emily to join them at a nearby hotel for soup and drinks. I stuck to tea, Mum and I a twosome on the edge of the green-carpeted room.

I overheard a young woman say, 'Did you see the arrangement Adam Mooney sent?'

'Quite right,' said another. 'Though a bit small...'

'Do you think? At least he showed the good sense to not send anything too ostentatious.'

'I kinda expected him to come to pay his respects. He's still in town, you know.' said a third.

'God, can you imagine? No. That would totally not be okay. Talk about upstaging the deceased!'

Mum nudged me. My cup wobbled on the edge of the saucer.

I glared at her. 'What?'

'Deb and Paul are waving us over. Come on,' she said.

Emily's parents had regained some colour in their cheeks. Whether it was because of the soup or the coffee — or whatever they'd spiked it with — was anyone's guess. It made them easier to approach. Less of the oppressing face of doom that caused me to be tongue-tied as we'd exited the chapel. I couldn't imagine their agony.

'Laura, my dear. Look at you all grown up,' Paul said.

It hit me that it was true: they hadn't seen me in years. Not since Emily's graduation. I didn't avoid Peebles — it was a fine place — I'd merely not been home for a long time. Too busy. Would I ever return? The cradle of my friendship with Emily unimaginable without her.

My mum gave them both a hug, and they shared words that passed me by. All the while I had an itch, something I needed addressed. And when I caught a lull, I asked, 'What are the police doing?'

They stopped talking, quizzical faces on me.

'Have they done anything?' I said.

Deb winced and leaned into her husband. 'Well, they've been kind. There's not much they can do, is there? I mean She... she was suffering. She did this... to herself.'

'But she was being harassed—'

'Laura...' Paul gave me a stern look.

Deb placed her hand on his. 'It's fine, Paul. We're all upset.' She looked at me and forced a smile. 'The Edinburgh police said they were looking into it, darling. Though they warned us not to expect too much. They said it was difficult to identify anonymous — what did they call them? Trolls. And, well, because Emily never made a formal complaint it apparently makes it even more difficult. To do anything.'

Paul nodded solemnly; a stereotype of Scottish stoicism: people who didn't speak, who never dwelled. Eventually, he said, 'We must let the wound heal.'

Heat rose in my chest. Let the wound heal? I'd pick at that scab as much as necessary to get the bastards that hurt Emily. 'How can you let it go so easily?' I asked. 'They committed *crimes*.'

The parents' shocked faces and Mum's bony elbow in the side told me I'd gone too far.

'How can we help?' Mum offered.

Deb shook her head and walked away, tearing at the tissue in her hands, mumbling something about more soup.

'The reason we waved you over, Laura,' Paul said, 'is about Emily's flat. Deb and I went the other day but...' He turned away from his coffee as though the mere sight of it made him feel sick.

'It's alright, Paul,' Mum stroked his arm. 'I can't imagine how difficult it must be.'

He sniffed, then sighed deeply. 'We opened the door. The place was in such a state. Deb fainted. I caught her just before she hit the ground.' He rubbed his forehead and grimaced. 'I put her down. Had to leave her there. I rushed in to get Emily a dress... for today.'

My heart sank at his lost face. Should I comfort him? Mum already had a hand on him. Would two be too much? I rubbed the handle of my teacup, clutching the saucer with my other hand. I looked down; a small scuff scarred my special-occasion pumps. 'Which dress did you choose?'

'Sorry?' I heard Paul say.

I raised my head back up. 'Which dress did you choose?'

His brow twitched. 'A blue one with flowers.'

A vision jumped into my head so suddenly I gasped: Emily picking me up from work one rainy afternoon, opening her raincoat like a flasher. *'Pssst, like my new dress?'* She'd quickly closed her coat again and let out a raucous laugh, her hand against the dress's high neckline.

I smiled at Paul. 'Perfect.'

He put his coffee down on a side table and cleared his throat. 'The thing is, we've hired a company to pack up Emily's belongings next week. The landlord is letting us break the lease early given... um... the circumstances.' He turned to me. 'But Deb and I thought you might want to go in first and choose some items to keep. For you.'

I recoiled.

Mum put a firm arm around me. 'That's thoughtful of you, Paul. I'm sure that means a lot to Laura.'

'We can get keys to you,' he said.

I shook my head. 'I have keys thanks.' I stroked the palm of my hand against my skirt, remembering the cold sensation of Emily pressing the cat-shaped key ring into it years ago, joking to Atticus that there was a new tomcat in town.

'In case of emergency,' she'd said. *'If I ever lock myself out there's only two places you'll be, work or home, eh?'*

I'd snickered because she was right. Me. Her ever-reliable Laura.

'Plus, I don't want to end up like that poor woman I read about in the Herald, who tripped in the bath and died. She was there for days before anyone found her.' She'd closed my fingers around the key ring. *'I mean, that's got to be the worst way to go.'*

I pinched the bridge of my nose, banishing thoughts of Emil's last moments.

How wrong she was.

A WOMAN SMILED at me from the corner of the room. She was roughly my age and wearing too much make-up, with thick, drawn-in eyebrows that were inexplicably all the rage. Blonde highlights snaked through her chestnut hair.

Did I know her from school? I didn't think so. Or had we all changed so much in seven years? My brown shoulder-length ponytail was the same as always — the incident with the scissors at nursery notwithstanding. Same face, with a button-tipped, straight nose and sunken brown eyes. My only change the peekaboo games played by my freckles between seasons.

When I smiled in return, the woman advanced, holding a half-empty pink drink.

'Hi.'

'Hi,' I replied.

She put her hand on her chest and said, 'Claire. From Pure Brilliant. You called me... that day...?'

'Oh, God. Yes. I'm sorry.'

'That's okay. It's a big shock for everyone.' She rubbed her lips together. 'You were close, right?'

Not knowing how to begin to describe the friendship of the ages, I nodded.

She took a sip of her drink. 'A lot of our colleagues came this morning. We'll miss her.'

We stood side by side, scanning the room, each waiting for the other to change the subject. I clutched my stupid empty teacup. Where the hell was Mum?

'You don't have to worry about your account,' Claire said. 'I've taken over the Empisoft conference.' Seeing my scrunched forehead, she said, 'I mean... Not taken over-over.'

I remained silent, which she must have interpreted as permission because she added, 'I want you to be confident it's all in hand. A lot of the organisation is taken care of. Emily did a great job.'

Pressure grew behind my eyes. Emily's squeals of delight filled my head. *This will be such fun, Laura. You and me working together.* Empisoft's inaugural conference had been a tiny affair, but it was her first. And she was dead proud. We both were.

'I'm focused on getting the media lined up.' Claire fidgeted with her glass. 'They asked about Emily. They liked her...' She sniffed and flicked her hair. 'They're still keen to cover it — it's always an exciting conference — but I am getting push back. They'd like there to be an announcement. Maybe a new product?'

How could she go on about the conference? When I shook my head in disbelief, she misunderstood. 'I know, right?' she said. 'You only launched the latest upgrade a few months ago, but they're like wolves. They travel in packs. Always hungry for more. So... no new product?'

I eyed Claire's hopeful face. This woman who was a stranger, and yet... We'd shared a profound experience, a common moment that would bind us forever. To each other ... and to Emily. She rubbed the rim of her glass with her thumb, her smile fixed. Was she nervous? I threw her a bone. 'No. But don't worry. The wolves will get fed something special. Be patient.'

Claire's eyes flashed open. 'What do you mean? Marketing has said nothing.'

People around us started to leave. The door opened and closed, yielding flickers of opportunity. But I stayed. The conference was Emily's baby, and my heart tugged at me to help Claire deliver it.

I took a deep breath. 'We haven't told Marketing yet. It's top secret, a last-minute thing. I'm only telling you to help you prepare better. Promise to keep this quiet?'

'Cross my heart.' Claire cemented her promise with an X across the chest.

'The company's being acquired.'

Claire's gasp made surrounding heads turn. 'When? Now? Who's the buyer?'

Her many questions made me regret I'd opened my mouth. Funny how that was always the way. 'I can't tell you who it is, but it's big. And bar any unforeseen circumstances, I'm told it's happening.'

'That's exciting!' Claire's exclamation prompted some disapproving stares. She cleared her throat and fished the memorial programme from her pocket. A signal she remembered why we were here.

The portrait of Emily on the front was taken somewhere outside, and the reflections of the sun in her blonde hair framed her head like a halo.

'Poor Emily.' Claire sighed. 'I looked, you know. When you called. I looked everywhere I could think of... I'm glad I wasn't the one to find her. It never occurred to me to check the gym. Darren can't step foot in it anymore. Such a weird choice, the way she went, the gym... We'll never know what was going through her mind, will we?'

11.
ME

The office had cooled. A more customary drizzle had replaced the radiant sunshine of the last week, and the dark clouds hanging low across the horizon made it clear this was only the start. I rubbed my upper arms on the way to the front of the building; I'd been cold all morning.

I spotted Suki outside. Her blue umbrella matched her elegant knee-length coat. Suki gave the umbrella a brisk shake and her hair a quick smooth before entering through the glass door. I watched her report to Liv. Suki spotted me staring and broke into an animated wave. 'Hey.'

I greeted her with, 'Let's go to the boardroom.'

'Give me a minute. I'm sore. I walked.' She stroked her calf and rolled her ankles in turn, her tan tights freckled with rain.

Her office was up in the New Town, a solid twenty minutes away. The posh part of the city. How did someone become a corporate financier anyway, a deal maker?

'Okay, I'm ready,' she said, straightening up.

I led her in silence to our room.

'You've been avoiding me,' she said.

'I've not.' I flipped on the privacy screen. 'I've not been here.'

'Are you all right? You look a bit peaky.'

'I'm fine.'

'Are you sure? I mean, I'd offer to come back later but I've been trying to get this meeting with you for days. And time is ticking on. But if you're under the weather...'

'I'm not sick.' A flush hit my cheek. Suki didn't deserve that bark. 'My friend died.'

'Your friend?' Suki's shocked face revealed she'd remembered our earlier conversation. My friend, my *one* friend.

I busied myself with cables; kept my eyes down. I'd run through my presentation on the wall-mounted screen and hoped that would be enough.

'Yes.'

'Oh Laura. I'm sorry. Was it an accident?'

The TV sprang to life. My skin prickled. The platinum-haired talk show host who'd berated Emily for making a mountain out of a molehill was speaking into the camera with a solemn expression.

'*Nobody knows what goes on in someone else's mind. Mental illness is a disability. And let me tell you this: every experience is legitimate; every pain is valid. Nobody should feel alone. On your screen is the number for the Samaritans*—'

'Too late for that, you soulless, slimy hypocrite,' I hissed, fumbling with the remote to make it stop.

Suki lifted an eyebrow. 'That girl. That was your friend? The one with Adam Mooney?'

'Yes.' I sat and navigated the file folder on the monitor.

'What they did to her.' She shook her head. 'It was horrible. Those Incel guys are the scum of the Earth.'

'Incel guys?'

'From what I've read. I could be wrong. It could be the technology discussion boards speculating — I have to read them to keep track of trends for prospective deals. The perceived wisdom is that she suffered from an orchestrated attack by various Incel groups.'

What was Suki on about? Facing my blank stare, she continued, 'You've not heard of them? No, of course not. You don't do social media.' Suki gestured for me to sit. 'They're called Involuntarily Celibates. It started innocently enough, with people bemoaning their sexless fate. Nowadays, it's dominated by men who can't get laid and who believe that it's the woman's fault. That women have taken the power and cut off their balls. Emasculated them.' Suki threw her hands in the air. 'It's insane. They cry, "Oh, the injustice! Everybody is having sex except for me". In their warped minds they blame everyone else. Ha! Not the fact they're not attractive, have no prospects, no chat. They hate the handsome, successful men because they hog all the girls. And they hate the girls for being sluts... just not with them.'

'They think they're *entitled* to sex?' I asked.

'Oh yes, and from the best-looking girls, too. That's what I find so weird. They're ugly, smelly losers who live with their mama and yet the plainer girls aren't enough. It's a really strange subgroup. They demand sex and woe betide any woman who denies it. That's when the violent threats come... when the misogyny slithers out in public' She made a snake-like gesture with her hands.

'Those attacks on Emily — that wasn't random trolling?' My heartbeat quickened. If this was orchestrated, what could that mean?

'That's what the word on the tech street is. We can't know for sure. Every time the Incel dudes find a new place to vent their anger, they get clamped down. The online platforms want nothing to do with their vileness; particularly since they've been caught inciting real-life violence. It's led to multiple suicide attacks in the US, you know. They just blow up innocent people. At schools, on campuses. Even the Vegas shooter was one.'

I rolled my finger in a backward circle. 'When you say "they've been caught"?'

'Oh, no. I meant that figuratively. They're great at hiding. Only those idiots who came out and killed people have been identified. And they've been turned to saints; left behind whole manifestos. No, for the rest it's all anonymous. Using decoy methods. They always find each other, though — online at least. Twitter still allows fake profiles, for example. I don't know of anyone arrested for being an Incel troll. Perhaps somewhere. But they're global. They could be anywhere, ganging up on a poor girl like your Emily thousands of miles away. A swarm of wasps that sting and disappear.'

I chewed the inside of my cheek. My mind whirred, pursuing scenario after scenario of different routes, different entry points to the Internet to find the bastards, hitting dead ends and starting again. I sensed Suki's worry.

'Listen, I'm sorry,' she said. 'It isn't helpful for me to discuss this with you. I can see you've got a lot on your mind. Once we concentrate on the acquisition and get things sorted, I can leave you alone. Okay?'

Having made little progress in my mental war games, I shrugged. Being left alone was always a good thing. 'Okay.' I grabbed the pointer from the table and clicked on a blue cloud icon, revealing a numbered set of folders. 'I've started gathering the information you mentioned and wanted to take you through how I thought we'd organise it.'

'Brilliant.'

'Here is the folder for our core software, which we launched three years ago. All it could do at the time is use the language in emails to grade employees on a scale of happiness, or job satisfaction. I have folders named *Documentation*, *Models* and *Validation*. We've produced five upgrades. The first one—'

'It's fine, Laura, you can skip through the description of everything you've launched. I'm already familiar with that and I recognise the names on the folders. Can I assume they each have the same content?'

'Yes.'

'Great. I got time with Justin the other day and we've gathered the documentation from your first investment and the follow-on funding round eighteen months ago. Man, I bet the rich guys who had a punt on your company back at the start will be delighted when they cash in.' She shifted in her seat. 'I can add the existing info to the central files, if that's okay?'

I was grateful for Suki's efficiency. I'd grown bored with giving the same presentation about our technology over and over these last few years. Suki got straight to the point. That was someone I could work with. 'Yes, that's fine.'

'Justin said you've got more things up your sleeve? That you've been reluctant to give him much of a peek. I teased him he shouldn't be peeking up sleeves.' Her face lit up when she heard my small chuckle. 'Just as well he didn't say you'd been keeping things close to your chest.' Suki's laugh lifted the room.

'I'm guessing you haven't succumbed to his charms yet?' I asked.

'Ha!' Suki's joyous roar reverberated against the glass walls. 'I'm afraid he's barking up the wrong tree there.'

'What do you mean?'

'I'm gay.'

'Ah.' Suki had thrown it out there, as if it was nothing. And of course it was nothing. It was new, that's all. I had to say something, though. Suki was watching me with those curious almond-shaped eyes again. 'Yes, I guess he'd be wasting his time,' I said, in my most casual voice.

'I also don't think a petite Thai girl is his type, judging from the blondes I see hanging off his arm at various events,' Suki added, a sparkle in her eye.

'Fair point.'

'And have you guys ever...?'

'God, no. He's like a brother.' I scrunched up my nose. 'That would be weird.'

'Good. Having lived through my share of workplace dalliances, I can confirm it's a terrible idea. Well... Now that's out of the way, can we return to your secret squirrel projects?'

'Fine. But it's early days. There isn't much written up.' I navigated through the folders and sub-folders again until I found a colourful web-like diagram.

Suki slid her chair closer to the screen. 'Ooh. What's this?'

'It's a tool intended to help companies find the heroes and villains at work.'

12.
CLAIRE

It was only eleven o'clock and Darren had already upset three people. Claire had seen the dark clouds hanging over each of her colleagues' heads as they exited his office. And now it was her turn.

She knew others had put his moods down to the stress of finding Emily, and down to the company — ironically — being on the receiving end of bad PR because of her blog post. It made sense: Pure Brilliant's reputation was sacrosanct to Darren. The pre-eminent PR and events company in Scotland. '*If you can't look good yourself, how will you make others look good?*' was his motto. Appearances were everything.

But to Claire, his moods were nothing new.

He'd always been an ass who didn't give a shit about her. Except this time, she was in charge of Empisoft's conference, a much more complex and high-profile event than the charity and minor fashion gigs she'd worked on these past two years. The next big thing they'd be known for. She might as well have a big bullseye on her chest. Screw up now and...

She didn't even fully understand what Empisoft did. What was data science anyway? She flicked her hair back. Who cares? An event was an event: people, chairs, rooms, screens, drinks, snacks, speakers, entertainment, audio and video, badges and — that which makes or breaks a conference — goodie bags.

And Empisoft's swag rocked.

She had this.

Even before the door closed, Darren barked, 'Where are we?' He reclined in his black leather executive chair and folded his hands behind his head, his short sleeves showing off the muscles he worked hard to maintain. A desk so empty you wondered if he did anything.

'I think it's going well. The venue has confirmed the catering requests made last week. The main logistics all seem on track.'

He leaned forward, his beady eyes on her. 'What's the bad news?'

Claire flinched. Why did there need to be bad news? Why didn't he have confidence in her? How about a little 'Well done, Claire' for a change? She'd never screwed up. Ever. Yet somehow, she was never as good as the others: the boys, Emily; the ones who got to work on what they loved. She pursed her lips and took a deep breath.

'Okay,' she said. 'There are a few small things. I'm having a little trouble with the speaker schedule and who goes where. And interactions with the council on the parking restrictions seem to have disappeared.'

Darren humphed. 'Did you check Emily's files? The parking can become a major issue — particularly with the band.'

Claire bit her lip. 'Yes, I've gone over the file folders and her email. Maybe the stuff is on paper. She was still drawing out the seating plans. Plus, you know how the council like their letters.'

He stroked his goatee, an interconnected tuft of hairs around his narrow-lipped mouth that reminded Claire of a dog's bum. He'd not had it long and Claire reckoned he grew it to make up for losing his hair at the back of his head. It didn't seem to put off other women, though.

'Where are the papers?' he asked.

Claire raised her shoulders. 'I think Emily might have left them at home.'

An awkward silence grew. Darren's hands fell onto the desk. He flexed his biceps as he seemed to ruminate on their options. Claire wanted to run away. After a while, he looked her straight in the eye. 'Get them.'

'What?'

'It's company property. We're entitled to get them.'

'I'm sure that's legally true, Darren,' she said. 'But what the hell am I supposed to do? Bother her parents? "Hello, I'm a colleague from work. Terribly sorry about your loss. Could you let me into you dead daughter's apartment for me to rifle through her things?" Surely you can't expect me to do that?'

'I don't care how you do it. Just do it.'

'I can't.'

He squinted. 'Is this too much for you?'

'That's not fair.' It came out as a whine. God, she hated it when that happened. She took a sharp intake of breath. 'I'm still doing my own job while taking over a huge conference. I'm having to juggle a real and a shadow schedule and keep the press fed with bogus information that will all be superseded on the day—'

'What?'

For a second, Claire regretted letting it slip, but it was too delicious keeping such a secret from him.

'Oops.' She feigned a guilty look. 'The client confided in me. All I can say is there will be a last-minute announcement, which means I have to manage two schedules. And hold the press interested without even telling them something will happen. But it's big.'

His chest puffed up. 'How big? Front-page news big?' Darren was undoubtedly counting the column inches, the new clients this might attract.

'It's big-big.'

'Now we're talking.' He grew a predatory grin. 'Come on, spill.'

'I'm sorry, Darren. The client swore me to secrecy.' Claire pressed her lips together and swiped three pinched fingers from side to side as if zipping her lips shut, but as she turned towards the door, her mouth unzipped into the largest of smiles. The first to exit that room all morning.

13.
ME

Liv popped her head around the door, holding an empty tray. 'Do you still need the room?'

'Hm?' I dragged my eyes from the dozens of squares on the screen; a collage of tweets I'd collected after Suki left, to see for myself what she'd meant. It was vile.

'I wondered why you were still in here. Can I tidy up?' Liv asked.

'Oh yes. I mean, hold on.' I flipped the monitor off, not wanting Liv to get the wrong idea. Brown concentric circles stained the table by my tea mug. I used paper to wipe them off. I pushed my chair closer to the table. 'All yours.'

What I'd seen on Twitter haunted me as I walked to my desk. I'd never been on it before — except for when I'd registered for an account to help Emily stay off the site.

What was the appeal of an online window into people's uncensored souls? I'd warned her more than once to stay away.

I shook my head. The worst thing was it was all fake — even more fake than the so-called reality TV shows people got sucked into. At least with them, you heard proper conversations. Not these fleeting, trite snips of text. This was not language. These were not human relationships. People should stick to real life for those. Or in my case, books.

But Emily's fascination with the reactions to her blog post became an addiction. Because it was about her, even if no one knew that, at first. I remembered her confessing how it gave her a thrill, a voyeuristic rush in watching the hordes coming out to celebrate, to condemn, to question, to like, to share, to fight because of her statements.

As upsetting as her experience with Adam Mooney had been, she loved the idea that she initiated a global debate on consent. She'd even joked she was today's Joan of Arc. She could live with people calling her names and making threats, because she was powering a movement. And she said it was worth it to her to enlighten a whole generation of young women and men, to give them each an insight into the other side.

Then it got ugly. And I'd just witnessed how ugly.

Once they lifted the veil from the actor's mysterious female accuser, the virulence grew. I guessed it became easier to threaten a person once they had a name, a face. An ugly face, according to the nameless, faceless mass. A face that should be grateful Adam Mooney paid it any attention. A fat, flat-chested, cow who should be begging for any male attention. A cunt on legs they'd gladly show what real sexual assault felt like. Bile rose in my throat.

Dozens of pictures of dildos had paraded in front of my eyes, tagged with Emily's name.

I'd worked out the women were no better, wretched jealousy inspiring insult after insult. Making her out to be a pathetic snowflake who'd just had a '*bad date*'. Adam Mooney fans had jumped to defend him. They, in turn, were attacked by those the men would call '*feminazis*' demanding an end to the patriarchy, an end to Adam's career.

I'd followed the news when in the office. Adam had kept a low profile initially. He'd seemed contrite in his public statements yet maintained that this had been a matter of miscommunication. That he believed they were having a nice time. That he had her consent.

My stomach churned. Although Emily admitted she hadn't spoken up until she texted him later to say the experience left her disgusted, he should have noticed her discomfort. He was not innocent in this.

Adam had been careful not to assign any blame to Emily for sharing her story. But when her name came out and she became the victim of such horrific attacks, he'd spoken out. Cynics suggested this was to keep his show running — it had another 3 weeks left.

After her death, he issued a statement that he'd met Emily days before. He said she'd forgiven him. But how could I be certain he was speaking the truth? Emily was no longer here to deny it.

I wracked my brain as to when this supposed meeting could have taken place. Would she have kept that from me? I knew I'd been less than supportive after a while, but it had been to protect her, to get to step away and forget the whole thing ever happened. Was I supposed to believe she gave this man a free pass?

The clock told me I'd spent two hours dredging through the swamp again at my desk. My shoulders were stiff. As much as I finally understood Emily's obsession, this was not the time or the place. I'd already neglected the acquisition and my new software model for too long. I'd been right all along to stay off social media, but now I wasn't done — which meant I would need to break another of my cardinal rules. I stretched my neck and got up.

Above the IT Help Hub in the corner of the office hung a bright blue sign: *Here to help.* I didn't recognise the bearded chap in a checked shirt manning the station. We'd been hiring new people at a ridiculous rate. How was I expected to keep up?

He was hunched over two mobile phones connected with a cable, white letters scrolling over black screens. Unlike other techies, I wasn't interested in how devices worked, hacking them to get better performance or more control. They were a tool. The beauty was in what you did with them.

He smelled of sweat and something sweet I struggled to place.

'Hi,' I said.

The guy jumped.

'Laura. Hi, what can I do for you?'

'Have you got a laptop lying around that I could take home?' I asked.

The look of surprise suggested he was aware of my reputation as a strange one.

'Sure. But if you're going to be modelling from home, you might need one with much bigger processing power.'

'No, it's fine. Make sure it has strong malware and virus protection, though.' He gave me a quizzical look, but probably knew better than to ask the boss what she was up to.

He stood up. 'Give me five minutes to configure it and I'll bring it to your desk.'

'Okay, thanks.'

Where did we find all these nice new people; all these young men and women equally eager to please?

As I stepped away, I caught sight of the news channel streaming on the rear wall. The demonstrators outside the Festival Theatre had grown in number and had gone from those accusing him of assault, to those accusing him of murder: a young woman had killed herself and it was his fault.

I spotted the yellow, high-vis waist coats of the police on the TV, keeping the demonstrators away from the theatre's entrance. Where had they been when Emily needed protection?

Then again, where had I been?

14.
ME

The computer model I'd been working on was buggy. I made some additions earlier in the day that seemed to have made things worse. Like a poet losing the ability to rhyme, my code came out clunky and inefficient. I'd been an early adopter of R, a relatively new way to code, but it wasn't working for me today.

I smiled at a joke I used to make with Justin. '*R: a pirate's favourite programming language.*'

I yawned. My concentration was shot. I'd even taken a little book break and re-joined those poor souls in the prison camp. It didn't help. Their fear in the face of the abuse from the guards left me drained. So much suffering.

And thoughts of suffering just pulled me toward Emily again.

The laptop rested on my desk inviting new investigations. How was it possible that so many threats, so much harassment be directed at someone, yet the instigators got away? I imagined what would happen if I tweeted back; raged about what they'd done to Emily. I shrugged. It was pointless. I'd spent long enough analysing the spats to know that trolls, when challenged by others, always said they were just having '*a little fun.*'

But they were all guilty.

Emily's parents had said the police would look into it, not holding out much hope. From what I'd seen, crimes had been committed. The police had to be doing something, surely?

I placed the new laptop in my rucksack. The way my brain was churning out nonsense, I was useless. I should just go home.

Outside, the cool wind woke my face. A lively group of Italians walked past; their words accentuated by their hands. They wore the yellow plastic ponchos that came with tickets to the Military Tattoo, unwilling to let impending rain dampen their festival spirits.

As I turned the corner into the Meadows, a young woman in a white-aproned, light-blue dress and black headband thrust a colourful leaflet into my hand.

'A modern retelling of Alice in Wonderland tonight at 5 o'clock,' she said. Too polite to refuse it, I glanced at the description, knowing full well I wouldn't attend the show.

The title in large yellow letters read *Down the Rabbit Hole*. They'd stapled a strip of paper onto the leaflet: a five-star review by the Scotsman. *'A dizzying journey into the world of societal expectations and interpersonal relationships.'*

I wondered what Lewis Carroll would make of this interpretation.

The leaflet said the play was staged in The Emplacement, a name I recognised as nothing more than a portacabin in the grounds of the Pleasance; an Edinburgh University-owned sandstone warren of bars, rooms and theatre venues that served as a student association during term time and exploded into a teeming hub of creativity in the summer. Queues of waiting audience members often snaked their way around the courtyard and onto the street.

St Leonard's police station sprung to mind. It was a stone's throw from there. Like Edinburgh's many sites glamorised by film and television, the station was marked on maps as a tourist destination for fans of Scottish crime fiction. I figured St Leonard's would have been put on Emily's case, since she lived Southside.

Why not pay them a visit?

I took a left towards George Street Gardens, another public space invaded by the Fringe and turned into, quite literally, a circus. A dazzling multicoloured, mirrored tent stood in the middle of the grassy square. Noise rose in stark contrast to the surrounding University buildings, which lay dormant. How many times had I walked across this square to go to lectures? I calculated an estimate for my four years studying computer science.

Loud music insulted my ears as I approached the Pear Tree. The sight of the outdoor beer garden — full of happy people — knocked the air from my lungs. I could still see Emily sitting there, with her friends on a sunny day. I'd watched, once, willing myself to join. The tip of her long hair had fallen into her pint. She'd raised it into a ponytail, shaking her head, and spotted me. Tears welled in my eyes as I remembered her broad smile and enthusiastic wave. Her friends had looked up like a multi-headed beast. Intimidated, I'd pointed at my school bag and my watch.

How could I have given up time with her?

I walked on. A blue-and-white checked sign hung outside the red brick Police Scotland building. I wiped a moist palm against my thigh; it was my first visit to a police station. The large glass façade invited me in.

Chairs lined three of the four walls, all occupied. I seemed to have hit upon a busy time. Perhaps it was always like this? I excused myself as I slipped through the various groups towards a booth in the far corner; a glass partition with a built-in microphone and a gap at the bottom for documents. The chair behind it was empty. The nerves on my neck prickled. I searched for instructions. A small bell protruded from behind a poster warning people about the dangers of drugs. I pressed it.

A young man with spiky hair appeared, his tie oddly formal against his casual short-sleeved shirt. 'How can I help?'

'My name is Laura Flett. My friend Emily Nairn died on the thirteenth.'

The young man's eyebrows shot up.

I gave him a small smile and said, 'I'd like to speak to the officer in charge of the investigation.'

'Nairn, was it? Like the town?' He hit his keyboard. 'Um, the investigation into her death appears to be closed. Was there something specific you needed?'

Closed. My stomach dropped. 'But there is evidence...'

'Are you saying you have new evidence in the case?' he asked.

I didn't like to bluff, but I wouldn't let them fob me off. 'Yes. May I please meet with the relevant person?'

He returned to his keyboard. 'DI Reddy was the last person listed.' He picked up the phone. After some unintelligible mumbles, he confirmed Reddy would be on his way down.

There was nowhere to sit. I hung about, trying not to eavesdrop on conversations of those I suspected from their dishevelled appearance and the wafts of alcohol emanating from their bodies weren't here for the first time. I paced, leaned against the wall, paced again.

When my name was called, I spun round and my eyes raced along a line of bodies, instinctively looking for someone white, middle-aged, with a receding hairline and in dire need of exercise. A man waved me over. I gasped and cursed myself for being so stupid. The policeman was tall and thin, his jet-black hair shaved neatly at the sides, his dark skin creased into even darker lines around his eyes pointing at the puffy bags underneath.

I walked towards the door where he stood, thinking I'd be taken through to a room. He introduced himself as Detective Inspector Raavi Reddy, crossed his arms and asked, 'What's this about?'

'Is there nowhere to go?'

'We're full up.'

'I'm enquiring about your investigation into Emily Nairn's death. She was my best friend and she died because she was viciously harassed. The officer at the desk said the investigation was closed.'

His face softened 'I'm sorry for your loss. You must understand, there wasn't much to investigate. Your friend took her own life. I was told you had new evidence?'

My chest burned and I hoped the heat wouldn't rise to my face. 'I have been looking at the online attacks on Emily and there were rape threats and threats of violence against her. Surely that's a crime?'

He sighed. 'Yes. Many people don't realise that anything that's illegal offline is also illegal online.'

'Why are you not doing anything?'

His eyes narrowed. 'It's more complicated than that. Much of it is anonymous, people hiding behind fake identities. We've examined the abuse directed at your friend. It was gruesome. It clearly impacted her heavily. We researched the IP addresses that we could find. That's like a computer address—'

'I know what an IP address is. I'm the founder of Empisoft. I'm a data scientist. That's why I think we could do more with what's online.'

His eyes shot open. He straightened up and pulled me into a quieter corner.

'You know as well as I do how difficult it is to get behind people's real identities. You're right, the crimes that were committed led to a heartbreaking and unnecessary death. And I'm truly sorry for her family and for you. If only she'd come to us earlier.' He caught himself when my jaw fell. 'I'm not assigning any blame, of course, but this is a very tricky situation. She never made a complaint. It's too late.'

'Shouldn't they still be punished? The guys who... Shouldn't she have justice?'

'I would love for there to always be justice. But even her parents aren't seeking that. We explained the situation, what it would take, the obstacles... They've been understandably shaken by the experience and would much rather move on than to have things drawn out, only to end up with at best an unsatisfactory result.'

'Why unsatisfactory?'

He used the little patience he seemed to have left to convey the hopelessness of his predicament.

'This isn't a simple case of harassment, with a single culprit. This was a loose army coming together with a single target. Even if we could list all the profiles whose threats had indirectly contributed to Emily's death, and even if we were able to get a court order forcing Twitter to disclose their whereabouts, what are we meant to do? They're scattered across the globe. I'm sorry but with the victim dead — and there being no direct danger anymore — we would never get the resources to go after them, let alone cross borders. That's "unsatisfactory". Even if we suspended their accounts, nothing would stop them setting up new ones.'

'What about local accounts? The person who identified Emily from the photo must know her, must be local.'

He raised his shoulders. 'It's not illegal to name someone on a photo online. We checked and neither that person nor the one who posted the original picture of Emily with Adam Mooney made any threats. The work associated with even filtering out the messages that cross the line — a fairly wide grey area in fact — is not something for which we could ever gather the resources in the current climate. Look around, we're struggling to police the streets of Edinburgh at festival time, let alone the whole Internet. I understand your frustration. Believe me, I feel it too.'

I clenched my fists. I opened my mouth, but Reddy put up a hand to silence me.

'Miss Flett, we looked at her emails; we looked at her Twitter; we visited her flat.'

'You searched her flat?'

'Yes, it took us a while to get officers allocated, so we'd had to ask her parents to leave the flat untouched. We got the keys from the landlord. We didn't find anything we wouldn't expect to find in the apartment of a single young woman going through a difficult time. We've been in contact with her parents in Peebles. We have jointly agreed to close the investigation. Now, if you'll excuse me.'

'What if I can help? I have skills. This can't be all.'

Reddy blew out a deep, nicotine breath. At least that cliché was intact, I thought. 'Your time is yours to waste, if that's what you want. I would advise you to move on, however. Find some peace. Let the grieving process run its course.' He fished a business card from his pocket. 'But if you can't let it go, and if you find something, get in touch.'

15.
ME

If cats had a built-in clock for feeding times, Atticus's was broken. The fact that I was home earlier than usual did not impact his routine of jumping off the sofa to greet me at the door and circling my legs meowing, ushering me to the kitchen.

Coming home early, I expected I might catch him in some energetic activity, sniffing around, playing with the many fuzzy toys lying around. It appeared not.

I placed my bag on the table and hunched down to give him a scratch behind the ears. 'Hi, buddy. I've still got some work to do.' Atticus cocked his head. 'Yes, I know. I've even got a new computer.'

The device's lead was tangled in some of the rubbish I carried around. I had to empty my bag to be able to plug it in. I moved a few piles of books — my normal evening companions — from the table onto the sofa to clear a working area.

The hinge was still a little tight when I lifted the laptop's lid. I powered up the machine, grateful to find that the Helpdesk guy had prepared it for immediate use. I punched in my login and password. An error message appeared: *No network access.* It asked if I wanted to set up a local profile. In the bottom right hand corner of the screen was a WiFi icon with a question mark. I always thought people were exaggerating when they slapped their forehead yet it's exactly what I did at this point. I didn't have any Internet at home. Why would I?

I clicked on the icon and saw that all my neighbours had WiFi. But they were all securely protected. Now what? I couldn't very well go round asking to piggyback on their network. I scrolled to the bottom of the list, to an open access point called Café Marchmont. The signal was faint, but it might do.

Fat droplets of rain were sliding down the window, making the prospect of walking to the café most unsavoury. What had started out as drizzle on my walk home from the police station had amplified into a torrent. As if the gods were conspiring against me.

Maybe the policeman was right? Maybe it was going to be a big waste of time.

Atticus jumped up on the table not best pleased at the new competitor for my attention. Once he felt the heat radiating from the computer, however, he seemed to decide the keyboard was the place to be. 'No Atticus, not here. I have to go.' I plopped my cat on the floor, closed the lid and grabbed my raincoat.

The café was only around the corner. I shot in and asked for an Earl Grey to go. The WiFi password was on a blackboard on the wall. *Marchmontguest*. Hardly secure. At least it was easy to remember. I paid for the drink and returned home.

Once connected, I was able to log in. I entered Twitter again, the viper's nest, and started to take a note of frequent harassers. The tweets led to others and to others again, each user replying to an ever-growing list of accounts. And Emily. They all tagged her, making her a party to every insult, every condemnation, every threat.

How would it have been at the receiving end? I examined the feeds of some of those who'd been nasty to Emily. They were filled with innocuous content: statements about upcoming movie releases, pictures of kittens, pouting selfies. How could seemingly normal people become such animals?

Would Emily have minded the assault from the women more than that from the men?

I continued my note taking. It became unwieldy. As the messages were replied to and shared, re-tweeted, and replied to again, I understood why the police would have struggled. It was too vast a network, with too many connections. How would you separate out those who threatened versus those who only shared? Those who spewed venom versus those who mindlessly shared things they vaguely agreed with?

My heart jumped when I recognised what I was looking at: a universe of words, with feelings. My expertise. If Empisoft could identify pockets of dissatisfaction and anger among employees, what was to stop me doing the same on Twitter — finding the most poisonous pools?

The tea had coursed through me, but a full bladder wasn't about to slow me down. All I had to do was get all that data into one place to let my software run on it: all those messages, their senders, the time, and who they'd tagged.

It was too much to gather manually. I opened the browser window and loaded Github. Thank God for this code-sharing site. It was bound to have what I needed. I rummaged through the building blocks developed by other data scientists. Nobody I knew ever started from scratch anymore, when so much code was available, free to use.

I checked the many entries for *scrapers*. I dismissed the majority of the programmes, which seemed tailored to help people fetch the various prices for a product from different retail sites. One entry seemed closer to what I needed: a script to fetch strings of text of a particular shape. But it wasn't quite right for letting loose on Twitter, with its vastness and unique structure. I thought of how I could configure the code to get me what I wanted. I sighed. There was a risk I would still end up with an immense amount of data because I would hoover up anything even remotely connected to the profiles identified. It would be a lot easier if I could enter from the most relevant point: Emily's account.

I was confident that if I set my mind to it, I would be able to hack Emily's password, but I realised there might be an easier way.

I reached for my phone.

Claire picked up on the second ring.

'It's Laura Flett.'

'Have you got news on the acquisition?'

'No, that's not why I am calling.' My pulse quickened. I adopted a casual sing-songy voice. 'I was wondering what happened to Emily's laptop. The police had a look at it, but I think it's been returned to the company?'

'Why would you want her laptop? If there are files you're after, I have access now. If you let me know what you're looking for—'

I didn't have a ready excuse; the truth would have to do. I plucked up the courage for the strange request.

'I want to be able to access her social media without her password. I'm looking into the harassment.'

'For the police? They asked you to do this?'

I hesitated. 'I'm seeing if I can give them more information,' I hoped I sounded natural. It wasn't a lie, and if my wording made Claire believe it was for the police, what harm was there?

'I don't know, Laura. Aside from the fact that I don't know where the laptop is, I'm not sure this is appropriate.'

She had a point, of course. You couldn't just access someone's social media just because they were dead any more than it would be appropriate to read their diary. Social media platforms would shut accounts down on proof of death but would only give someone else access if there was evidence of a living will; if in life you had appointed someone you wanted to give access to once you'd passed.

While I was trying to come up with some convincing reasoning, Claire said, 'Let me ask you this... Can you get into Emily's flat?'

Why did Emily's flat matter? Could Claire know where Emily had written down her passwords?

'Yes, I have the keys. Why?'

Claire's voice went to a whisper. 'I need to find some papers which I think are at her place. If you meet me there, I'll try to get my hands on her computer. Deal?'

The trade-off seemed fair.

'Deal.'

After hanging up, I went to the toilet and fed Atticus in preparation for a long night of coding.

16.
NOW SUKI

The Madainn office was at Rutland Square, tucked away behind the busy intersection of Princes Street and Lothian Road. It was one of the many discrete pockets of wealth management in the city; understated Georgian architecture reassuring the old money it was safe while giving the new money the opportunity to feel part of the institution. To have arrived.

After the walk from home that morning, Suki's feet were killing her. Her heels didn't suffer the cobbled street of Edinburgh well, but she was damned if she was going to be treated like a short arse. Besides, her Louboutins had become her trademark. She thought of the other pair she'd been seduced by — crocodile, with thin ankle straps — but her bank balance didn't allow it. Not yet.

Her pointy heels sank into the plush yellow carpet of the corridor to Angus's office. She could sense his insincerity leaking through the ornate mahogany door; the brass knob's ridged motif smoothed by a hundred years of clammy hands. Why had he summoned her for a progress report? She knocked.

Diane, the firm's other partner, sat in one of two armchairs opposite Angus's large desk. With all the other projects Suki had worked on, she'd only ever dealt with one partner, but Empisoft was a biggie.

And it was hers.

'Come sit, Suki.' Diane patted the back of the empty chair, her diamond solitaire casting bright rainbows on the walls.

Angus sat at his desk, positioned so as to be regally framed by a tall window with blue velvet curtains. By Suki's side stood a bar, a stand supporting a nineteenth century-style globe that opened to reveal three bottles of whisky and a set of tumblers. Suki didn't know if he used it often — perhaps only with clients — though a faint peaty scent always hung in the air. Angus's porous nose and surrounding ruddy complexion alluded more to lunchtime port than to whisky.

'Diane and I were looking at this month's numbers and wanted to get an update on the PeopleForce deal,' Angus said. Sweat glistened on his forehead.

Always about money. Corporate finance was a funny business, with lumpy, unpredictable revenues. There could be months without sufficient fees coming in to cover the exorbitant overheads of a fancy office and the staff of twelve. Summer was invariably tricky. If you hadn't completed the deal by the end of June, chances were it would drag on well into September by the time all the players had returned from their holidays. December on the other hand, usually provided a giant kick up the arse — with the financial windfall to match. Everybody was incentivised to put in the hours night and day to avoid working over Christmas. It also marked the end of the tax year for foreign investors, so there was no option but to get it done.

Suki didn't need the notes she'd brought. She was fully in control. 'The amended Heads of Terms have been verbally approved by both parties,' she said. 'PeopleForce's lawyers are looking through the files we've uploaded into the data room holding the details of the previous investment rounds. There are a few pieces missing, nothing major.'

'Are we still looking at early September?' asked Diane.

'Justin is keen to be able to announce the deal at the conference,' Suki replied. 'PeopleForce's CEO has been lined up to fly over for the event. I think they want to get as much PR out of this as they can.'

'Yes, we know,' said Angus. His brown eyes bored into her. 'The reason we're getting a little nervous is that there's not much time left. We should be past the due diligence by now. What's the hold-up?'

What's with the questions? The partners' conspiratorial glances suggested they knew something that she didn't. 'The main thing that's been delayed is the details about the R&D projects. We'd given them some info early on. With the latest write-ups, they're getting a better look at it. If anything, the product pipeline still looks as if it has the potential to increase the company's valuation.'

Suki straightened her shoulders. It was important to remain confident and bullish at all times. Doubt was for the weak. And once you're weak, you're dinner.

'Smashing,' said Angus. 'However, if we're going to change the terms of the deal, we'll have to act quickly. Has this all been documented?'

'It's in hand. Kind of. The R&D lead, Laura Flett has had... let's call it a personal crisis.'

Diane threw her arms in the air. 'Great timing.'

Suki squirmed. Nice empathy there. Although empathy was not what financiers were known for.

Never missing a chance to take the bull by the horns, Suki asked, 'Is there anything else going on here? In my mind, everything is under control.'

Angus wiped his forehead with a handkerchief and folded the fabric into small squares. 'Diane has told me about a conversation she overheard in London, in the lounge of the Institute of

Directors on Pall Mall. Some Americans talking too loudly. Damn fools. Apparently PeopleForce have also been courting Yellowsoft.'

Suki took a breath. This was bad news. If PeopleForce's lot were also talking to Empisoft's biggest competitor, this could mean she was being played. She'd have to up her game.

'Do we know how far along they are?' Suki asked, ready to talk war tactics.

'No,' said Angus. 'It may be that they're only plan B. It's essential that we get there first. I don't need to remind you that this is a hugely valuable deal for us. The price stands at $100 million. These are not the kinds of valuations we see every day in Scotland.'

'Our fee could keep us going for two whole years, after our bonuses.' Diane drew a circle with a finger between the three of them.

Suki didn't need reminding of the bonuses. This was the first deal in which she would get a share of the pot. She was the first senior associate to ever get a percentage of a fee. But she was the one who'd introduced the firm to some of the bigger players in Silicon Valley, including PeopleForce. It was *her* network, carefully cultivated during her MBA that persuaded the suitors to come in with the bids they got. With a one-hundred-million-dollar deal, Suki would take home two hundred grand — over one hundred and sixty thousand pounds in real money. And for every thousand more, she would get ten percent of the firm's commission.

Well, if those fuckers in San Francisco thought they could get one over on her, they had another think coming.

'I'm on it. I'll do everything I need to get this over the line. I'll sit on Laura's desk if I have to.'

Diane patted her knee. 'Good girl.'

'Apparently we're meant to call you "women" now,' Angus said, no doubt referring to Justin's rebuke.

Diane threw her arms to the heavens once more. 'Oh, for fuck's sake!'

17.
ME

The key ring lay on the café table, its metal cat winking as sunshine flickered past. I kept a firm watch on the main door to Emily's tenement across the street. I hadn't wanted to wait for Claire inside; it was too painful.

A dried tear track tickled my cheek. I sipped at my tea.

I started to worry I'd gotten the time wrong. The clock and my watch both showed 8:10. We'd agreed to meet before work — hardly my favourite time of day. But today was always going to be horrible.

Finally, I caught a glimpse of Claire from behind, looking up at Emily's first-floor window. I sprung from my seat and sprinted across the road. 'I'm here.'

'Hi, Laura. Are you ready for this?'

I shrugged. 'As ready as I'll ever be. Emily's parents asked me to go in and pick anything, any mementos that I might want to keep before they send some packers in. I haven't had the courage. Maybe having you here will make it easier.'

A look of panic crossed Claire's face. 'I haven't got much time. I'm only here for the papers.'

I stepped forward and inserted the key in the door. 'It's fine. I just meant, you know, not being alone going in.'

Claire placed her hand on my shoulder. 'Okay.' I twitched.

We climbed the stairs in silence, my heart speeding up with every step.

When I opened the flat door, we were met with the stale smell of neglect. Claire hesitated before following me in. I cracked open a window.

'I've never been here before,' she said.

'It didn't use to be like this.'

Claire scanned the room. 'I can imagine. I know she'd been holed up here for some time before...'

'I did visit. I visited a few times. I never thought she would do what she did.'

I didn't know why I needed to justify myself; Claire was only here for some files. Had she even been friends with Emily? I stroked the ribbed top of the sofa, dents marking where our heads had jerked back in laughter so many times.

'I'll have a look around in between the papers, shall I?' she asked.

'Sure,' I said. Not that it was my job to give permission.

The rottenest stench drew me to the kitchen.

Jesus, what a state. I'd swear Emily had been hoarding ready-meal packaging. I followed my nose to the sink, where green rolling mounds of mould covered decomposing teabags and breakfast oats. I looked in the lower cabinet for rubber gloves and fetched the grey compost bin. I scooped the putrid pile out, holding my breath. A splash of cold water took care of the rest.

How did it get so bad so quickly?

I felt compelled to restore order, as if undoing the decay might reverse time and bring Emily back. I gathered the empty plastic tubs and opened the tall stainless-steel bin. A purple dildo stared at me with a bulbous eye.

A hot flush coursed through my chest and up my cheeks. This wasn't the sort of thing friends should see. Why would she...? When she was planning...?

Claire appeared out of nowhere. 'I've got the files.'

I let go of the bin's lid. It snapped shut with a clang, making me jump.

'Are you okay?' She frowned. 'You look like you've seen a ghost.' She raised her hand to her mouth, eyebrows arched. 'God, sorry, I mean... is everything okay?'

'Yes, it's nothing... There was a dead mouse in the bin.'

'Ew. Lemme see.'

Before I could stop her, Claire lifted the lid. 'Oh...'

'Please leave it,' I said. 'I don't think we should—'

'Why are there two?'

'Two?'

Claire took a fork from the worktop and pushed the purple dildo aside to reveal the tip of a pink one lower down. 'I'm all for a girl's best friend, but *two*? And why would Emily throw them away?'

'I don't think we should—'

She kept poking at the thing with that fork. 'It's light. Like there's no batteries inside,' she said. 'And they look brand new.'

I desperately tried to blank the idea of what a not-so-new sex toy would look like. None of this made sense. I needed it to make sense. 'Emily was fanatical about recycling. She would have removed them.' I cringed. 'Please, leave it alone.'

Claire stepped back. 'Okay. Speaking of recycling, shall I throw away the magazines?' She gestured to the living room.

'Yes, thanks, the blue box is over there.'

I distracted myself by emptying the fridge, and burying my shocking find with whatever rubbish lay about. Sod the environment.

'Hey Laura, check this out.' Claire stood over the blue recycling bin that held a neat row of flattened cardboard.

'What is it?'

She fished a box out and held it up so that I could see the writing on it. *The Bitch*. 'I think some asshole sent her a gift.' She nodded towards the bin.

My stomach churned. 'You mean the...?' How could the police have missed this? Reddy said they'd visited... Did they not do a full search? His voice echoed in my head: *'too late'* ... *'no complaint'* ... *'no resources.'*

'There's no address or anything,' Claire said. 'It's a recycled Amazon box. There's a torn-off barcode. My sense is this was hand-delivered.'

My heart raced. 'We have to tell the police. How could they have missed that?' I remembered Reddy's *'nothing we wouldn't expect to find in the apartment of a single woman.'* I felt ashamed for Emily. The assumptions they obviously made...

Claire handed me the box. 'I agree. If that bastard made it to her flat, they might be able to find him.' She placed a hand on the worktop and sighed. She peeked into the chaotic living area. 'Poor Emily, having her name and address on the Internet like that. I can see why she felt vulnerable, desperate. And then this... I wish she'd realised it would never last. This would have blown over in time.' She turned away. 'These things always do.'

'It didn't sound like a flash-in-the-pan kind of thing when I last looked online.' I said, then remembered why she was here. 'Did you bring the laptop?'

'No, the IT guy said the police still had it. Something about forty-two days? I thought you would've known that.' My stomach fell. 'But I got you the next best thing,' she said.

Claire walked towards the chair that held her bag. 'It's lucky the chap has a crush on me — he wouldn't stop talking. He said that once she'd been identified, Emily received lots of emails. Really, really disgusting ones. She'd gone to him and he set up a filter, so the emails got blocked. They were purged every day, meaning the only thing he'd been able to give the police was the last day's worth. He said he doubted they'd make any sense of it because he'd had a nosey himself and the email addresses were all untraceable. Gmails and suchlike.' She pulled an iPad from her bag. 'Ta da! Emily had brought it for repair weeks ago. It was only when I spoke to him that he remembered he had it waiting for her.' She handed it to me. 'No one can find out, okay?'

I stuck the device under my arm. 'Is there a screen lock?'

'No, I asked him to take it off. He wasn't happy. He's worried he'll get caught. He's already had the boss on his case because the company's website crashed after people started attacking it. It was down for two days. I managed to calm him down. Convinced him it would help Emily. I think he liked her, too.'

'Why did they attack the website?'

'Who knows,' she shrugged. 'I guess they wanted to attack Emily any way they could think of. Darren was furious, spitting that it made the agency look like amateurs.' Claire shook her head. 'Anyway, I promised to return it in three days. Okay? Though it doesn't sound like you'll find much.'

I clutched the iPad to my chest. The police may not have found anything, but they didn't have my skills, my determination. I would find the harassers. I would find the trolls responsible for Emily's death. She deserved that much at least.

18.
ME

A green sticker on the conference phone in front of me read *Salsa room*. It was the furthest meeting spot from Empisoft's open plan office and backed onto the kitchen of the restaurant next door, originally a Mexican *cantina*. Justin and I had been inspired by the pervasive smell of lunchtime burritos when baptising the room. But with the Mexican now a vegan café and Empisoft hiring people at such a furious space, hardly anyone knew. I smiled as I remembered overhearing Liv explain to a newcomer it was meant ironically: the space being so small you could hardly turn around in it, let alone dance.

Closing the door, I felt a pang of guilt. I should work on the acquisition. It was our priority. But it was hard to resist the lure of Emily's portal to the data I was itching to collect.

I pushed the phone to one side of the desk and positioned Emily's iPad to face me. I'd wanted to hole myself away at home with it, but my lack of broadband would have slowed me down. I pressed on the home button, grateful for Claire's foresight in removing the screen lock. A lack of icons revealed they'd also removed access to Emily's corporate files and emails but that wasn't what I was after, anyway.

I opened the browser and went to Twitter. Emily's profile loaded without a hitch, her password loading automatically. Pure

Brilliant were clearly laxer in their security: that would be a sackable offence here. No wonder their website had been an easy target.

My stomach fluttered. I'd rewritten my scraping software to run on Apple's mobile operating system rather than a laptop but wasn't sure it would work. My plan was to use Emily's Twitter account as a starting point. Once in, I could also check if Emily had received direct messages, though I couldn't imagine her having been stupid enough to follow those who were attacking her — and you couldn't receive messages from anyone you didn't follow.

An error warning flashed at the top of the screen.

Your tweet was not sent.

Intuitively, I clicked on the unsent message. It was dated the morning of Emily's death and showed a stock photo of Adam Mooney. Above it, Emily had written:

Leave Adam alone. We spoke. All is forgiven. #peace.

A chill ran over my shoulders.

Peace?

Had Emily wanted to grant forgiveness before ending her life?

I scratched my scalp. We hadn't been raised particularly religiously. Perhaps the vicar's speeches at school assemblies and the obligatory singing of hymns had a bigger influence on Emily than I'd have expected. My heart sank. Perhaps I hadn't known Emily as well I thought. Perhaps if I had, I could've stopped her. Maybe if I'd popped round the night before... read the signs more...?

I swallowed to hold back tears. I had a job to do.

The Hollywood star's face stared back at me, smooth skin masking the monster inside. Why hadn't Emily told me about meeting him again? It must have been a big deal. What could they have said?

I knew from his statements that he'd been mortified when he'd read Emily's version of events on the blog. His recollection of the truth was entirely different.

Was there even a single truth? I wondered.

That horrible blog had laid out the goings-on between them that night in graphic detail. I remembered Emily calling me, shocked at just how graphic. She'd expected her interview to have been edited, sanitised by the blog's author. And she'd been so ashamed.

I could still picture Emily curled in the corner of her sofa, biting the corner of her cushion, saliva darkening the blue silk in an ever-expanding semicircle. '*They found my name. And now Mum has read it all too,*' she'd howled.

Her mum. Only I could understand the immensity. Deb was not the most liberal women at the best of times, turning a blind eye to any 'boy stuff', pretending sex didn't exist. What had it done to her to witness her daughter's debauchery there, in Technicolour, for all to see?

That damn blog. I grimaced recalling its salacious title: '*The unwanted dick of Adam Mooney*'. Its vile paragraphs were etched into my memory. How they'd described Adam pouncing on Emily like a lion the minute she entered his hotel room. How, being simultaneously exhilarated at being in his presence yet shaken by his sudden advances, she went to freshen up in the bathroom — a move it seemed he'd misinterpreted. When she returned, he was on the sofa, his trousers off, his penis erect, waiting expectantly. Emily jokingly called him cowboy and told him he might want to slow down. He covered up and they kissed for a bit. But his caresses had grown more insistent, his tongue more probing, and before long he slid down to the floor and buried his head between her legs.

It asked, *Was it at this point she should've said 'no'?*

I shook my head. If it was up to half the Internet, she shouldn't ever have agreed to enter the room. She should have known what messages she was giving off. Yet this implied male ability to mind-read signs of seduction seemed to conveniently stop when Emily was trying to transmit other, non-verbal messages.

How could they blame *her*?

She'd squirmed. She'd wriggled. She pulled him back up to her eye line. Yet as his lips smothered her face in her own juices, his heavy body writhed against her. She held her two hands against his chest, pushing him away gently.

Adam had ignored her. The blogger had clearly relished in describing how he climbed onto the sofa and straddled her, his knees locking her thighs. He'd stretched his tall body upwards until his throbbing cock reached her mouth. With both hands, he smoothed her hair and flipped it behind her ears — a detail no one needed. He'd kissed the top of her head and pulled her forward.

At this point, it read, Emily didn't think she could say 'no' anymore, even though she wanted to: he'd gone down on her — even if she hadn't wanted that.

So yes, she sucked him off. It took no more than a half-hearted attempt for him to orgasm — this revelation had delighted the online trolls. Emily had said good night then and left.

Only then.

'LAURA?' JUSTIN'S deep voice startled me. 'What are you doing in here? I've been looking everywhere for you.' He wormed his body around the door of the tiny room.

I failed to shield the iPad in time. He stuck out his lower lip. 'Twitter? You?'

He searched my face. I had never lied to him. Not in all these years. And I didn't particularly want to start now.

'Yes, sorry.' I stared at the iPad mounted on the stand and fiddled with the wireless keyboard. 'I wanted to check something... About Emily.'

Justin crouched beside me and swivelled my chair to face him. 'I know you're hurting.' His voice softened. 'I can't imagine what you're going through. But we're worried about you. *I'm* worried about you. You don't look so hot.'

'I never look hot.' I quipped. 'And definitely not compared to the girls you take out.'

Justin laughed, gave me a small slap on the knee. His smile faded. 'Seriously, Laura, what the hell are you doing? I don't want to be an ass, but we're waiting for you to finish documenting the R&D projects.'

'You're right. This can wait.' As I moved to shut down the machine, I spotted a detail I'd overlooked. 'Hold on. There's a tweet Emily planned to send the morning she died, but it didn't go.' I pointed at the small lettering at the bottom of the message. 'The time stamp. It was *after*. See? 8:40. She couldn't have sent this...' I pushed myself back from the screen, my pulse throbbing in my throat. 'Who sent this?'

'Hey, calm down. Let me see.' He leaned forward. 'She might have programmed it to go at that time, and it failed. No biggie.'

'Can you do that?'

'Yes, there's a thing called TweetDeck. Here, scoot over.'

I rolled my chair to the side while Justin took control.

'Do you want to sit?' I asked.

'No, I can't stay. But now I'm intrigued.' He tapped through various screens like a pro. 'Oh my God.'

'What is it?'

'Here. There are six scheduled messages that never went out.'

The screen showed a list of greyed-out snippets of text with little red exclamation marks. Justin stepped away and pulled his phone from his pocket giving me the opportunity to examine the iPad.

I clicked on the first message. An animation of a beating heart appeared underneath Emily's words:

_I'm sorry, my darlings. Love you always @RachelB75, @Shalini_G26, and my bestie @LFP. Forgive me._

The room swirled. Was this Emily's way of saying goodbye to her friends? Her bestie... me. I'd had to choose something when I set up the account and couldn't come up with anything better than Laura Flett from Peebles; @LFP. Transfixed, I clicked on the next one. An image of a pointed gun, its deep, dark barrel dripping with menace.

You are NOT forgiven. Burn in hell #slutshamers

This was followed by a long list of names in blue, all starting with @. She was outing those who'd shamed her, shaming them in return. The next four messages were all the same, listing more names, more anonymous trolls. Was this the list I should be looking at? The men who had pushed her over the edge? Had Emily deliberately narrowed it down for me?

'Mystery solved.' Justin pointed at his mobile. 'TweetDeck had a service outage that morning. For about an hour none of the programmed tweets were sent.' He shook his head. 'My God, what are the odds?'

'All these messages... Her last words... Not spoken. I can't believe it,' I said.

Justin put his hand on my shoulder, still staring at the screen. 'Look at that list. Those bastards have blood on their hands.'

I clicked on the last unsent message. A photo of the purple dildo in the bin popped up, catching Justin off-guard. 'What the...?'

'Somebody brought that to her. There were two in the bin in her apartment. I'm going to tell the police.'

'Good. Leave it to them. I don't think you should be digging anymore, Laura. It's not good for you. You'll never catch whoever it is. They're all anonymous; hiding behind their keyboard. Small pricks wanting to feel big, each showing off in front of the other. You won't bring her back. Don't let them eat you up, too.'

I stared at him. 'What about her last words? Don't we owe it to her to send them out?'

His jaw fell. He cupped my chin in his hand, like a concerned father. 'We can't do that. That's ghoulish. Can you imagine what would kick off? No, let it go.'

I shook my face free. 'I guess you're right.'

'Come with me. Let work distract you. And when we've made our millions, you can spend them on the best hackers money can buy to get your revenge.'

He stepped towards the door, pulling at my limp arm. I had just enough time to call up my software on the screen with my loose hand and press *Enter*.

19.
ME

'I still can't believe you got us a meeting with Adam Mooney,' I said to Claire.

I shielded my eyes from the sun bouncing off the glass façade of the Festival Theatre across the street. Posters of the many plays that would grace its stage over the coming months hung invisibly suspended behind the clear panels in a colourful matrix, a giant portrait of Adam bang in the centre.

Eight doors placed in an arc made up the entrance. Each door was wide, with curved brass handles. Wide and inviting. Why was I afraid to go in?

Two women with square-shaped, pink, woollen hats were all that was left of the angry protest mob. Who knows what new injustices the others had gone on to battle? The two sat on the concrete steps, pouring themselves a steaming drink from a flask while half-heartedly holding up signs. My eye was drawn to the bigger one.

Go home, perv.

Perv was scrawled in white on a piece of black duct tape whose length suggested they'd started with a longer insult. What would it have been? Assaulter? Rapist?

I scoffed. The authorities might be unable to cope with hateful online harassment, yet the slanderous slogans of peaceful protesters... *that* they knew how to censor. Or perhaps Adam had threatened to sue, as was often the case with Americans.

'There are some perks to working in PR,' Claire said, gently nudging my elbow to take advantage of a lull in traffic on busy Nicholson street. 'Pure Brilliant was involved in the gala opening of his play. I pulled a few strings.'

I fell back as Claire bounded up the steps.

'What is it?' she asked.

It was difficult to explain. Adam Mooney wasn't fully real before. Not just because he was a big, famous movie star, but because through this whole nightmare, he had become larger than life, a mythical beast to be slain — or protected depending on whose side you were on. Emily had forgiven him, but what did that mean for me?

'It's okay, Laura.' Claire waved me over. 'He's expecting you. When he found out you were Emily's best friend, he told his people to make it happen. I'm not saying it was easy...' She paused. Was she expecting a compliment? My gratitude? I stayed quiet.

She added, 'In fact I have a small favour to ask in return.'

I joined her. 'Really?'

'You know I'm having to maintain two different programmes for the conference: the public one, and the secret one, for when the acquisition is announced. I don't have a problem with that in principle, and I've kept it to myself. But it would be *so* much easier if I could speak freely to your marketing peeps because I don't want to be making all the decisions myself.'

'You can't do that. They don't even know about the deal,' I said.

'What about Justin? Can I talk to him?'

I shook my head. 'He'd have a fit if he knew I'd told you. Besides, he's got enough on his plate.'

She pointed at me; one bony finger extended 'Which leaves you. I need you to keep me completely informed of what is going on —

and I mean completely-completely informed. Because I'm proceeding on the assumption this deal is going to be announced at the conference. And if anything changes, that could cause some real problems for me. I only have a *fake* plan B at this stage.'

I shrugged. It wasn't an unfair request. 'Fine.'

Deal done, Claire pulled me towards the building.

I was glad that at least this wasn't where Adam and Emily had met. I wasn't sure I'd be able to face that. The opening party had been held in a nearby hotel. Emily had told me she could go because her electronics client had sponsored the event and were milking all the PR they could out of Adam using their smart watch in his latest film. She'd been drunk with excitement. A proper A-list party. If only she'd known.

We entered the foyer and were ushered up the grand central staircase by a waiting staffer, her angel-curled blonde hair swishing along her back like a metronome as she climbed. A uniformed cleaner hoovered the steps. I moved aside, my hand grabbing the bannister still tacky with what smelled like citrus Dettol. We followed the woman to the left, past the wine bar, past a row of framed photos of the sets of yesteryear, and into a corridor that led us backstage. The amber carpet was a lot scuzzier here. I noticed the walls were bare, too.

'It's still a few hours to showtime,' Blondie said. 'Adam likes to get there early to soak up the atmosphere and energise his live performance.' This was delivered in a Californian accent and imbued with respect for his great art — with a capital 'A'.

Claire seemed giddy with anticipation, tapping the tips of her fingers together in miniature applause. She'd relayed the latest gossip about Adam on our way to the venue, gleaned from celebrity magazines. By now, the publications cared less about passing judgement one way or another on what had happened with Emily.

Their focus had turned to whether it was fair that Adam had to leave his Cockapoo in the USA due to our strict quarantine laws.

'Laura, you come with me. Claire, is it? Please could you wait in here,' said the woman opening the door to a small, empty room.

Claire and I exchanged a look. Was that woman nuts? Did she live in a bubble where her boss could do no wrong; where a private audience with Adam Mooney was every girl's dream?

Except it hadn't ended up that way for Emily, had it?

'No, I would like Claire to stay with me,' I said.

The woman pursed her lips. 'Very well. This way'

She opened another door, which led to a much larger room. Racks of costumes hung on one side, covered in plastic sheeting, looking freshly pressed. A bank of mirrored counters stood opposite, stacked with an invasion of pots, sponges and brushes that I imagined would soon transform the actors into character.

At the far end stood a surprisingly patchy, green velvet sofa that had seen better days. The production's no doubt lavish budget had obviously not extended to a decent one. Perhaps it had sentimental value. Weren't actors all superstitious?

'Sit,' the woman said before sliding away.

Claire smoothed her skirt and ran her hands through her hair. I wished she'd stop fidgeting.

The door opened. I stiffened. Was it him?

Adam Mooney's six-foot-four frame filled the doorway. His radiant tanned skin accentuated his green eyes. He gave a sheepish smile. 'Hi,' he said.

He sat down, choosing a plastic chair like mine, rather than sit next to Claire on the sofa. 'Laura?' he asked, eyeing us both.

I half raised my hand. 'Me.'

He turned to Claire. 'And you are?'

Claire opened her mouth.

'This is Claire, she's with me.' I said hurriedly, getting a cheap thrill from the suggestion I needed a chaperone.

He twisted the cap off a water bottle and took a large gulp while gesturing for us to help ourselves. We didn't.

'So.' He leaned back, one hand on his thigh, the other holding the drink. A slightly bigger smile this time, with a hesitant curl at the edge, exposing his trademark white teeth.

'I want to tell you something,' I began. 'And this is going to sound weird. Before Emily...' I took a breath before continuing. 'On her final morning, Emily programmed some tweets to go out. Except they were never sent. There was a system failure. I've seen them.'

A look of horror flicked across Adam's face. Claire's mouth fell open. I hadn't shared that information with her yet either.

I wiped my palms on my thighs. 'Don't worry. It's not bad. It was her forgiveness. She told the world she forgave you. She'd wanted you to know.' I handed him a small slip of paper; a printed screen shot of the tweet.

A deep sigh fell from his lips. He hunched forward, rubbing his forehead. Claire craned her neck to see the paper, but he folded it up. She turned to me and raised an eyebrow. I shook my head. She crossed her arms like a petulant child.

Adam shifted in his seat and inhaled a giant breath that inflated him back upright. 'Thank you for bringing this to me.'

'I thought you should know.' I twirled my ponytail around a finger. 'I was surprised to read that you had met. I hoped you would tell me about it because Emily didn't. I don't know why.'

Claire's pout faded and she perked up again.

Adam stroked his shoulder, as though he were cold. 'I don't know why either. There wasn't anything to it. I mean, I'm not saying that it wasn't important. It was. Very important. And it was great. I couldn't believe when I heard... I thought we were good. I thought she was okay.' He rolled the paper into a thin cigarette and rubbed it with his thumb. A watery film clouded his eyes.

'What did you talk about? Where did you meet?' I pressed.

'She didn't want to talk to me at first,' he replied. 'My publicist wanted us to make a joint statement, to quieten down the attacks. I told him that seemed unfair on her, but he convinced me to try, given that by then, everyone already knew who she was. I wanted it, too. A show of unity would be like pulling the extinguisher on those intent on fanning the flames of divide.'

He had a way with words, you had to hand him that. He scratched his chin and continued. 'Eventually she agreed to meet in private. I got the hotel to set up afternoon tea in one of their small function rooms, for privacy. I apologised. I apologised a lot. Maybe I had misread the signs that night, but I had no idea she wasn't having fun. She never said anything.' He sipped his water. 'I told her although I'd already made the public statement, I didn't want her to think this was only to save my ass. I needed her to believe that.' He looked from me to Claire, back at me again, his eyes pleading for us to believe him.

He leaned back. 'Don't get me wrong,' he said. 'I was angry. She could have talked to me rather than go running to a blog. Or kept quiet. There was no reason for her to throw me to the dogs like that.' He leaned forward, palms open. 'I didn't rape her.'

I bit my lip.

'She started crying into her tea,' he said. 'I wanted to comfort her but figured I would be the last person she wanted to touch her.' He winced. 'She said she felt dirty. Used. And she didn't want anybody else to have to go through it. That's why she gave the interview. As a warning to men that women are scared to speak up. She wanted to tell guys to listen out for the non-verbal cues.' He wrung his hands. 'She told me she regretted it. She apologised. Nearly as much as I did. She said hurting my career had been intentional, but she hadn't expected it to blow up the way it did.' He rubbed his nose. 'She'd predicted a quickie scandal and that was all. She hadn't expected the backlash. And she definitely hadn't anticipated people figuring out who she was.' He frowned. 'Whoever leaked that photo is an asshole. They deserve to rot in hell.'

'Yes, they do.' I didn't want this to sound like I was excusing him. At the end of the day, if he had left her alone, none of this would have happened — yet he seemed genuine in his remorse, in his belief that his actions had been terribly misinterpreted. Or was he just a good actor?

Emily had forgiven him. I felt forced to do the same. But my itch for justice needed scratching and the more I thought about it, the more it made sense that the person who *identified* Emily was the true culprit. They'd opened the floodgates to the personal abuse... and her being targeted at home. 'Did you ever find out who did it? Did you have anyone investigate?' I asked.

His eyebrow arched, as if this was the first time it had occurred to him he could've helped. 'I... No. I'm sorry. It was a chaotic time. We were fighting fires.'

Fire again. Is that how he'd experienced it?

I looked him straight in the eyes. 'And of course, your publicity team had you to protect... more than her.'

He squirmed.

Claire uncrossed her arms. 'The photo was taken at the party, but there was no press allowed inside. I remember my colleague who organised the event telling me that. He'd been surprised at how insistent your people had been there should be no photos taken by anyone other than the official photographer.' She turned to me. 'And I mean *anyone*. People even had to hand in their mobile phones at the door.'

'This may seem excessive to you,' Adam said, 'but when you are me, when you can't open your bedroom curtains in the morning without somebody snapping a picture of you in your robe, when you can't leave the house without hordes of paparazzi throwing themselves at your car, hoping these antics will annoy you enough that you get out and throw a punch, when people are constantly stopping you for selfies, you long for a chance to party in peace.' He leaned forward. 'This play means the world. What's wrong with wanting to let my hair down without worrying whether a sneaky lens was pointed at me?'

'Why have a photographer at all?' I asked.

'For publicity. And the sponsors,' Claire said. 'Guests had to pose in front of a wall covered in logos when they arrived. The professional photographer's work would always be approved before being released, though, so no unflattering shots made their way out. Isn't that right, Adam?'

'Yes. We always have control.'

A surge of adrenaline spiked through me. 'Where are those photos now?' I asked. 'We have to check if he took that shot.'

'The guy must have taken hundreds of pictures. We only get the good ones. As do you,' Adam said nodding at Claire. He slapped his thighs and sprung to his feet. 'Okay listen, I'll get my publicist to give you the guy's details. No. Better yet, I'll make sure she phones the guy and tells him to give you anything you want — anything at all. It's the least I can do.'

He said something else, but I couldn't hear him through the blood pulsing in my temples. I was finally going to catch a break.

20.
ME

When Adam Mooney says jump, you jump, I thought as photographer Craig McBen introduced himself on the phone only half an hour after I'd left the theatre.

'Do you want to meet right now?' he asked.

'No,' I said, without even thinking. It came out a bit harsh but after all, this was possibly the guy who'd framed Emily. I'd also just arrived home. 'Let's meet tomorrow.'

My stomach rumbled. I went to the kitchen where I heated a tin of *chile con carne* in a copper pan. As it bubbled, I fished a red onion from the net. Out of habit, I opened the drawer and inserted my hand, feeling around for the swimming goggles I used to prevent my eyes watering. My fingers reached the smooth surface of the rubber band. A giant sob overtook me.

Emily.

I sank to the floor and cried. I stretched the band and let go, making it flick against my thigh, like she'd done when she'd given the goggles to me. The snapping sound took me back in time.

My Emily standing in the doorway, her brown work dress creased after a day of sitting. She takes off her knee-high boots and throws them in the corner of the kitchen.

How that had irked me. I'd forgive her anything now.

I rubbed the plastic lenses with my thumb and heard her voice in my head. *'Here, I brought you these.'*

Snap.

A sting.

My '*Ouch.*'

Her laughter.

'*What are these for? I don't swim,*' I'd asked.

'*I'm hungry and after some chilli. It's cold outside. But after your blubberfest last time slicing the onions, I thought I'd play it safe. I don't want any snot in my food.*'

She'd stuck the goggles on my eyes and placed the band around my head, gently removing strands of hair squashed against my face. '*There you go.*'

I'd blinked inside the plastic cups to get used to the kitchen distorted into angular shapes around her smiling face. '*I don't think I need these.*'

She'd batted my hand away when I tried to remove them. '*Yes you do. Cause you're a big softie.*'

She wasn't wrong.

Still anchored to the floor, I wiped my nose with the back of my hand and sniffed. I heard the hiss of distressed flames.

Shit.

I pulled myself up. Clumps of burnt chilli coated the pan black. I turned off the gas. The splatters had even reached the worktop. I grabbed two sheets of kitchen roll and wiped; first my face, then the hob.

I replaced dinner with ginger biscuits. I had work to do.

As I drew diagrams and documented explanations of my new software, my mind kept wandering to that photo: Emily and Adam sneaking out a side door beside the bandstand during the opening party, other guests in the foreground clutching champagne, deep in conversation. Adam was instantly recognisable, his tuxedo adding to his classic good looks. His arm hung loosely around Emily's shoulder; her favourite blue-sequined, floor-length dress flattered her curves. Her blonde wavy hair draped her nude shoulder and only partially hid her delighted face.

Did Craig release this?

The only way to find out was to go and ask. Hot prickles rose form my chest to my throat. Could I ask Claire along? No, I'd already imposed enough on her — though getting to meet a Hollywood star was probably no imposition. Plus, it wasn't as though we were friends; there was always a professional angle with Claire.

I called Craig back. Could I come after all? He gave the High Street address and explained I'd need to go through the close marked 107 to reach his courtyard entrance. I thanked the heavens it would still be light for a few hours; those narrow alleys could get creepy at night.

I WALKED through the grey stone arch on the Royal Mile that marked the entrance to the close. Moisture seeped down the sides of the short, dark tunnel. Cigarette butts and an empty, mud-splattered bottle of Buckfast littered the ground. It reeked of urine. I held my breath until I reached the rear of Craig's building.

I strode up two flights of external stairs. He'd called it his 'studio,' but as I examined the labels on the doorbells, I realised his studio was in fact his home. My shoulders tensed up as I pressed the button.

A buzzing sound released the door. Through the intercom, Craig instructed me to go up two more flights.

Oh great, a mansplainer. Anyone in Edinburgh would know 2F3 meant the third flat on the second floor. I looked down at the metal staircase I'd just climbed and gave him the benefit of the doubt. The building's entrance was already two stories up from a seriously sloped street. He'd probably had his fair share of disoriented visitors to make him want to explain.

Craig stood by his open door when I reached his landing. The first thing that struck me was not his friendly round face, not the baggy jumper with which he drowned his rotund frame, nor the oversized hand I instinctively shook; it was that he was barefoot.

'Come in,' he said. 'I'm glad you could come after all. It's not every day you get a call from Adam Mooney's people. And they said it was urgent, that you need to see *all* the photos of opening night. Is there something wrong?'

I gave a curt nod. 'Thanks for seeing me.'

He led me down a tight corridor, further narrowed by a row of bookcases I would've loved to spend time examining. I caught a flicker of a Robert Harris collection — hardbacks, no less. I noticed his taste for history extended into the framed, black-and-white photographs of Edinburgh's Gothic buildings that lined the walls.

'Did you take these?' I asked.

'Yes, a long time ago.'

'They're beautiful.'

'Thank you.' He gestured ahead. 'Here we are.'

The studio was a small, beige-carpeted office with a strange collection of mismatched standing lamps — some without shades — clustered around a workstation with three giant screens. He moved two up-lighters out of the way and pulled a chair up next to his.

I took it all in.

'A lot of lamps, huh?' he said. 'I sometimes get commissioned to take photographs to hang in offices or homes. I like to get a feel for how they might look, given how different the lighting can be. I bought these in charity shops. I put all types of bulbs in them and change the angles to check the images out in different conditions.'

I nodded. 'Makes sense.'

'Please, sit down.'

I slid the chair a little further away from his. So far there was nothing alarming about him, but I didn't know this man.

He turned on his middle monitor. It showed the interface of sophisticated-looking photo editing software. 'Okay. What is it we're looking for?'

'I guess it's easiest if I come clean... I'm trying to find a particular photo of the opening party. It's the one that—'

Craig leapt out of his seat. 'Hold on.' He bent down and popped back up, holding a wriggly furry creature in his hand. I gasped, thinking it was a rat.

'Sorry, I forgot to close the kitchen door. I spotted her about to crawl up your trousers and I didn't want you to freak out.'

A face sneaked out from a curl of black and white fur, dark, shiny eyes on me, a gradient of wide stripes between its pointy nose and rounded ears. 'Is it a ferret?' I asked.

'Yes, this is Scout.' He presented the animal face-forward and held its hind legs as if it were a machine-gun. 'Don't worry. She's harmless. You can touch her if you like.'

I recoiled.

'Maybe not,' he said, laughing as he pulled her away. Her pink tongue darted over her nose.

'No. I'm sorry. That was rude. I do want to. I've never seen a ferret before. Not up close. Scout? As in *To Kill a Mockingbird*?'

A grin spread across his stubbled chin. 'You're the first one to have guessed that.'

'I have a cat named Atticus,' I said, smiling. His face lit up. I ran a tentative finger along Scout's rump. Softer than expected.

'Let me go and shut her in again,' he said. 'She could give Houdini a run for his money.'

'They have ferrets at NASA for that reason.'

'What?'

A blush tingled on my cheeks. Why had I said that? I was always blurting out random facts and quotes. 'I read somewhere that they have ferrets at NASA. They train them to run cables where people could otherwise not get to.' I shrugged. 'They probably use robots for that now.'

He stood in the doorway, a goofy grin on his face. 'And here I was thinking I was the ferret expert. I'll be back in a minute.'

He stepped away, leaving me unnerved — but in a good way?

To fill the time, I glanced at the long list of folders lining the side of the screen. One was labelled *Empisoft March 2016*. That was years ago.

'Right, let's get to it. You were saying?' He dropped into his chair again.

I cleared my throat. 'I'm looking for the photo of Adam Mooney leaving the party with a woman.'

'His accuser?'

'Yes, Emily was my friend. I — we — want to find the source of the photo, that's all.'

'And you think it's me? That I put the photo of your friend online?' His voice reached a distraught pitch and he brought his hands to his chest. 'It wasn't me. I would never... I'm sorry about your friend. It's awful what happened to her. She didn't deserve that. I can assure you it wasn't me.'

Watching him protest, he didn't strike me as the sort. But what would be the sort?

'There's only one way to find out,' I said. 'Let's start with whether you took the picture.'

His movements quickened. Was he keen to show me he was innocent?

'Okay.' he said. 'I don't think it's mine. And even if it is, loads of people had access to it.'

'How so?'

'I put all the ones that were of sufficient quality in a shared folder, which I made available to Pure Brilliant and Adam Mooney's publicist.'

I found it hard to believe that any of Emily's colleagues would do this. And it certainly wouldn't have been in Adam's interest to fuel the fire.

'I have a print-out with me, so you can see what I'm looking for.' I reached in my jacket pocket and unfolded the paper.

He examined it. 'Hm...'

'What?'

'That one's taken at a completely wrong angle. No way that's me.'

'But you were the only photographer on site.'

'Let's go through them if you don't believe me.' His indignant tone made me want to reassure him, but I held firm. He wasn't out of the woods yet.

He opened the relevant folder on the screen. The monitor filled with thumbnails of people enjoying themselves, wearing their glad rags and posing like pros, duck faces and all. The colourful images scrolled up as Craig ran through the collection. I asked him to pause a few times, thinking I'd found it, but it was never the one.

'See?' he said, dropping his hands on his thighs.

'Is that all of them?'

He pointed at a little icon underneath each photo. 'Yes. And all the ones marked with a star were shared with the client.'

I sank into my chair, disappointed, but also relieved: at least the man whose home I found myself in wasn't a total creep.

'Who took this picture? Could somebody have smuggled in a mobile after all?' I asked.

'I don't think that was taken on a mobile.'

'Why not?'

Craig opened the browser window and searched for an electronic version of Emily and Adam's photo on the Internet. It wasn't hard to find — it had gone viral. He zoomed in and pointed at the crowd in the background. 'See how fuzzy these people are? A mobile would have a different depth of field. This has DSLR written all over it.'

'You mean, a proper camera? Who could that have been? They needed to have been in the room.'

'I don't know. And there won't be any way to find out from the photo's metadata. Has anyone looked at the Twitter account?'

'Anonymous. And the police won't do anything more.'

'Well that's not so surprising. There's nothing illegal about posting a picture of fully dressed people. The guests even signed photography waivers when they received their tickets. Of course, they would've expected only me to take them.' He looked again at the original tweet. 'And all he said was "Who knows this woman?" The only law broken here is his copyright, by the hundreds of people who re-tweeted it and websites that used the image. I doubt he would've minded. He wanted her identified — and he wanted his fifteen minutes of fame.'

I sighed.

He added, 'If you ask me, the person who's most to blame is the one who *named* her, not the one who shared the photo.'

I'd thought of that, too. But that person's account had disappeared the day after the news broke about Emily's death. Did they fear of reprisal? Probably justified. 'We won't find him either.'

He picked at the hairs above his lips. 'Come to think of it, the blogger who interviewed Emily is also to blame. What a warped understanding of journalistic ethics. I remember thinking, when I read the blog —'

I shivered.

'Sorry,' he said. 'It was all anyone could talk about. There was way too much gratuitous detail in there. A proper journalist wouldn't do that. It was unnecessarily sensationalist.'

It was a culprit I hadn't considered. 'Isn't that what everything is like at the moment? I know Emily had chosen the Woke Poke because it was a new blog for millennials that wanted to discuss big things. The woman who interviewed her had assured she'd be safe.'

He shrugged. 'Sure, she protected her as a source, but I still feel the story could have been written very differently.'

I stretched and rubbed my neck. This had all been in vain. 'I don't want you to take this the wrong way. I had so hoped it was you. Because now there's nowhere to turn.'

Scout scuttled between our legs, giving us both a jolt. Craig scooped her onto his stomach. 'How did you get out again?' He shook his head at me. 'She's a little demon, this one.' His big hands flattened Scout as he stroked her. 'Sorry you didn't get what came for. But I'm not sorry that I am not the man you were looking for... if you know what I mean.'

I did. Something pulled at me to stay. I gave Scout a quick stroke, then pointed at the folder labelled *Empisoft* I'd seen before. 'What's that?'

'March 2016. I think that's a product launch. Possibly your first?'

I didn't know why but I felt rumbled. 'You know who I am?'

'I wasn't sure you'd be *the* Laura Flett when Mooney's people called, but then you walked in.' He smiled, gesturing toward me with his right hand.

'I don't remember you being there.'

'You shouldn't. My job is to lurk in the shadows.'

'Like this one,' I said, tickling Scout's nose. 'Let me see them. That feels such a long time ago.'

Craig put on a slide show that stayed on each image two seconds before skipping to the next. A young start-up proudly demonstrating their innovative creation. Justin in his element. A crowd of colleagues, investors, journalists whizzed by. Me standing in a corner, a cup of tea in hand. And another, zoomed in on my profile. Another, closer still, each fine eyelash catalogued.

I stiffened. Craig squirmed. His hand hovered over the mouse.

'Why did you do that?' I asked. 'Take photos of me?'

He winced. 'You looked interesting.'

'Interesting? This is more than interesting.' Before he had a chance to respond, I wiped my hands on my jeans. 'I think we're done here.' I stood up and headed for the door.

Craig followed, keeping an obvious, measured non-creepy distance. 'Please don't think I'm...' His voice wavered.

I looked back. He stopped and smiled, hope spreading across his features. He held Scout to his cheek and together they gave me a big-eyed look. 'We're harmless.'

'You said Scout was a demon.'

'Touché. Seriously, I'm one of the good guys.'

I stepped outside. 'If you say so.'

21.
ME

The cloying dough of a Tesco ham and salad sandwich stuck to the roof of my mouth. Moist crumbs fell from my chin onto the guest keyboard in the meeting room.

On the wall, the screen was filled with code, folder directories and diagrams. Sighing, I thought of how incredibly behind I was, even though I'd stayed up late after seeing Craig. I stifled a yawn. Men in grotesque masks had infiltrated my dreams last night, lurking in the shadows, gradually surrounding me like I was prey.

I rubbed my eyes and tried to focus, intent on completing the mind-numbing task of documentation — made all the more excruciating by the R&D projects still being in their infancy, and their logic still residing mostly in my brain.

The thick glass door swung open. It was Suki, her strength belying her petite frame. As usual she was dressed immaculately, her blouse the kind of pure white I'd learnt during seven years of doing my own laundry could never be maintained. I looked down at my uniform of black top and blue jeans and shrugged. Besides, even if I tried, I could never pull off Suki's elegance.

'Hey. It's good to finally catch you, Laura.'

'I'm sorry I've not been around.'

'That's okay. You're here now. Hopefully we'll get through the bulk of it today.' Suki placed her briefcase on the table, pushing my discarded sandwich box away with a raised eyebrow. 'You do know processed meat causes cancer?'

'I know,' I said.

'So what have you been up to?'

'Not much.'

'Any progress on the data room?'

'A bit.'

Suki's eyes shone with mischief. 'I see we're our usual talkative self today.'

'I'm tired.' I yawned for effect.

'Out on the town with a new beau?'

I scoffed. What was she like? Tenacious Suki. She wanted in, no matter what — and I was starting to warm to it. 'God no, men are the last thing on my mind. Creepy bastards.'

'You can always defect.' Suki threw her head back and let out a joyous, guttural, contagious laugh. 'What have the stinky boys done this time?' she asked.

'It's a long story. Let's just say, the sooner I have cash from the sale, the sooner I can escape to a desert island and not bother with them anymore.'

'Now that's what I like to hear. Let's make some money.' She clapped her hands and pulled up a chair beside me, casting her jasmine and sage smell around. With a sideways glance, she said, 'You know, hiding isn't the answer. Don't get me wrong. I hear you, sister,' she said, raising her arms like a gospel singer. 'Men can be real pricks, but I strongly advocate developing thicker skin. My trick is to be more like them and not give a shit. It makes life a lot easier. Someone ogles you in the tram? Ignore it. When they ask you to smile on command when you walk past? Ignore. If they call you a bitch because of it, hey ho, let it go. I could write a book about sexual innuendo at work.'

'You get harassed at *work*?'

'Ha! I'm in finance. I play in the big boys' pen. And it's diiiirty.' She rolled her shoulders. 'It doesn't help that white men seem to have an Asian conquest fantasy.'

Part of me wanted to stop her talking about sex. How could she be so open with someone she'd only just met? But my curiosity won. 'Does it upset you?'

'I'm used to it... It's the price I pay. Mostly I choose to treat it as a sign of weakness. They're intimidated by me. Insecure man-babies can't handle smart women who went to Stanford.'

'You went to Stanford? Why are you back in Edinburgh?'

She pointed her thumb at the grey sky, raindrops sliding down the window. 'Well, not for the sunshine.'

I shook my head. 'It's inconceivable to me that you would just leave Silicon Valley. It's the dream. I mean, I know Edinburgh is becoming one of the world's great centres for data science and all, but that's still not the same as being at the heart of the revolution in artificial intelligence.' She looked at me, her head cocked, her closed lips curled in a smile. I brought my hands back to my lap and cleared my throat. 'And yes, the weather.'

'I did my MBA there. On a scholarship. But my parents are here and like a good little Thai girl, I came home to be with them.' She gave me a wry smile. 'They were already upset I didn't join them in the restaurant.' She sat up straight, breathed in and said, 'Besides, unlike London or New York, here I can be a big fish in a small pond.' She waved regally at her surroundings. Seeming to remember what had started this conversation, she added, 'Anyway... the sexism there is five times worse. At least in Edinburgh I don't have to take our clients to strip clubs. The dingy places on Lothian Road don't quite have the cachet of Mayfair...'

I scrunched up my nose. 'Ew.'

'Wherever I choose to be, I'm an intruder in a man's world. Hell, I can't even use my real name.'

'Your name's not Suki?'

'No, it's Sukhon. It means "pleasant smell".'

'What's wrong with that?'

'It's so puerile: you tell a guy your name is Sukhon and next thing you know, he's inviting you to "suck on" this and "suck on" that.'

'Oh, for crying out loud.' I rolled my eyes.

'I swear to God. Every. Single. Time. And this one bloke, a real shit, calls me Ping. Short for ping-pong. Sexist *and* racist.'

'Because ping-pong was invented in China?'

She hooted. 'Oh bless you, sheltered child.' It's a reference to showgirls in the sex trade in Thailand. They're known to shoot ping-pong balls into the audience from their... what shall I call them? Suki pointed at her crotch. 'Hoo-hoos.'

I spluttered. 'That's disgusting. Is this guy in your office? You should have him sacked.'

She shook her head. 'It's not that simple. He's the boss's son. The stupid thing is people think I'm Japanese because of Suki.'

'Can't you tell the guys you're gay to make them stop?'

'That would make matters worse! If you think they have an Asian-chick fantasy now, wait until they imagine me with another woman. No, my dear, lesbians are by no means excluded from male persecution.'

'Oh.'

'Don't worry about me. I'm more worried about you.'

'Why?'

'This all started when you said men were creeps, and I can't help but think I've made it worse. Sorry and I'm not just saying this to change the subject. I'm honestly worried — this is what you eat?' she said, holding up the sandwich packaging. 'I have a feeling you don't know what good food tastes like. I'm going to take you to my parents' restaurant tomorrow night.'

I opened my mouth to object.

She put up a hand to silence me. 'Not taking "no" for an answer,' she said. 'It will be a reward for all the hard work you're going to be doing for me this afternoon. So let's get cracking.'

It seemed futile to argue. I swept the crumbs from the keyboard and pressed a few keys. 'Fair enough. What do you want to see today?'

'I want you to tell me more about your new invention.'

'Which one?'

'The one about finding the people in a group who have the most influence in terms of how others feel, the heroes and villains you mentioned. I've called it "Network Impact" since you didn't have a name for it yet. Do you like it?'

'Sure. Why not.'

Suki turned to face the big screen, poised to be presented to. 'I don't think we have factored in the value of the R&D portfolio sufficiently in the price we're getting PeopleForce to pay yet. But I need to understand it better.'

'I don't know. It's awfully early stage. It's not been tested on any sizable data.'

'Is there a data set you could test on quickly? It would be great if we could show it in action.'

I exhaled deeply. 'There's a lot involved in that. I don't think our existing sets would work because that's not what they were created for. And we can't use any of our real-life client data without their permission. I'll think about it. I suspect the models won't be good enough yet anyway.'

'From what I have seen to date, I believe that's you being modest, Laura. Now, show me.'

22.
ME

The stone steps to Craig's main door were slippery with rain. I clung onto the steep wrought iron handrail, cold water sliding into my sleeve. Nearly-black clouds hung low in the sky, the moon just peeking through.

The door buzzed open the minute I pressed the bell. No identification required; he was expecting me.

I wiped my feet and climbed to the second floor. Was this a mistake? I'd hummed and hawed about coming when he'd called earlier.

I stopped in my tracks. Craig was standing two steps from the door frame. No shoes again. He waved me in with a warm smile. 'I'm glad you're here.'

'I'm sorry it's late, I've had a lot of work to clear off my desk first.'

'No worries,' he said leading the way. 'Come on through.'

Inside the studio, Scout lay curled around the base of a standing lamp, near the radiator. She raised her pink nose as she spotted me and sniffed the air expectantly

I couldn't help but think it was a strange sort of pet. A dog, a cat, a goldfish, okay, but a ferret? Although not traditionally cute or fluffy, weirdly, it fit. I couldn't imagine Craig with a kitten. That would have looked ridiculous in his oversized hands. And a dog might have been too difficult to keep with that many stairs. I glanced again at Craig's round shape and nondescript clothing. Like me, he didn't look like he went out much.

I walked straight past him to his desk. 'You said you had a lead on the photographer that took Emily's picture?'

'Yes, I could have sent you the photos, but it's a little complicated and I find it easier to point.' He brought my chair in. 'Take a seat.'

My shoulder was so close to his, I could feel the warmth of his body. Craig woke his three monitors with a single shake of his mouse and three distinct images from the opening party appeared. My heart jumped as I saw Emily's shot with Adam on the left.

'Okay. The first thing I want you to see is that I definitely could not have taken that picture.' He hovered the mouse over the image and right-clicked to show its properties. 'See here? Make a note of the time. It's twenty-nine minutes past nine and thirty-two seconds.' I nodded. He brought up the properties of the photo on the middle screen, that showed a few guests whispering to each other in what looked like the corridor. 'And here is a photo that I took at exactly the same time. I couldn't have been in the main room to take the other shot.' He searched my face, looking for my reaction.

Given the trouble that he'd gone through, I didn't have the heart to tell him I'd believed him on my first visit — even though he'd taken those close-ups of me. What was it that made him so non-threatening? Maybe it was the copy of Anna Karenina on the console table? Or the way he let Scout jump on his lap, jump down, and up again without showing any sign of losing his patience? I also couldn't really blame him for doing his job, photographing one of the company's founders at their launch event.

'Okay, you're off the hook,' I said. 'What else did you want to show me?'

He moved his finger to the screen on his right, to a heavy gold-coloured curtain beside a floor-to-ceiling window at the far end of the party venue. It hung behind a smartly dressed smiling couple, him in a green velvet suit and her in a silvery dress, posing with champagne glasses in their hands. 'See that dark patch?' he asked.

I shook my head. He zoomed in. I saw something black, a shoulder, an arm. 'Who's that?'

'I don't know. I went over all the other shots.' He called a new image onto the middle screen, the gold curtain in the background again. 'Do you see that little flash of light? It's a camera lens reflecting the chandeliers. Now this...' He hovered the mouse over a more visible, black-clad, male with dark hair.

'Do you know him?' I asked, leaning in. I caught a whiff of Craig's earthy scent and my stomach fluttered. What the hell was that about? I shuffled in my seat.

'No,' he said. 'But whoever this person is, I'd bet he is behind the leaked photo of your friend.'

'Press?'

He shook his head. 'I doubt it. First off, that would have been unethical. And secondly, why send someone and not use the material they shot? There were loads of famous people there.'

'So who could it be?'

He shrugged. 'Someone who wasn't supposed to be there. Someone who wanted to sell these pictures. Someone who probably couldn't find a market for them in the end. This has amateur written all over it. Any experienced photographer would know none of the publications would run this, too many restrictions for a start.' He took his hand off the mouse and stretched his fingers. 'I called the security company. They said they hadn't seen any trespassers.'

I smirked. 'Would they tell you if they had?'

'I guess not. It would do their reputation no good at all if word of this came out.'

I placed my hand on the desk. 'I want to take this to the police.'

Craig looked bewildered. 'What for? All this guy did was gate crash a private party. Plus, this was weeks ago. I can't see them looking into this. They'd say there was no harm done.'

A flash of anger spread across my forehead. 'No harm? That bastard leaked the photo that led to Emily being identified online and bullied to death.' I jumped up. 'All I want is justice for Emily. Why else would I be here?' He frowned. I hit my fist into my other hand. 'Somebody needs to get nailed for that. Yes, the trolling had been horrific.' I pointed at his screen. 'But it hadn't been *personal* until Emily was identified from this shot.'

'I'm sorry about Emily. I can't imagine what she went through. And I can completely understand that you want to blame somebody.' He reached for my shoulder, then changed his mind. 'And yes, this guy jumped at the opportunity to show off his secret photo, knowing full well the Internet would blow up.' Craig rolled his chair back and shook his head. 'But I don't think you're going to get any closure on this, Laura. You can't pin her death on him, even if we find him.' He swallowed hard. 'I know we don't know each other well and forgive me if I'm speaking out of turn. I worry you will make yourself crazy trying to find the culprit. Maybe it's time to find another way to deal with what happened?'

The kindness in his voice chipped at my resolve. But I wasn't done, I couldn't be done. Every single action had led to another and collectively built into an avalanche that was too much for Emily to bear. I couldn't let everyone get off like that.

'I want you to give me the photos,' I said.

'Why?'

'I don't know yet.'

He watched me for a moment, head cocked. Then he got up and rummaged through the drawer, pulling out a USB stick still in its packaging.

'Technically I can't give these to you. They belong to Pure Brilliant. The only other person who has the rights is Adam Mooney. Please don't get me into trouble.'

'I won't. I'll take care of Pure Brilliant — and Adam Mooney.'

Craig transferred the files and handed me the stick.

'Thank you,' I said.

He escorted me to the door. 'I hope you get what you need. And if I can help you in any way, you know where to find me.'

23.
SUKI

Suki strode to work the next morning, skilfully avoiding the grooves between the city's cobblestones. She ran her fingers over her eyebrows and tapped at the puffiness under her eyes. God, working with the West Coast could be a pain. She remembered the words *'serious concerns'* in the middle-of-the-night emails from PeopleForce. They'd changed in tone, too. What if it all falls apart?

She knew they'd be expecting instant answers, but she needed to play it cool. She'd chosen a strategic *'out of office'* reply to buy a few hours to discuss matters with the Madainn partners. No harm done. She figured the Silicon Valley *bros* would still hear back in time for their company-sponsored healthy breakfast.

She yawned. Why hadn't her morning coffee kicked in yet?

When she arrived at the Rutland Square office, the support staff were scuttling around like worker bees. Suki headed straight to Angus's office and knocked. A deep grumble replied.

The door handle had smears of pink cleaner between the brass grooves. She turned it with three carefully placed fingers.

Diane's bob peeked from over the back of the leather armchair. Noticeably blonder. Suki wondered how grey the hair underneath really was.

'Good, you're here too, Diane,' Suki said. 'I was hoping to have a word about Empisoft. Am I interrupting?'

'Are we done?' asked Angus, glancing at Diane tight-lipped.

'Yes, for now,' she replied icily.

'Great,' Suki said in the perkiest voice she could muster. She sat in the other armchair, her legs neatly crossed. 'Empisoft shared their management accounts with PeopleForce yesterday and this has caused a bit of a... not sure what to call it... a ripple.'

Angus's eyes darkened and his forehead creased. She'd expected that: he didn't like surprises. And even less surprises involving Americans, having had a giant deal explode in his face at the last minute last year. '*Damned yanks*,' he'd cursed. But what did he expect? In corporate finance, nothing was certain until it was signed off. Although to be honest, any significant issues would normally be smoothed out well before the due diligence phase they were stuck in now.

'What's the problem?' Angus asked, rubbing his temple.

'There's been a slow decline in revenues in the last few months, which PeopleForce were aware of. However, Justin and I had talked a good game in terms of how this was a blip and nothing to be concerned about.' Suki curled her toes inside her shoes. 'But with another month showing a downward slope, they are understandably underwhelmed by this explanation.' She cleared her throat. 'My sense is they're most concerned about the latest upgrade having lost its initial momentum, and there not being enough in the R&D pipeline.'

'Do you think it's a negotiating tactic or is there a reasonable basis for their concern?' Diane asked, fingering her pearls nervously.

'I suspect a bit of both,' Suki said. 'Given what we know about their chats with the competitor, I wouldn't put it all down to bluster.'

'I agree,' Angus said, slapping the table. 'We need to take this seriously. Worst case scenario? The deal falls through, which I'm not anticipating. However, there's a possibility of losing valuation over this. I don't need to remind you, Suki how important this deal is for the firm.'

'No, you don't.' And yet he always did.

Suki sighed. If he'd just give her a minute... She prided herself on never bringing a problem to someone without at least one solution, no matter how half-baked. It was one of the tricks to maintain the appearance of authority she'd learnt in her classes on 'Interpersonal Influence'— which her fellow MBA students cynically called 'Manipulation 101'.

She smiled sweetly. 'The good news is they haven't seen everything. The headline valuation of one hundred million was based on the work their corporate finance guys had done on the basis of the two research projects that are the most advanced. I've spent time with Laura Flett. Although she's dragging her heels on completing the data room, she's proving to be quite the innovator.'

'Why is she dragging her heels?' Diane turned her upper body towards Suki, clutching the arm rest of her chair with both hands. 'Has she not sorted her personal problem out yet? Please tell me the company isn't hiding anything and you only just found out.'

Lay off, bitch.

As if she'd be naive enough to have the wool pulled over her eyes — and by someone like Laura. She might not have been a financier as long as Diane, but Diane wasn't a patch on her ability to read people.

Suki locked her fingers and rested her tightly clasped hands on her lap. 'No. Her best friend died. She's distracted. I'm dealing with it.' She took a breath and exhaled slowly. 'What I was trying to say is that Laura developed a new tool that I think could exceptionally exciting to PeopleForce, and bigger than the other two projects combined.'

'Really?' Angus perked up, never one to venture far from thoughts of money. 'Could we get more for the company?'

'I might,' said Suki, using none of that '*we*' shit. This was her deal and she would bring it home.

'What's the tool?' asked Diane, relaxing back into her seat, her legs swept to one side.

'It's extremely clever, if she can pull it off. It's untested but has huge potential. Rather than mapping where in a company people are feeling engaged, or stressed, or downright depressed, she's working on a network-based analysis that can identify the people that are *causing* and *amplifying* those feelings the most.'

'I don't understand,' Angus said. 'Wasn't the point of Empisoft to help coach managers of unhappy teams to improve their performance?'

'Yes, the importance of management cannot be discounted. However — and this is where it gets interesting — their current software only scores people's communications on a set of emotional indicators *at a particular time*. Here, Laura's looking at what — or more accurately who — could be causing *changes* in people's emotions.'

She waited, palms open.

Angus blinked.

Diane squirmed.

Good God, people, still no? No wonder they'd hired her. What hope would those two have in making this firm have any kind of reputation in the city's growing technology sector?

An image she liked to use in her phone messages popped into her head: a large woman in a gospel choir robe rolling her eyes, arms to the heavens. *The Lord is testing me.*

Suki gave a single clap. 'Let me give you an example. If I were to complain about my boss — not that I would.' She smiled jokingly at Angus. 'And Frank in Accounting said to me "There, there, everything will be fine," I'd probably leave happier than when I came. But if he said, "You're right. That's totally unreasonable," I would be more resentful than before.' Diane listened intently. 'It doesn't matter whether Frank himself is happy or not, it's what he causes in *other* people. This software is trying to find the Franks, the colleagues you wouldn't expect to have much influence, but who do. And if you could coach them — or get rid of them — you would have a healthier company.'

Diane stroked the outline of her mouth with her index finger, a smidge of her trademark *Allure* by Chanel transferring, revealing the concentric circles of her fingerprint. 'So, the opposite could be true also? That there might be someone that you wouldn't recognise at first glance who could have a positive effect on employee engagement?'

'Exactly.' Suki nearly bounced in her seat. 'You track all the communications inside the company and score how people's moods are affected after engaging with someone. You take all that together, put it in a big model, and the next thing you know, it turns out there are a number of people in the organisation who have a positive effect. Either they reduce people's negative feelings, or, better yet they amplify positivity. These are the ones you want to keep, the ones you should be giving pay rises to.'

Angus shifted in his seat. 'Okay. Let's say Laura gets this to work. How do we use it to our advantage?'

Suki lifted her thumb. 'I'll make new financial projections for PeopleForce to get them comfortable that there is growth in the company beyond what they've seen, to make up for some of the recent disappointing revenue numbers.'

'Best to make it as look as rosy as you can,' said Diane.

'We can't overdo it,' Suki replied. 'This new Network Impact tool hasn't even been tested. Besides, what I can do depends a bit on where we are with the agreement. Angus, you're still dealing with the existing shareholders... are they all lined up yet?'

'No.' He scratched the top of his forehead. 'Two of the original high net-worth investors are complaining they will lose their tax relief because they won't have held the shares for three years.'

'Are you shitting me? How greedy can you get?' Suki was all for lining your pockets whenever you could, but this was ridiculous. 'They're making over ten times their money!'

Angus nodded. 'I know. These guys hate paying taxes. They will already have claimed the relief two years ago. It will feel like losing money. What they're asking is to extend the timeline by a few months so that it's three full years and they can benefit from tax-free capital gains.'

'If PeopleForce gets spooked by this, we're left with nothing,' Suki said. We can't give into this.' She squinted. 'Did Pam not deal with these investors before on a similar matter? Can she advise on the best way forward?'

She caught Diane glancing nervously at Angus. 'What?' Suki said.

Diane straightened her back. 'Pam isn't with us anymore.'

'Why?' Suki asked.

'She's been under a lot of stress and decided she needed time off.' Diane bit her lip. 'She's going travelling, I believe.'

'A bit sudden, isn't it?'

Angus stood. 'I'll see if I can have another word with the shareholders. Is there anything else?'

Suki shook her head, the signal she was dismissed well and truly received.

SUKI EAVESDROPPED by the door for a few seconds, sadly not catching anything. Damn mahogany.

She returned to her desk and scrolled among the contacts in her mobile.

'Pam, hi. It's Suki. I hear you're no longer with us? I never got to say goodbye.'

A breath. 'I... I... needed a change. You know what it's like. Once you set your mind on something, you want to get on with it.'

'Come on, Pam. What's the real scoop?'

'Nothing. I'm going travelling.'

'Bollocks.' Suki cupped her hand around her mouth and the microphone. 'Did you do something wrong?'

'No. Absolutely not. Leave it, Suki. I can't talk about it.'

'Pam, we go back a long way and I know for a fact—'

'I've signed a Non-Disclosure Agreement.'

Suki groaned silently. She wouldn't get any further, that was for sure. The partners had made sure something wouldn't come to light. Whatever the hell that was.

'Keep in touch, Pam,' she said. 'You were an amazing team assistant. We don't seem to be very good at holding on to you guys.'

'Yes, well... You might want to think why that is.'

'What do you mean?'

'Look, I'm sorry but I have to go.'

Suki ended the call and stared into space. Could it be fraud? Some financial shenanigans? She wouldn't put it past Angus. Those old-world, entitled men believed the laws weren't written for them.

She patted her mobile against her pursed lips and imagined all sorts of crimes.

Diane's creepy son Robert approached from the side, swaying side to side like a slithery snake. He perched his saggy bum on her desk. 'Hey, Ping, if you're looking for something nicer to press those lips against, I could make a suggestion.'

'Bite me,' she said, lifting her middle finger.

What a fucking place.

24.
ME

'I'm going to hang up now,' I said to Justin, while reaching inside my kitchen cupboard with my free hand, feeling for the new pack of tea bags. 'I *know* I need to get the documentation done. No need to call at home.'

I moved the phone away from my ear to hang up but still caught, 'Time's ticking on and PeopleForce are growing impatient, Laura.'

Didn't I know it. Suki called with the exact same message only ten minutes ago. It was as if they were ganging up on me. Them and Craig. His stern face had stayed in my head since my visit. Who was he to lecture me about letting go? It wasn't *his* only friend who died. He never even knew Emily.

I sighed; a bubble of air lingered at the back of my throat. Emily would've liked him... She would probably have called him a big teddy bear. I poured boiling water into my favourite green mug. The steam formed a moist circle around my chin that made me think of the cute white patch of fur around Scout's mouth — then Craig's stubble. I wiped the heat from my cheeks with the back of my hand.

Was he the good guy he claimed to be? Why else would he spend all those hours trawling through images for me?

I stirred the tea into the perfect amber-coloured cuppa and pulled out the bag. What would Craig have made of Emily?

Through the open door, I peeked at the unpacked boxes of books in the living room — the ones I'd salvaged from Emily's flat.

I put the phone in the cutlery drawer and shoved it shut with my hip.

No more distractions. It was time.

The cardboard in the lower corner of the first box was scrunched from the weight of its content. I sat on the floorboards and crossed my legs. I pulled out *Angela's Ashes* — a gift from me — and I swallowed, a lump in my throat. I remembered Emily turning her nose up at the weighty drab coloured tomes with abstract titles I brought her from time to time, only to gush after reading, *'You have such talent for finding the perfect book at the perfect time for me.'*

I dusted the dog-eared novels, releasing specs of Emily's home into mine. If only I could have found a book to reassure her to hang tight when she was under attack, that it would all pass. I kicked at the box. I'd been a terrible friend. Why hadn't I done more? Was it any surprise she hadn't confided in me about the dildos — when all I'd done was berate her to stay off social media?

I reached Emily's romance novels and stacked them on top of each other; one bare chested man after another; the *Fabios, Jamies* and *Patricks* that made Emily's heart swell, helped her to believe that someday she too would be swept away. I shook my head. That category didn't feature in my bookcases. But I made room for them anyway, smiling as I carefully aligned the spines into a hunky line dance.

I took one of the books to bed; read a few chapters of a story that promised blushes and thrills, and an obligatory love triangle — this one involving sexy twins. Some time later, my eyelids heavy, I lay with the paperback on my chest, feeling as close to Emily as I could ... which would never be close enough.

I COULDN'T remember the last time I'd had peace and quiet. Proper peace and quiet; the productive kind. Perhaps getting up early wasn't a bad habit to get into after all? Headphones on and for once undisturbed, I caught glimpses of colleagues arriving and settling in. By the time the row of desks in front of me was full, I'd been at my station for a solid hour and a half, a long row of code debugged.

Sally appeared by my side, quietly calling my attention with her rocking hips.

I looked up. 'What is it?'

'I was hoping you could help me with one of my data sets,' she said. 'I think it might have been corrupted. It's causing my algorithm to go loopy.'

'Sure. But it'll be at least an hour if that's OK?'

'No problem.'

She hovered like a summer's wasp.

'Anything else?' I asked.

'I'm just really glad I caught you. You've not been at your desk lately. Some of us were starting to worry.' Sally cocked her head. 'Everything okay?'

Is this what they talked about in the break room? Nerves pricked at the base of my spine. Did they all know about Emily? Or was it just because I'd been away or hiding in meeting rooms so much for the acquisition?

'I'm alright. Just busy,' I said.

'Great, because I know a few others want to come to you for advice too. We come a bit undone when you're not around.' Sally smiled sweetly.

'Fine. Could you ask them to email me first?'

'Will do. See you later.'

Now, where was I? I checked the code on my screen but didn't remember where I'd stopped. I'd have to look it all over. I sighed and stretched. I couldn't face it. Instead, I searched my bag for the policeman's business card.

The chap who picked up the phone offered to look for DI Reddy, no questions asked. Maybe they were finally taking me seriously?

Reddy came on. He sighed, then said, 'Miss Flett, what is it?' My stomach dropped. So much for taking me seriously.

'It's about the items I told you to get from Emily Nairn's flat,' I said. 'You know, the... erm... sex toys. I thought you might have run through the CCTV in her area to see who delivered them?'

'Miss Flett — Laura —whilst I appreciate your efforts and remind myself that your heart's in the right place, I think you may have been watching too much television.'

'I don't watch TV.'

'Well, wherever you get your information on police activities from, I'm afraid it might be somewhat fictional.'

'Look, Detective, I was her best friend,' I said. '*I* told you about this, *I* sent the photo of the trespasser at the opening party... I'm like a witness. All this evidence —'

'If you want us to open this case again, you'll need to pick it up with her parents.'

I stiffened. 'They're grieving. I don't want to disturb them.'

'Which is why I would suggest you leave it. There have been no new developments.'

I sank into my chair. 'You're not even trying?'

'Trying what?'

'To find the people who bullied Emily. Bullying is a crime, isn't it? Aren't you there to fight crime?'

He sighed again. 'We've had this conversation before. We do not have the resources to do an international search for people whose harassment may have contributed to your friend's state of mind when she took her own life.'

'What about the photographer? He was in Edinburgh. That's your turf.'

'Possibly. But he committed no crime in publishing his photo online, although admittedly he had dubious means of obtaining it. Nevertheless, we've asked Twitter to flag his account for monitoring. We can't do anything more without a court order—which we won't get. We are satisfied there was no crime there, Miss Flett.'

'What about the person who named her on social media? He must be Scottish, if he knew her? He must have known identifying her would cause her harm. That's malicious—'

'Not a crime. Besides, he — or she — closed their account. I think they got their comeuppance on Twitter already. Don't you?'

I remembered the hundreds of abusive tweets that person had been subjected to. Served them right. But at least that meant Reddy had actually looked at the case. Done some digging.

'Surely there's more you can do?'

'We've done all we can,' he said.

My hand hurt. I noticed I'd been squeezing the receiver. 'But the ... um ... sex toys. That wasn't online. That's physical.'

'If Emily had reported them at the time, we could have looked into it,' he replied. 'But we can't say for sure she didn't buy them herself. And if someone did indeed give them to her, as a form of torment, we have no idea where or when that happened. I'm sorry, but as I've said, the case remains closed.'

'No.'

He softened his tone. 'For me to re-open this case, I would need to make the Nairns aware of the dildos. Is that what you want? Because they'd already found it extremely difficult to talk about Emily's experience. They're keen for this chapter to be over.'

I rubbed my face with my open palm, trying to scrub away the picture of her parents that formed in my mind; pale and anguished, facing the stares of a world that branded their daughter a harlot. They deserved peace. I sighed. 'No, you're right.'

I threw the handset away from me and let out a big, frustrated grunt. The coiled cable stretched into the void in front of me and the receiver came flying back, swung under my desk and hit me on the shin.

'Ouch,' I yelled.

Heads popped up from behind their computer monitors. Sally rushed towards me. 'Laura! What's wrong?'

Feeling twenty pairs of eyes on me, I pulled at the cord and placed the receiver gently on its base. 'I got frustrated with a piece of code,' I said. 'Sorry. Let me save what I've got, and I'll come help you with yours.'

I navigated my file directory to save my work and I came across the giant file I'd taken off Emily's iPad after my scraper had done its job. My heart fluttered. It would contain all the abusive tweets, their tags, the writer's profiles, the timings — everything.

I pictured the data in my mind's eye; a giant web of gruesome interactions. Account holders that kicked things off; those that jumped on the bandwagon; those who agreed and disagreed; those who called for her head — and that of the offending movie star — those who debated between each other; those who amplified the beating of the drums; the ones who incited others to keep up the noise and threats.

All those connections...

Adrenaline coursed through me.

That's it! It wasn't enough to just run Empisoft's existing product on the data. This was a network of people egging each other on.

Sally leaned over my desk and waved in front of my face. 'Are you coming?'

I held up my hand 'Give me a few more minutes.'

She walked away.

As I loaded my latest R&D project to run on this file, I felt guilty being distracted again — not to mention using the company's resources. But I was finally going to get what I wanted. And hadn't Suki asked me to find a test case for Network Impact?

Well, here it was.

25.
CLAIRE

Claire pulled her tights up in the office toilet and let her skirt drop. She applied some lippy from a miniature tube and checked her teeth weren't red. She clipped the lid back on, the golden Dior logo facing her. Ah, the joy of samples.

She checked her watch. Late. It was only the weekly lunch with Sarah and Jo, her closest friends, but better get a move on.

After a short walk, she reached the entrance to *A New Leaf,* the bustling vegetarian bistro on Teviot Place. Looking left, past the *27* bus going in the direction of Lauriston Place, she gauged it was only a few hundred metres to the Empisoft office, where she was due next.

Plenty of time.

Claire stepped inside the restaurant and nudged her way through the annoying group just standing there. She spotted the girls and gave a little wave. She couldn't believe she'd been sworn to secrecy about her meeting with Adam Mooney. I mean, she met Adam Mooney. SHE TOUCHED HIS HAND. How was she supposed to hold that inside?

She slid into the booth and placed her handbag on the floor. She suddenly remembered the horror story her neighbour told of having a rat jump out of her handbag on returning home from a night at the manky Barrowlands concert venue, where she'd left the bag on the floor. Of course, that was Glasgow and this was a nice clean place in Edinburgh, but still. Claire picked hers up again and squeezed it between her and Sarah on the bench. Better safe than sorry.

The girls each had a big salad in front of them, served in a bright blue bowl with herbs painted on.

'Well hello there, stranger,' Jo said. 'Quick, let's get the waitress before she gets pulled in all directions.' She looked around and raised her arm.

'Sorry I'm a little late,' Claire said.

'At least you're here this time. It's been weeks,' Sarah said, filling Claire's glass from the carafe of water.

Claire noticed a new bracelet on her wrist. Probably that sleazy boyfriend. What did he do this time? She took a sip from her glass. 'Ah. I needed that. Thank you. It's been completely hectic.'

'How come?' asked Jo, still trying to get the server's attention.

Claire felt her stomach rumble. 'It's like I'm doing two jobs.' She stole a crouton from Jo and chewed quickly. 'You know my colleague Emily died, right? Well, I've taken over her work, while Darren is taking his bloody time figuring out how the agency will work without her.'

'Do you know what you want?' Jo interrupted.

'Well, I don't want to be doing Technology,' Claire replied.

'No, I mean do you know what you want to eat?'

I scanned the menu. It looked new. They now made a big feature of the green smoothie, whose secret recipe of fresh fruits and vegetables apparently kept people guessing. 'I'll have the chickpea tacos.'

'Don't you also have the Tartan Gala to work on?' asked Mia.

'No, that was a few weeks ago. The fashion and charity gigs are pretty much over for the summer. Next up will be food and drink season, though. Soooo dull.'

'Speaking of which. Have a try of this.' Jo passed the feta salad to Mia. 'I think it's under seasoned.'

Claire pricked a piece onto her fork. 'I feel like I'm not being appreciated at all in doing two jobs. Darren doesn't treat me fairly.'

Jo rolled her eyes. 'So you've said.'

Claire pursed her lips. She licked the sticky, sour cheese from her teeth. 'It's like Darren doesn't want to make any decisions and expects me to get on with it. It's not right. Whenever there's a problem, it's my fault, but if things are going well, it's thanks to him or Emily's planning.'

'I'm sure your boss will recognise your talents soon enough,' said Mia.

'Hm. Ever the optimist, Mia. It's hard to get motivated by software. I mean, who understands data science? What even is that? At least Emily got to work on things she liked — and is apparently still getting credit for it.' Claire groaned, ignoring Jo's raised eyebrow. 'And there aren't even any more glamorous events to go to, with the festivals coming to an end.'

Jo winced. 'Yeah but look where that got Emily...'

'I'm obviously not meaning that. I only meant—'

'You know, jealousy isn't very becoming,' said Jo.

Claire fell silent.

'She did get to snog Adam Mooney,' Sarah said with dreamy eyes.

Claire wriggled in her seat. How was she supposed to keep quiet about her encounter? But she'd promised Laura and Laura was her best client. She bit into her taco, fragments of fried maize shell falling from her hand.

'Bloody hell, Mia,' Jo said.

Sarah raised her arms in defence 'What?'

'That's a bit tasteless. That's Claire's colleague you're talking about.'

Sarah shrugged. 'Well yeah. And it's shocking how much crap she got. That was horrible. But if you ask me, she did ask for it by going public with her story. So he was a little too insistent... So she didn't enjoy the sex all that much... Haven't we all had that?'

Jo nodded. 'I've certainly had my share of bad dates.'

'And they weren't even with a movie star,' said Sarah, poking Jo in the shoulder.

Claire watched the surreal exchange as if detached. Were they serious? How could they be so callous? Then again, they kinda had a point.

Sarah continued. 'I'm frankly surprised he didn't sue. His reputation is in tatters.'

Jo sat up. 'I read he got to stay on for the new series, whereas there are plenty of other actors who have suffered much greater consequences for being lecherous monsters. I could name a few.'

The waitress refreshed the water carafe and stacked the empty plates on one arm. A man walked through the door with his toolbox and stood by the side of their booth.

He smiled and asked the waitress, 'Did you call about the boiler, hen?'

Claire did a double take: his rows of perfect teeth clashed with his Glaswegian accent.

'Right this way,' the waitress said.

Jo turned her head and ogled his muscular body as he strode to the rear of the room. 'Oh my God, I wish my plumber looked like that.'

'There's something about a weegie accent, too,' cooed Sarah.

'Listen to us,' giggled Jo, 'Just as bad as the men.'

26.
ME

After work, I caught the number 2 bus in the direction of Haymarket station. It was one of those distances that you could bus or walk in approximately the same time — about twenty minutes. But the heavens had opened, and despite having an umbrella with me, I reckoned the horizontal rain would have drenched my legs by the time I arrived for dinner with Suki.

I'd looked up the Fragrant Orchid on the map because I didn't know the address Suki had jotted down. It turned out to be a small alley off Morrison Street, directly behind the train station. The reservation was for seven o'clock. I checked my watch again. I'd left in good time.

The windows steamed up as more people hopped on the bus, their breath mingling and hitting the cold glass. Passengers who looked like train commuters started to gather their things. I wiped the condensation and looked outside. Almost there.

As the bus slowed down, I held onto the metal poles while people moved me towards the exit on the wet, slippery, rubber floor. On the street, I stepped away from the crowd and opened my umbrella. The freezing wetness on my shoulders made me shudder.

I navigated to the restaurant using my memory of the map. The alley wasn't well lit and smelled of the chip shop on the corner.

I peered inside the restaurant, noting I was the first to arrive. I hesitated. I didn't know whether to ask for Suki or Sukhon. Would I offend her parents if I got it wrong? Best to stay outside and wait.

The place was cute, with colourful transfers of orchids pasted on the window and lotus-shaped hanging lamps outside. There were two rooms, and both were reasonably busy. A couple exited, making me step aside on the narrow pavement.

'Hey, crazy lady. Whatcha doing outside?' Suki's voice came from inside a corporate-logoed umbrella.

It had made sense only minutes ago, but now I felt a bit dopey. I followed Suki inside.

An older woman, dressed in traditional Thai clothing, rushed to our side with the largest of smiles. She embraced Suki and chatted away in their language before turning to me, her arms outstretched. 'Hello! Welcome!'

I hunched down a bit to let the stranger squeeze me. I hoped to God this was Suki's mother and not a random over-affectionate waitress.

'Come, come,' she said.

She seated us at a reserved table by the window. Oh good; Western cutlery. I'd never mastered chop sticks — though worst case the deep green tablecloth would have forgiven spills.

I breathed in the delicate aromas of lemongrass and ginger that made a nice change from the smell of fried batter outside. I picked up the menu and a bright-red drink was instantly plopped in front of me, two fat shrimp perched over the side of the glass.

'What's this?' I asked.

'It's a Siam Mary', said Suki. 'It's like a bloody Mary with a Thai twist. Careful, it's spicy.'

I sniffed at it. 'I don't normally drink much.'

'Come on, live a little.' Suki raised her glass in salute and took a sip.

I brought the glass to my lips. Here goes nothing.

The tomato juice was delicious. I was thirsty from the bus and it didn't feel like there was that much alcohol in there, so I gulped it. I could feel my tongue swell up from the chilli Suki warned me about.

The menu was a heavy brown binder containing laminated pages of beautifully presented dishes with complicated names and a jumble of options for sides. What *is* all this? My mum only ever cooked the classics and aside from the occasional curry takeaway, we hadn't ventured far into the global cuisine. There wasn't much choice in Peebles. Plus, no money to eat out.

Suki must have noticed my bewilderment, because she took the menu off me and said, 'Let me.' She seemed to telepathically beckon her mother who arrived with a notepad in hand.

They chit-chatted away, pointing, arguing, eventually agreeing. I couldn't understand any of it, though I did recognise the subject changed from food to me, when Suki's mother elbowed her daughter's shoulder, cocked her head towards me, said something and cackled before turning away.

Suki rolled her eyes and gave me the wide smile that appeared to be a family trait. 'I'm sorry. My mum's obnoxious. She is all excited because she thinks we're on a date.'

I smoothed my ponytail. 'Oh.'

'I haven't set her straight yet because it means we'll get the full feast. She can get a bit arsey when I bring people from the office. She thinks I work too much.'

'And is your mother okay with you being gay?' I asked.

'I'll admit it wouldn't be her first choice,' she said. 'Both my parents have grown okay with it. In Thailand people are a little bit more fluid about sexuality and gender. It's not just an exported fantasy.' She motioned towards the pile of leaflets on the windowsill for the Ladyboys of Bangkok, a Vegas-style extravaganza featuring transgender performers, that had been a sold-out fixture of the Fringe Festival for nearly twenty years.

'Besides, her goal in life is to have grandkids — by whatever means necessary.'

Suki's infectious laughter loosened me up. She asked if there was anyone special in my life and I was, for a change, willing to answer.

'No. Emily used to try to set me up,' I said. 'It was always a disaster. The guys seemed more interested in her, which was perfectly understandable. Who wants a data science, book-loving nerd who never goes out?'

'Well, you're out today.' By magic, another Siam Mary appeared.

The starters followed, and I marvelled at the effort made in the decoration of the dishes. Carrots carved into floral shapes balanced on leaf-shaped cucumber slices. Was I meant to eat them?

'I know you and Justin met at Edinburgh University, but what's the story?' Suki asked, chewing her food.

'We studied computer science together. We were paired for an assignment and I told him about the project I was working on for my master's thesis. He got very excited. He'd been taking some classes on entrepreneurship, venture capital, that sort of thing.' The spicy pickled cucumber brought a flood of saliva into my mouth. I coughed. 'I thought it might be a bit of a rebound project. He'd tried to sell a multi-player war game idea to a few companies in Dundee but failed.' I shrugged. 'Something with armies and a new type of commands. I can't really remember.' I stirred a spring roll into a light green sauce. 'Anyway, he liked my model and ran with it. Pitched the business at a competition and got us our first twenty thousand pounds.'

'So it was your idea, but he took the lead?' she asked.

'Yes, we made a good team. I didn't want to be the face of the company and deal with business matters. That became his role. I only wanted to do the product development. We would each get fifty percent of the company. It's worked well.'

The second courses came and took over the entire table with their side plates and dipping bowls containing mysterious liquids. Suki instructed me on which bit went where and with what.

As I devoured one delectable dish after the other, I noticed the smile on Suki's mother had shrunk. Perhaps Suki had told the truth in their last exchange? My suspicion was confirmed when she replaced my empty cocktail with a Singha beer.

Suki drank, chatted and laughed freely. I felt lightheaded already, but her interest in me awakened an alien desire to be liked. To have a friend. A new friend.

'How did you get the idea for the software?' she asked.

'I did an internship at an online retailer in the north of England that was growing its data science department. The executives were keen to extract value from the enormous amount of data they held on their customers. You know, like automated product recommendations.' I put on a robotic voice. 'You bought this blue dress, so you might like these blue shoes. People like you bought this barbecue.'

'If you like these unicorn slippers, you'll want to furnish your entire house in pink.' Suki guffawed.

I snickered. 'Indeed. Despite being high-tech when it came to the customer's experience, they were using a simple questionnaire internally to gauge employee satisfaction. I just thought of a way to make that smarter. People lie on questionnaires, but not in everyday emails.'

'And here we are, one hundred million dollars later,' she said. 'All from your mind. Wow.'

I averted my gaze and buried myself in dessert, a satisfying combination of cold and sticky. The accompanying white drink caressed my throat with sweetness.

Suki doled out a few tales of deluded friends at Stanford who bet everything on ridiculous products nobody needed. I laughed as she told me about a programmable dog collar and how she'd seen the demise of that particular innovation a mile away.

She beamed. 'Did you know there are people who actually bought pouches of chopped-up fruit and vegetables for a four-hundred-dollar machine to squash into juice?' she said. 'And the stupid machine couldn't even squeeze it better than a human!'

Maybe it was the alcohol talking, but this was fun. Thoughts of Emily kept slipping through, but I sent them to the back of my mind. Emily would understand I didn't want to put a dampener on my night. She'd be delighted for me, wouldn't she?

It was time to leave. I almost pulled the tablecloth with me as I got up. Despite not being a future daughter-in-law candidate, I still received a generous send off from Suki's mum. Maybe she'd seen us have too much of a good time for this to just be work?

As we stepped outside, it was still raining. Suki and I simultaneously opened our umbrellas. They got entangled and made us laugh.

'Here, share mine,' Suki said. She pulled me close and wrapped an arm around my waist. I told myself it was to steady herself as she set her high heels on the uneven street, but the closeness, and the smell of Suki's hair caused confusion to stir inside me.

Were we having a *moment*? How was I meant to respond? What if I didn't? Would Suki still like me?

I let myself be swept back to the station. A drove of festival-goers rushing to catch the last train home pried us apart. Over the heads of a gaggle of young women, I shouted, 'I'm going this way,' and pointed in the direction of my home.

Suki waved and yelled — in the most casual and ever so slightly disappointing of ways — 'See you tomorrow.'

27.
ME

The letters on my monitor jumped around. I closed one eye and tried to make sense of them. My head throbbed and my mouth was dry. I licked my parched lips with my swollen tongue.

No alcohol, ever again.

The model Sally asked me to review kept getting stuck in the same place. I tried a few tricks but I was probably doing more harm than good in this state.

I saved what I'd done and put the model in the queue to be run on the company's servers. While there, I noticed that my new code, Network Impact, had completed its run on the Twitter data.

I tisked. About time. If this was going to be a valuable new product, I'd need to make it work more quickly. I clicked through.

The interface wasn't pretty; a boring grey background and a font only data nerds would find appealing. It would be the design team's job to fix that before we marketed it. I didn't do slick, I did functional — and as I read the screen, the functional looked good.

Clusters of tweets by the same account cast off red lines that scattered to other nodes and onward again. These highlighted accounts were the ones who were influencing and amplifying the negativity in the other people. A few obvious hotspots had taken shape.

With my mouse, I dragged the giant 3D web-like structure in different directions, zooming in and out to explore these red blobs.

But where was the green? I frowned then realised it made sense: the data was a representation of a global outpouring of hatred and anger. It would look very different if I ran the model on a company's internal communications, where there would be positive influencers and happier emotions, too. In a corporate setting, the dissatisfaction would never be as extreme as I was seeing here, but at least this proved the principle worked.

I made a note of the accounts that were showing the biggest influence and compared them to the list I compiled manually before, of those that had directed the clearest threats and abuse to Emily. I also cross-checked the names that Emily wanted to publicly shame in the tweets that never went out.

Nothing matched.

My heart sank. My model was rubbish. But as I continued checking through the big red hotspots, I grew more confident. I found the strong agitators who indirectly influenced the actions in other people. I leaned back in my chair, my hands on my head as I realised I'd been right. Those at the forefront — the ones whose opinions we saw the most — were only unwitting puppets of a few in the background, urging them on.

Excitement bubbled in my stomach. I chuckled. Suki's eyes would be lighting up with pound signs if she saw this.

I searched for the account of the secret photographer. Surely he'd be a big red node? But as I followed the lines emanating from him, it was clear that releasing Emily's image did nothing to increase the wave of hysteria directed at her. It was merely a new weapon picked up by the already frenzied warriors. If anything, the release of the photo had made some people abandon their tirades, now they could see she was a real person.

The person who named Emily, as guilty as I still believed him to be, had also only fed an unstoppable mob. It frightened me to see how quickly a small grumble, a little hint of heat, could infect others, building up the temperature, until the whole thing reached boiling point. It was no wonder it exploded into the real world, them looking for her at work... at home.

Hampered by the size of the data and unwieldiness of this early prototype visualisation, it took a good few hours to scan the network of clusters and line. But then I found him, the deepest red, the master inciter.

The profile name was *Chosen One*, with a Twitter handle of @*chosenone2*. I snorted. Trust there to be at least two chosen ones.

I scoured his tweets. He might be talented at picking the words with which to agitate others, but grammar was not his strong point. I wondered, out of professional curiosity, whether misspellings actually increased the sense of camaraderie among the uneducated. Maybe bad grammar made these Incel loser guys more readily adopt you into their clan?

It had the absolute opposite effect on me. I winced at some of the writing on display —word salad, frankly. People needed to read more. I pursed my lips when I twice saw him bastardise the word '*insolence*' into '*insolance*'. It made me wonder about him. Such a rarely used word. Even misspelled, it perfectly captured the sense of superiority in its author, the warped view that women had no right disobeying — or denying — men.

Despite two degrees in computer science, with plenty of tricks up my sleeve, I was, as before, unable to trace the account owner. The IP address jumped from the UK to the USA to New Zealand in a pattern any hacker would recognise as being someone who used a Virtual Private Network; a simple way to pretend you were in another country, set to randomly select locations.

I sank into my chair. Here he was — and it was most definitely a male calling for *the bitches* to burn — and there was nothing I could do. There was no point bringing any of this to the police; I'd get shown the door again. What were they meant to do with this mysterious inciter?

Inciter.

The word stuck in my head. Wasn't inciting hate a crime? I perked up at the prospect of having found a possible rebuttal to DI Reddy's anticipated objections. A quick Google search revealed that being female was, however, not one of the minority categories covered by anti-hate speech legislation.

I did learn that it was a crime to incite others to commit a violent or illegal act. If the police didn't even have the resources to go after those who actually made the threats, I could just imagine Reddy's response at my arguing — scientifically sound though it was — this person in the background was to blame. Never mind that someone sneaked into Emily's tenement to deliver a package meant to harass her; I could prove that they would not have done that were it not for this Inciter building up the frenzy that propelled them into action.

I buried my head in my hands. It was pointless.

The police might be interested in my work if I were looking for terrorists, jihadists who influenced others to convert to Islam and wreak havoc on the infidels, but not for this. Not for the hateful bullying of a young woman whose only offence was to try to heal publicly after an upsetting encounter.

No, there was nothing more I could do for Emily.

Life was unfair. And it broke my heart.

28.
SUKI

Who did Justin think he was? Suki picked up the yellow coffee cup Liv had handed her twenty minutes earlier. It wasn't very nice then and it was cold and horribly bitter now.

'Will he be much longer?' She asked Liv for the second time.

'I'm sorry. I'll check on him again. He knows you're waiting.' Liv straightened her cardigan and turned towards the long corridor in her soundless ballerina flats.

Suki crossed her legs and dangled her shoe from her toes, patting it to her heel in tempo with the song she couldn't get out of her mind: *I will wait.* She reached for her phone, but there weren't even any urgent emails left to process.

On the wall, the TV news covered the closure of the Woke Poke blog, describing it as a short-lived attempt to woo the millennials. Everybody was chasing that generation — the advertisers demanded it.

Suki paid special attention in case there was anything new to share with Laura. Woke Poke was the blog that hosted Emily's story and Laura spent a lot of time trying to make sense of her friend's death. From their conversations, Laura seemed to have a slightly unhealthy obsession with some of the folk on Twitter — surprising, as she'd disavowed any knowledge of social media when they first met.

One of the analysts on screen said the owners were closing down Woke Poke to protect their share price. The blog had been lambasted for posting an ill-advised, graphic piece of click-bait dressed up as a thought-piece to invite debate about feminism and sexual assault. Suki couldn't disagree with that assessment.

Liv returned with an apologetic smile. 'Justin is ready for you in the boardroom. More coffee?'

'No thanks.' Suki grabbed her stuff and made her way through.

She found him on his phone, his feet on the table, chuckling to himself. Yoda socks peeked from under his trousers.

'Having fun?' she said.

He raised one finger. 'Wait a second. This is a good one.' He tapped the screen in a typing frenzy, then put the phone down. 'Okay, I'm done.'

Suki approached the table he'd at least given her the courtesy of taking his feet off. 'While you're playing games, I've been ploughing through the draft acquisition agreements. They seem to be getting longer by the day and I need to make sure we're not being taken for a ride.'

'Speaking of rides,' he said, picking up his mobile again. 'Look at this beauty.' His eyes shone with excitement. 'I've put my name on the waiting list.' Justin turned his phone towards her to display the image of a very red, very large, expensive-looking motorcycle.

'That's some crotch-rocket,' she said. Her eyebrows shot up as she saw the price. 'Did you have to put down a deposit?'

'Peanuts, in the grand scheme of things.'

She gave him a fake smile. 'Well if I can have your attention, I might be able to help you not lose it.'

Justin put the phone down and asked, 'What do you need?'

'We need to talk about Schedule Four—'

Justin's device pinged and he rushed to pick it up. 'Hold on.' He chortled and moved his fingers across the screen.

'What are you doing?' Suki asked in her most glacial tone.

'Gimme a second. I'm having a bit of fun,' he said. 'The rumour mill has gone crazy about the acquisition. I'm just teasing my followers a little.'

Suki reached forward and pressed his phone onto the table, face down. 'I don't think that's a good idea, Justin. PeopleForce are trying to keep things confidential. It could affect their share price'

'Don't worry,' he said, waving her away, 'the PeopleForce guys love me. I can't wait to join them in California.'

'What's this?'

Justin grinned from ear to ear and held his arms out. 'You're looking at the new Global Director of Digital Labs. They want me to come head up the group from Silicon Valley.'

'I hope they know what they're getting,' Suki muttered under her breath.

'What did you say?'

Nerves pricked in the back of her neck. She'd started; she may as well continue. 'Well, I hope they're not expecting you to be the technology wizard. We both know that's Laura. You wouldn't have this business, if it wasn't for her.'

Justin seemed taken aback. 'I'm the one who made it a success. She chose to stay in the shadows. Somebody had to be the face.' He re-emphasised his trademark dashing smile by waving his hands underneath his chin.

Suki tasted bitterness in her mouth. 'As I understand it, you also agreed to go fifty-fifty. But you didn't, did you? You've got growth options she doesn't have.'

'And?' Justin's face clouded over. 'There was nothing in the small print about getting something extra for pulling that last investment through.'

'I think you should tell Laura before she finds out... She's going to have to sign a whole stack of documents and it's going to be there, in black and white. Not hidden away in the minutes of some board meeting, this time.'

'It was never *hidden away*, Suki. I don't know why you're bringing this up now. These growth options were awarded years ago. Compared to the amount of money we'll be raking in when the sale goes through, it's nothing. I don't remember asking your opinion about our past. Your job is to look to our future. You would do well to remember who you work for.'

She squeezed her fists.

Justin grabbed his files and started flipping pages to Schedule Four. 'Now, what seems to be the problem?'

29.
CLAIRE

'Claire, a minute please.' Darren half-leaned out his office door, his expression serious. It wasn't their normal catch-up time. A series of knots formed in Claire's stomach. Had she done something wrong?

She put aside the proofs from the conference programme she'd been reviewing, smoothed her hair with her fingers, and walked over. Was it hot in here, or was that just her?

When she entered his room, she braved a bright smile. The sun hit her through the window on the side causing dark spots to dance in her eyes. Framed motivational posters lined the walls, urging her to '*Be the best*' and '*Make it happen*,' and declaring that '*Hard work pays off.*'

Darren was at his desk, fiddling with his mouse, a sleek silver unit with a blue LED stripe that looked tiny in his muscular hands He removed and replaced its battery and gave it increasingly agitated shakes. 'Damn thing. Keeps skipping around the screen.'

Claire stayed standing, not knowing whether he'd really meant this would be a 'one-minute' exchange.

Darren gave the mouse another shoogle on its mat. 'Ah. There it is.' He gestured for Claire to sit down.

'What's up?' she asked as nonchalantly as she could.

He pulled at the sleeve of his dark grey Armani polo shirt, the cuff lining up with a red-speckled ring around his sinewy bicep. Claire had seen him heading for the gym before with an iPhone strapped to his arm. Could this be some sort of reaction to trapped sweat?

He caught her staring and let go of his sleeve. 'I'm letting everybody know... Because I don't want any rumours kicking about. Jacob's going to London.' He clasped his hands together. 'I've put him on immediate gardening leave. I can't risk him working out his notice when he's going to a competitor.'

A fanfare of excitement rose in her chest. Jacob owned the Culture portfolio. She'd have to play the part of sad colleague but sensed the opportunity within her grasp.

'That's a shame,' she said. 'I didn't expect that. Where's he going?'

'He's going to Embers. I tried to keep him.' He hit his fist into his other hand. 'Always hard to compete with the lure of the big city. I'd be grateful if you could keep this to yourself, while I tell the others.'

'Sure thing.' Claire made a mental list of who she'd seen exit this office already that day and whom he had left to see. She wasn't going to blow her shot.

When she didn't leave, he raised his chin. 'What is it?'

From the wall, a black-and-white weightlifter instructed her to 'Push yourself—because no one else is going to do it for you.'

She sat up straight. 'With Jacob gone, I want to pitch for his job. I've always made it clear that Culture is where I want to be.' She stopped, remembering her interview training from years ago: it's not about *you*, it's about what you bring to *them*. She rephrased. 'It's also where I could best use my skills to the benefit of the agency. And I know everything there is to know about what's going on in the arts world. Got some connections—'

'I'm going to stop you there, Claire. I'm giving the job to Otto.'

Her shoulders dropped. So much for *'Be a leader, not a boss.'* Claire tried hard not to let her voice turn into the shriek she was hearing inside her head. 'But I'm more senior than he is.'

'I'm well aware of that. But with the profiles of staff we have now with both Jacob and Emily gone, this makes the most sense. I can't have him working on fashion and charity gigs as a bloke. Most clients are women, and they like the feminine touch. You've always handled them well.' Darren lowered his head to catch her downturned eyes. 'Even though you're not getting your dream job, I was thinking about making you responsible for Technology permanently.'

He put on a smiling face and nodded. She should smile, too, but she didn't. He started scratching his arm. The rash reddened.

'Here's another way forward,' Claire suggested. 'Otto gets Technology and I get Culture. Why is that not an option? I'm not interested in technology.'

Darren's scratching became more insistent. 'Yes, well, it's your level of interest in popular culture I'm worried about. The thing is, I don't want you running Culture because frankly, the last thing I need is another one of my people with a girlie infatuation throwing herself at a movie star.'

'I wouldn't... That's not fair. Don't tar us all with the same brush.'

'I don't see what you're complaining about, Claire. I'm giving you Technology. That's a bigger brief. If you don't like it, stay where you are. It's straightforward enough to find someone eager to do this job. We've got the hottest technology client list in town. I could easily poach someone from Rebel Agency who would love to work on the juicy stuff.'

Should she complain? Was this enough to claim sexual discrimination? Darren was shrewd. He'd probably thought it all through. What would she have to complain about? He'd given her a promotion, hadn't he? That would be his defence. And in all her time at Pure Brilliant, she was still to see Human Resources do anything other than side with the boss.

'Does it come with a pay rise?' she asked.

'What?'

'Technology. The promotion.' She made sure to place an accent on the word *promotion*. Two could play this game — although she wouldn't be able to push too hard. On paper, Technology was a great job and she knew it. And it was doubtful she'd get anything better elsewhere given her limited experience.

He sighed and stroked his goatee. 'Maybe there is scope for a raise. I'll get back to you later today, okay?'

As satisfied as she was ever going to be, Claire grumbled her acceptance and left.

30.
ME

Suki and I pored over a stack of documentation. Empty cups littered the table. Our breaths mingled with the aroma of freshly baked cookies Liv had brought in to keep us going.

My initial awkwardness following our after-dinner moment had faded. Over the last few days we'd developed a work routine. I knew to always be available for Suki when needed, recognising increasing nervousness as her speech sped up. I didn't mind so much. The sooner this deal was done, the sooner I could get on with my life.

Suki for her part, seemed to have learnt that I needed regular breaks and quiet when I'd spent too much time in the company of others. Like everyone else in the company, Suki respected my 'book time'.

The frosted privacy glass in the boardroom was always turned on when she came. She'd told me that with rumours swirling on the Internet, and the markets responding to that by betting on PeopleForce's share price, it was imperative to keep the deal under wraps.

I looked over at my companion, reading her papers, a red pen in her mouth to scratch out or circle a whole new vocabulary: legalese and finance speak I'd only ever encountered in Grishams or financial thrillers without understanding what they meant. There, it didn't matter: it was enough to catch the gist to follow the story.

But in real life, it was a matter of millions, of risk and lawsuits, of a carefree future.

A shadow grew on the opaque glazed door. The figure swayed, then knocked.

I switched off the wall monitor with the remote control. 'Come in,' I said.

My colleague Grant stepped inside, his wiry frame straight as a pole. He held the side of an open laptop in one hand, the other folded below the machine for balance. 'I'm sorry to interrupt, Laura. I know you guys need to be left alone. This can't really wait.' He nodded at Suki politely. Everyone in the office had seen her at some point, but nobody but Liv knew who she was.

'What is it?' I asked.

'We've been having some serious performance problems lately, and I've been struggling to find the cause until today.' He chewed his lip. 'It looks like it may be something you did.'

'What do you mean?' I turned to Suki and said, 'Sorry. I need to deal with this. Grant is our systems man, heads up all the network side. I'll be as quick as I can.'

Grant shuffled one foot over the floor, smoothing the carpet. 'The guys have been complaining that our email and fileshares have been frequently grinding to a halt. It's only on and off so it took me a while to find what was happening. I eventually spotted a process consuming a large amount of resources ... and it has your ID on it.'

I chewed my lip. 'Has it been impacting our clients?' I asked.

'No, thankfully only our internal systems,' he replied.

I waved him over. 'Let me see. That doesn't make any sense. I've only been working on the Development servers.'

Grant approached the table and set the laptop down. Suki moved to the side to give us space. In the corner of my eye, I could see she was only pretending to continue with her reading, her gaze discreetly on us.

Rows of white letters travelled across a black background on Grant's display. They represented all the activity on the company's systems, each line showing a piece of code running, its technical characteristics and the level of processing power it was using up. It was Grant's job to monitor this and make sure that the company always had a sufficient level of processing and storage capacity.

I knew what I was looking at since, in the early days, I'd fulfilled all the technology roles, including this one. Of course, it had become significantly more complex as the company acquired new customers and grew into a multi-million-revenue business, but the basics stayed the same.

'I don't see anything strange,' I said.

'That's why it's been hard. Wait for it...' Grant leaned forward. His aftershave was overpowering.

'You know what,' I said, pushing my chair back. 'Put all this up on the screen. I want Suki to see too.'

Suki looked up from her reading, bemused. I pointed secretively to Grant, scrunching my nose. She gave me a subtle nod in reply.

She set her pen down like an eager schoolgirl and clasped her hands in front of her. 'Yes, please,' she said to Grant.

'And you'll need to explain like she's an idiot. She's just a banker,' I teased.

Grant took the cable and plugged it into his computer. The screen jumped to life with the new content. 'I didn't see anything strange at first, either. Yet we were having some hard spikes that were locking resources and causing everything else to queue. Eventually, I started to see a pattern. Just wait. It will come in a few seconds.'

We sat in silence while the jumble of letters and numbers on the screen darted about.

'There.' Grant jumped out of his seat and ran to the screen. He pointed at a line that hadn't been there before, which seemed to be consuming eighty-five percent. 'This model called *TwtrNetImp* pops up like that every so often wreaking havoc.'

My stomach churned. It was mine, yet it had no business being there. 'And it's running on our live server?'

'Yes, which is why I needed to see you urgently. It's crawling over all our data. At first, I thought it was some sort of attack I needed to shut down, but once I figured out it was yours, I didn't want to kill it off. Because it may have been, you know, important?' He alternated his gaze between Suki and me, no doubt searching for some insight into our secret activities. Suki maintained a neutral face.

'You did the right thing, bringing it to me, Grant,' I said. 'Don't kill it just yet, though. I'll have a look and take care of it. I promise.'

'Okay... If you're sure.' Grant pulled the cord from his device. 'Let me know when you're done, will you?'

I nodded.

The minute he left the room my hands shot up to up head. 'Oh my God.'

'What is it?' Suki asked.

'It's my new tool. The Network Impact. I was testing it on some... never mind. I was running it on some data. Only on my R&D part of our systems. I don't understand why it would...'

I typed furiously and jumped across multiple screens. Suki left me to it. I stopped. 'Crap.'

'Is it bad?'

'I made a mistake in the security settings. Instead of constraining it to the development server, it had the freedom to run everywhere.'

'Wait, you mean while you were playing with Network Impact on test data it went and started using your live data?'

I grimaced. 'Yes. It ran on all the emails and messaging from my colleagues. What I can't work out is—'

'This is great,' exclaimed Suki, paying more attention to the screen. 'What's it showing?'

'No, you don't get it. The security implications of this—'

'I know, I know. You'll need to fix what happened.' She slapped the table. 'It's you who doesn't understand,' she said. 'It's working! And not only have you run it on some test data you still need to tell me about, but you've run your new product on a live company test case.' She whooped and clapped her hands. 'You said you couldn't run it on a live company, a client, because you'd need consent and all that. We never thought about doing it on Empisoft itself.' Excitement lit up her face. 'If it's showing you what are expecting to see, we can take it to PeopleForce and secure the full value of it before we sell the company.'

'Okay, okay. Fine. Let me stop it, contain it, and we can look at the data.'

Suki got up. 'I'll get us some drinks while you sort this out.'

I quickly skipped through a series of programmes and settings. How did this happen? I'd directed it to run on the stuff I'd scraped from Twitter, but it seemed that when it ran out of data, it just ventured onto a new source.

By the time Suki returned, I'd managed to disable the tool and retrieve what it had produced so far.

'What have you got?' she asked, balancing two cups in her hands.

I scrolled through the screen in a flash. Having spent hours and days analysing the Twitter results, I had grown more adept at handling the giant 3D web of connections to find what mattered.

'I've got the preliminary results,' I said. 'It was nearly done, in fact.'

Suki joined my side. 'Could you not let it finish?'

'No. It's jumped one wall already. I don't know what damage it could cause.' I felt a twinge of guilt seeing Suki's shoulders slump.

'Once we contain it, and plan for it in terms of our systems, we should be able to run it again. We would need to get the lawyers to check and Justin to consent...'

'Ha! I'm sure he'll be jumping up and down as much as I am to parade this in front of PeopleForce. Plus, this is all about showing who is the most influential in a group, isn't it? He'll be super eager to show them how important he is.' Suki chuckled. She'd regained the colour in her cheeks after the dreariness of the last few days' documentation work.

I, too, felt a surge of excitement. Here was my newest creation beautifully doing its job.

'How does it work?' Suki asked, half-sitting on the table facing the screen.

'You need to come sit here with me. I can't move the structure around and point at the screen at the same time.'

'Did you still want your tea? I don't need my coffee anymore — I'm buzzing.'

I pulled a chair up beside me and slid my laptop in place for us to share. She tucked her hair behind her ear. Her skin glowed in the screen's glare.

'Now this is obviously only a prototype,' I began. 'We'd have to do an awful lot of user interface work to make this something that a non-technical person can work with and get the insight from they need. Here's what you're looking at. This jumble of lines and knots is a 3D representation of how a group of people impact each other. These little nodes are people. See? If I hover over a node you will see their user ID come up. Their colour, green to red, you've seen before in our core product. That's their current state of mind. But the colour of the lines *between* these people shows how they influence each other. And the size of the line shows you by how much.'

Suki pointed at one of the lines. 'This guy seems to piss off this guy a lot because the line is bright red.'

'Yes and no. There's a way of looking at that too. In this mode, it's showing you that the guy is amplifying the feelings of discontent, not pissing him off directly. It's an important distinction. And it's also critical to look at this data over a longer period, not only the one event.' I pulled at the web of lines with my mouse, zooming out. 'We're scanning here for people who are consistently stirring up aggravation in others, without necessarily being the cause of the initial resentment. Maybe they don't even know they're doing it because they're not necessarily annoyed themselves. This could be the one that people go to to complain, who agrees with them and makes it worse.'

'Frank!'

'Huh?' I asked.

She fanned her hand dismissively. 'Nothing, it's the example I used for Angus when I explained your tool.' Bringing her attention to the screen again, she said, 'It looks like the interactions within Empisoft seem to be quite positive on the whole. I mean, it's all fairly green or light amber.'

I was reminded of the angry red, thick-lined structure I'd examined before: the clump of nastiness that was Twitter's reaction to Emily. In comparison, this was an oasis of calm.

'Yes, and I would expect that to be the case for most clients. At least that's what I hope. We'll need to calibrate the colours to get the scale optimised. At this stage what you are looking for are the biggest influencers, with the most and fattest lines.'

'Like this one.' Suki pointed at a bright green blob, thick branches growing out of it.

I zoomed in to this seemingly extraordinarily positive connection, the main influencer of happiness at the firm. The name popped up as I swept my mouse over it. I quickly let go and it disappeared.

'So?' Suki's eyes lit up.

I rubbed my forehead. 'Remember this hasn't been validated yet at all. I'm not even sure the data was set up in the correct way for the analysis since it wasn't even supposed to go there. We don't have anything to compare it to—'

'Oh, shut up already.' Suki leapt on the mouse and clicked on the mass of green. 'Ha! It's you. Of course, it is. I knew it.' She clapped her hands and bounced on her chair.

'We can't show this,' I said, turning the image away from her. 'I need to spend some time looking at it first.'

'You mean, in case Justin looks bad?' Suki arched an eyebrow. 'I actually agree. Let's do a quick check to make sure he doesn't come off too badly, but Laura, you need to stop erasing yourself like this. I knew it all along and this confirms it. You, my dear, are what's valuable in this business. And I think we need to right some wrongs.'

'What wrongs?'

Suki turned my chair to face her. She grabbed the arm rests so that I could only look her straight in the eyes — eyes that turned serious, above a set of pursed lips.

'You told me you and Justin had agreed that everything would be split fifty-fifty when you first started out. That you'd always have the same salary and the same number of shares.'

I nodded. 'And we do.'

Deep grooves formed on Suki's brow. 'Well, you've only ever looked at the share structure that had the ordinary shares on it. And there, yes, you both have equal ownership. But you're wrong overall.'

I squeezed my armrests, not quite knowing where to set my hands in this enclosed position. Where was this going?

Suki sighed. 'Because you've never wanted to be a director on the board of the company, you weren't involved in the decisions that were made on different forms of remuneration. Justin has a boat load of growth options that you don't.' She must have recognised my puzzle expression as she went on to explain. 'An option is when you have the right to buy a share in a company for a discounted price in the future. When an employer gives you options in the company, it's an incentive to stay and work hard. Because tomorrow, you might be able to use your option, buy shares at, say, ten pence and immediately sell them again for a pound.'

'Making an instant profit.' This was less complicated than I expected.

'Right. Options are particularly valuable in start-ups. People tend to exercise them — that means to use them — when the company is sold or if it goes public. Now, a *growth* option, like the ones Justin has, is the same as any other option, except you only get to exercise it when the company's share price has grown by a predetermined amount. With me?'

'Yes.'

'In Justin's case, the company needs to be worth *ten times* more than when he got the options. I've never seen it be that high before. The investors who granted them to Justin at the last investment round must have thought they would never be worth anything. But because of the valuation I've managed to get you in the sale to PeopleForce, they'll actually be worth close to one million dollars.'

A bubble grew inside my throat, an empty vessel of missing words. My memorised dictionary failed to crystallise my feelings. I swallowed. It hurt. I wrestled free and took a few steps back, rubbing my lips to condition them to adequately express... what? Disbelief? Betrayal? Grief? Anger?

Suki was quick to jump in. 'I told Justin it wasn't fair, that he should tell you.'

Her voice sounded distant. The surrounding light dimmed. The meeting room was moving away from me, and I was left alone.

I'd always thought I liked being alone but for the first time, I realised that being alone when I had friends was not actually being alone. I didn't need to see my friends often, or interact much, to know they were there. And now Emily was dead.

It had been long clear to me that all this work, the search for the culprits, someone to punish, was my way of keeping her alive. But I was failing. Soon there would be nothing left to cling onto.

Justin.

I'd trusted him...

I felt hollowed out, like my inner life had been ripped away. No longer me.

'Laura? Laura!' Suki waved her hand inches from my face. 'I said, what do you want to do?'

'I don't know.'

31.
SUKI

It stayed dry the whole way back to Suki's office, despite the dark clouds hanging ominously low in the sky.

She hadn't wanted to leave Laura, who seemed in shock — more than she'd expected given Laura's limited interests in the money side. But once that girl went into one of her dwams, with her mind somewhere else, there was no point hanging around.

Suki's knee-length skirt stretched over her thigh as she climbed the steps that led to the rear door of the Standard Life headquarters, past which there was a convenient shortcut between busy Lothian Road and the stillness of Rutland Square.

With her hands full of papers, she used the side of her wrist to press the doorbell. Many of the other buildings in the square had sophisticated intercom and code-entry systems, but the finance houses liked to maintain a sophisticated air of tradition.

The old-fashioned ding-dong summoned the receptionist, just like it summoned the help when the wealthy merchants lived here.

The door opened and the young chap greeted her with a smile. Was it Alisdair? Chad?

'Hey Suki. Forgot your key?'

She was tempted to tell the truth, that she'd been too lazy to look for it with her hands full, but manners required her to lie. Particularly since the temps they'd been getting for the receptionist role didn't seem to last long. 'Yes, I'm sorry.'

'No worries,' he said, his Australian accent making Suki half expect to be handed a beer. 'Angus was wondering where you were, by the way.'

Suki lifted her chin towards the rear. 'Is he in there?'

'Uh-huh. He's been on the phone all morning.'

Suki dropped her cargo on her desk and straightened her hair. The cushiony carpet in the corridor to the rear office provided a welcome relief from the outdoor stones she'd been treading for the Empisoft deal. She wouldn't normally handhold her clients quite so much, but these guys were one seriously inexperienced management team.

She knocked.

His gruff voice sounded through the door. 'In.'

'You were looking for me?' she asked.

Angus removed his reading glasses and closed the folder he'd been holding. His rosacea had flared up into a furious red pyramid over his nose and cheeks. Had he been drinking?

'I got a call from Justin Travers last night.' He let that sentence linger for a while longer before frowning and adding, 'I'd like to hear your side of the story.'

Sweat gathered on Suki's palms; she rubbed her hands. 'I suppose you're referring to the conversation I had with him yesterday about the share structure?'

His arms were crossed. 'What were you thinking, challenging him on some historical arrangement?'

'Is that what he called it? "Challenging"? I was only pointing out, at a critical time in the company's existence, that he had reneged on a verbal agreement with his co-founder. It's not something I wanted to see blow up at the last minute.'

'No, you thought you'd let it blow up now. Did Laura whats-her-name ask you to do this?' Angus rose from his seat and leaned on the table with both fists.

'No,' Suki said. 'But she would've found out eventually.'

'Would she? And what was there to find out? That she hasn't been paying attention for years? That she shouldn't be signing things blindly? This happened eighteen months ago. It's completely irrelevant. What we need to focus on is getting this deal with PeopleForce over the line. And the last thing we need is for the Empisoft management team to fall out.'

He was right. The Americans would run a mile at the merest hint of discord, particularly with rumours intensifying of them courting the competition.

But it had sat like a brick in her stomach, the inequity, the blatant disregard for who was actually creating the value in the company. And not just at the start, with the product that put them on the map; still today, every day. Laura, with her mind-blowing innovations.

Suki reflected on the images of Laura's latest influence model. She wished she'd seen Justin's node. What colour lines would come out of him?

There was no question Justin had been essential to the company. Laura would never have pursued the opportunity as relentlessly as he did. It was his charm and salesmanship that got them their initial investment, followed by their first reference client. He was the one who had wooed and hired a superstar sales team — skills that were in short supply in Scotland. Yet without a product there would've been nothing to sell. And all the while Laura had beavered away at it, trusting that she would be treated fairly.

Suki had learnt long ago trust was for losers.

Angus slapped the table. 'Hellooo, are you listening?'

Indignation spewed bile into her mouth. He couldn't speak to her like that — she wasn't his daughter.

She breathed to steady herself. The deal was at risk and she needed to save it. 'They've been friends for years. They must be able to come to an agreement. It's the last chance to do anything before he can cash these growth options in. I think I'll—'

'Remember who our client is: the Empisoft board. And your little friend isn't on it. If she's not on it, she doesn't count. Are we clear? We are *this* close to signing a deal that will make us, you and me, an enormous amount of money. I will not have you endanger it with some emotional crusade. I am in two minds whether to take this deal off you.'

Suki's whole body stiffened. It was her knowledge of the technology sector that had allowed Madainn to win the pitch to represent Empisoft. It was her Silicon Valley network that had attracted the bidders. It was she who'd managed the auction, manipulating each of the players into bidding more than they had intended to. She wasn't about to let this stuffy, old-world, out-of-his-depth partner of a medium-rung corporate finance boutique take the credit for her hard work. This was exactly what the Justin and Laura thing was all about.

But he wouldn't care about any of that. His firm, his rules. They were here to make money — and, truthfully, she was too. 'I wouldn't do that, Angus. I suspect taking me off this deal would spook the Americans even more, don't you?'

He humphed. 'You need to make this go away. Make peace with Justin, because he is asking for your head. Maybe he can give the girl a big bonus or something to even things out a bit. I don't know what she's complaining about. She stands to make a life-changing amount of money. Why cause a fuss about a little bit more? Besides, she could walk away the day after, cash in hand. Whereas Justin, being the Key Man as far as PeopleForce are concerned, will need to stay on for two whole years before he gets his full reward.'

To her annoyance, he was right again. When companies were acquired, it was common for agreements to include conditions that incentivised the most important people to stay on. It would otherwise be too tempting to cash in and ride off into the sunset, leaving the buyers in the lurch. In this case, Justin was the one they wanted to keep, and he would be tied into them for two years before he got his millions. Suki thought back to the red motorcycle he was lusting after — it would be his sneaky growth options that would pay for that. Coupled with his new cushy job in California, there wasn't much to pity.

Angus returned to his seat and held his mobile phone with an extended arm; the reading glasses on his nose clearly not doing their job. After a few, slow taps of his index finger, he looked over the lenses at Suki and said, 'Can I trust we will have no more of this ra-ra equality nonsense and that you will get this fixed?'

Suki nodded curtly and retreated, a ball of fury in her stomach. This was not over.

32.
ME

Atticus tapped his paw against my forehead repeatedly, the blanket over my face protecting me from his claws. It was past dinner time, but I couldn't face getting up from lying on the sofa. He stomped onto my wool-covered head, over my shoulders, into the well created by my chest, my thighs and the settee's back rest. His weight pulled the cover firmly over my mouth and nose.

I flung an arm outward to let in some air. I flinched. My eyes adjusted to the brightness and I wiped the drool from the side of my mouth. I'd hoped to sleep, to shut the world out entirely. All I'd managed was an hour and a half of enclosed, humid breathing.

I hoisted myself to a sitting position and brought a reluctant Atticus to my chest. I buried my face in his tummy, the soft down helping to avert the tears I desperately wanted to hold in — in case they wouldn't stop.

'It's just you and me, buddy.'

He purred.

I'd wanted to run home straight after I left Suki in the boardroom but needed to first make sure my rogue software code hadn't affected anything else on our systems. It had taken until 5PM.

When Justin had walked past my bank of desks and given me a quick wink, it had taken all my might not to throw my keyboard at him to silence that blinking eye once and for all.

How could I have been so stupid, to think we were a team of equals? He'd changed over the last few years. The company's success had gone to his head. Fond memories of late-night scheming filled my mind. We'd been chums at the start, each respecting what the other brought to the party. And we had a good time along the way.

Had I misread him all along?

I rubbed my thumb over Atticus's cheek and he flicked his rough tongue over the palm of my hand. 'At least with you, I know where I stand.'

Why had Suki told me about his growth options? Curse her. What game was she playing? I thought of our time spent together, wracking my brain for signals I might have missed of a betrayal that could be around the corner. I couldn't work it out.

One thing I knew: Suki was motivated by money. Her excitement when the Network Impact tool worked proved that. It was all to do with the price they could sell the company for. Why bring Justin's options up when all it could do was cause problems? Could she really care that much about me getting my fair share? Was that what this was?

Suki's laughter echoed in my head and raised a cautious smile. You couldn't fake that laugh. We'd been having fun, hadn't we? Suki toying with her mother at the restaurant as she placed her hand on mine. Her snicker when her mum had replaced cocktails with beer when our amorous cover had been blown. The way she'd even managed to make a joke of the horrible things some of her colleagues did to her, and her description of how she'd squash them all like bugs when she reached the top.

The giggles under the umbrella.

I felt a tug at my heart. I'd only ever giggled like that with Emily before.

My gaze crossed the room to settle on our childhood photos. Sparkly eyes and gummy mouths against the backdrop of familiarity, love and a carefree, small-town upbringing.

I clenched my jaw. Had I been a good friend to Emily? I thought I had — had certainly always meant to be. Could my good intentions of fighting Emily to stay off social media and ignore it all have made matters worse? Maybe if I'd been more supportive, more willing to listen rather than lecture... I hoped to God that it wasn't me who'd made Emily feel alone.

Like I was feeling.

Atticus stepped on my bladder and jumped off the sofa towards his water fountain. It was Emily who'd convinced me to get a pet. '*You can't live with only fictional beings for company,*' she'd said. '*Like training wheels on a bike, maybe a cat can help you learn to open up your life to others.*'

When I named the tiny jumble of fur 'Atticus', for his role in supporting a social outcast, just like the lawyer, Emily didn't recognise the literary reference and just shrieked, '*Atticus the Catticus! I love it.*'

Lost in my memories, I only noticed my phone ringing on its third chime. I wiped the tears sliding along my nose and checked the screen before answering. Trust Mum to call at the right time.

'Darling. How are you?' she asked.

Where would I start? 'I'm... okay.'

We'd spoken frequently straight after Emily's death. That had slowed, no doubt caused by my unwillingness — inability? — to talk at any length about my feelings. I didn't mind the long pauses, the two of us at either end of a line, connected, breathing, alive. How could I explain I only wanted her quiet company?

Forever trying to fix things, Mum had suggested journaling — what with my love of words and all. But I'd stared at the blank pages of the flowery notebook she'd sent, and it had made me feel worse. Again, a clumsy good intention causing more harm than good. They seemed to be everywhere.

She tried to coax more out of me. 'And the big business deal? How is that going?'

There was little point sharing the ups and downs of something my waitressing mother could never get her head around. 'That's going okay, too, Mum. Not long to go.'

'That's exciting. Well, I have some exciting news, too. Oliver and I are getting married!'

It was as if the cord had been cut. My head felt light and I clasped the blanket in my spare hand.

Happy.

I should be happy.

Be happy, damnit.

'Wow, Mum. That's great. Congratulations.'

'We're going to have it at Drill Hall. It won't be a big affair. We're thinking February. There's something romantic about a winter wedding, don't you think? I think we'll have enough saved up. We won't be able to have much of a honeymoon...'

Drill Hall, the Peebles community centre? That cold place where I used to go to Cub Scouts? No, that wouldn't do. Not for Mum. Not if I had anything to say about it. And for once, I did.

'Yes you will. You're going to have the honeymoon of a lifetime. You're going to have the wedding of a lifetime, like at Cringletie House or the Hydro. You'll have the dress of a lifetime. I can pay for it.'

'What? No. How?'

'I insist, Mum. That deal I've been telling you about. What I haven't mentioned, is that it's going to... it's going to make me very rich.'

'How rich?' I knew Mum's idea of rich didn't even come close to the eight figures that would soon be landing in my bank account.

'More than rich enough. And I can't think of anything I would rather do with that money than to make you happy. I mean it.'

'But darling, it's too much. I mean, a little contribution would help... Don't feel like you—'

'Please, let me do this.' I cupped the phone with both hands, holding it close to my cheek. 'You've done so much for me. You've worked hard. You've made this success happen, too. Go think about your dream wedding and tell me what you need. Anything goes.'

Mum took quick little breaths. 'Oh darling, I can't believe it. Thank you. It's hugely exciting. I'm going to tell Oliver straight away.'

'You do that,' I said, as I lost my heart's last connection.

33.
ME

My noise-cancelling headphones weren't fully blocking out the colleagues standing close by. On their mid-morning break, they were retelling some of the jokes from the comedy show they'd seen the night before. I watched them, distracted, out of the corner of my eye; a little group of young, healthy-looking, like-minded men and women enjoying life. No drama. No tension.

I admired the ease with which the conversation flowed, the wordless passing of the baton for the next person to build on what had been said before and delight further.

Sally's laughter was raucous and before long, I caught myself chuckling along, even if I hadn't heard the actual gag. I imagined myself party to this warm, good humoured exchange. I could be like them; open, accepting, gregarious even. Making friends, casual conversation. Why not?

I took my headphones off to join them, but the group dissipated before they noticed me, each one returning to the work I'd set for them. I was the boss, and probably not a person they'd want to spend time with socially anyway.

A green bubble popped onto the screen of my new mobile.

Suki insisted that as the representative of a pioneering technology start-up, it was unacceptable for me to not have the latest, highest-spec phone when the Americans came to town. Plus, she'd teased, there was no way she was going to hang out with a Nokia-waving dork.

So I'd taken the bus into town that morning and entered the bright, white Mecca for gadget lovers, where I'd been overwhelmed by the choice laid out on row after row of long pine tables.

I almost ran when a smiling, bearded chap skipped my way, iPad in hand. But I knew if I wanted to get what I needed quickly, I'd have to engage with this stranger.

Fifteen minutes and many, many hundreds of pounds later, I was the proud owner of a surprisingly light, sleek black device. I might have been new to smart phones, but I was no fool, and quickly disabled the tracking and all except the most necessary privacy-intruding features while I walked to work.

A message from Suki flashed at me.

Meet me for lunch. 12.30. A New Leaf.

Was this the kind of 'hanging out' she meant when she'd dissed my phone? Hanging out — such a friend thing to do. I took a sip of water to neutralise a spark of excitement. It would only be a work thing. Didn't bankers 'do lunch' all the time?

Nevertheless, I watched the clock on the lower right side of my screen intently until it was time to set off the few blocks to Teviot Square.

Outside, the sun had returned after a few days' absence, a last hurrah for the Scottish summer. It hit the top of my head and I pulled my ponytail loose to feel the warmth spread across my scalp.

A queue spilled onto the pavement outside the bistro. My step quickened. What if there was no room for us?

I slunk past the bodies on the pavement to peer inside and was relieved to see Suki already seated, deep in concentration. Her manicured thumbs danced over her phone's keys at a dizzying speed, the tip of her tongue squashed between her lips.

The place was packed, and the smell of coffee punched me in the face. I shifted my weight from one leg to the other by the side of her table, subduing my shortness of breath. No reaction. 'Hello.'

Suki kept her head down and raised her index finger while she continued swiping with her right thumb. After a few awkward seconds, Suki put her mobile down, and looked at the empty bench opposite.

'What are you still doing standing there?' She laughed and said, 'Sit! Sit!' sounding like her mother. 'Sorry. I was in the middle of a complicated email.'

I slid into the booth and grabbed the plastic-coated menu. I'd heard about their mysterious green smoothies, but I was after something more substantial — something that would take a little longer to consume. 'What are you having?' I asked.

'Chickpea tacos,' she replied. 'They're awesome. You should have them too. Or you can get something else and have a taste of mine.'

It was as if sharing food was the most normal thing in the world. I blinked. 'Okay.'

Suki looked around for the waitress who darted around the venue like the target at an arcade shooting game.

'Listen, I wanted to talk to you outside the office because... Well, because of Justin. Let's just say I'm not his favourite person at the moment,' she said.

'You can say that again.'

'Let's just say I'm not his favourite person at the moment.' Suki chortled. 'Sorry, I couldn't resist.'

'Laugh all you like. He had a huge go at me.'

Her eyes widened; the fun gone. 'When?'

'Last night. He phoned me at home. It was the last thing I needed.'

'I'm sorry.' Suki hunched forward to grab my hand then jumped upright again and shook her head. 'No. Sorry, not sorry. You know what? He's not entitled to give you a hard time over... what? The fact he's been caught? What he did was wrong. Full stop.'

Suki's fieriness disoriented me, as her unclear intentions had the day before. 'Why—'

She interrupted. 'I know I messed up — we can't have this impact the acquisition. I'll fix it. But he needs to know he can't wipe the floor with us.'

'Us?'

'Him. Them. Us. Women. I'm sick of men lording it over us, disrespecting our work. Behaving like we're some *thing*, a second rate—' Catching my bemusement, she deflated. 'God, listen to me. Like I'm on some sort of feminist crusade. That's not it. I discovered the injustice and it was so... Ugh.' She wriggled like she'd been covered in worms.

'Why did you do it?' I asked.

She cocked her head. 'Why did I accuse Justin of cheating you?'

'Yes.'

'Because it was so glaring. There hadn't even been an attempt to justify it — or to hide it. I did it because I knew you wouldn't have stood up for yourself if I'd told you first. And because... I don't know. I like you. You're smart. And nice. You deserve better.'

My heart skipped and I turned away — outwardly to look for the waitress, but really so that Suki wouldn't see me blush.

Instead, it was Claire who did. She was standing right next to us. I pressed the back of my hand against my cheek and smiled meekly.

'Hello, Laura.' Claire let her eyes drift from me to Suki and back. 'And Suki. What a nice surprise.'

Suki gave a small wave. 'Oh hey, Claire.'

'You two know each other?' I asked.

'Yes,' said Claire. 'Suki and I worked together at a Madainn-sponsored awards ceremony last year.'

'I needed to stay close to Claire to make sure we'd win the prize for best corporate finance house of the year.' Suki laughed.

Claire held her hands up in defence. 'You got me... you've uncovered the deep dark secret of PR.' Her mobile pinged. She read the message. 'Oh. I get lunch here with friends every week, but I've been stood up today.'

Suki skooshed sideways. 'Why don't you join us?'

I clutched the tabletop. What was Suki doing? We were having a nice time. Had she not wanted to talk about things?

Claire hesitated.

Suki patted the seat beside her. 'The more the merrier.'

'Okay. Don't mind if I do. Have you ordered?' Claire looked around the café. 'It can be a bit tricky when it's busy like this.'

Suki finally succeeded in waiving the waitress over. 'Not yet.'

After we placed our orders, I watched the two make expert small talk. About the smoothies, the weather, Claire's lovely new highlights. All smiles. Easy for them. Had they been this chummy when they worked together? Is that what Suki did? Charm you until she didn't need you anymore?

I jumped in. 'Claire's taken over the organisation of Empisoft's conference from my friend Emily, who was a real fan of technology.' The little dig went unnoticed as the dead friend reminder stopped the conversation cold. Suki cleared her throat and sipped at her water. Thankfully, the waitress came with our plates, giving us something to do. We chomped on our greens in silence.

Suki eventually asked me, 'Are you doing anything for the conference this year?'

I shrugged. 'Not much. I tend to just show up in case there are questions.'

Claire tried to catch my eye. She was pointing at her own teeth. What did she want? Suki joined in, wiping her teeth with her finger. I wondered if it was a game. I supposed I should do the same, and that was when I realised I'd been talking with a shred of spinach lodged between my teeth. A hot flush ran across my cheeks. Such a dope. My goofy chuckle released laughter from the other two. I glowed inside.

'Laura's being modest,' said Claire. 'She runs a technical breakout session which is in high demand. In fact, it's got a waiting list.'

Suki smiled warmly. 'Yes, I've discovered "modest" is Laura's default setting. I'm on a mission to shake that out of her.'

I looked down, brushing focaccia crumbs off my lap.

'What are you two doing together?' Claire asked Suki, whose eyes darted straight to me.

'It's okay, Suki,' I said. 'Claire is the only other person who knows about the acquisition.'

'Oh good,' Suki said. 'Because I wanted to mention something about PeopleForce—'

I winced. 'She didn't know who Empisoft's buyer was...'

'Oops.' Suki grinned. 'Well, you do now, Claire. You'll keep that quiet, won't you? However hard that must be for a PR person.'

'Sure thing. It'll be our little secret.' Claire raised her glass and Suki clinked it. They held their glasses in the air, waiting, until I realised what was expected. Our three glasses chinked in tune. I couldn't remember the last time I'd felt included like this.

Claire picked the coriander from her falafel pita. 'What were you talking about when I arrived?'

Suki replied before I could. 'Funnily enough it's about Laura being too bloody modest.'

I buried my hands in my face. 'Suki, stop.'

'No. Claire will appreciate this, won't you?' Suki grabbed my hands and pulled them away. 'Here's Laura with her brilliant mind who set up this company with Justin fifty-fifty. And guess what?'

Claire's eyes glistened with interest. 'What?'

Suki rubber her fingers together, the international sign for money. 'Turns out he's finagled some secret share options worth a million.'

Claire's hand flew to her mouth. 'Shut up!'

I flapped my hands to make it stop. 'No, please. It's okay. It's not as bad as it sounds.' But I waved, I wondered: wasn't it? Why was I defending him? Force of habit?

No. It's that it wasn't about the money. Him getting a million more would make no difference to the fact I was about to be seriously wealthy. I just wasn't sure if it was worth the trouble, the fall out. How on Earth could I make that point without sounding completely obnoxious?

'It's not okay,' Suki said firmly. 'But we'll need to find a better way to fix it than what I've done.'

Claire raised her eyebrows. 'Oh?'

'I've caused a bit of a rift between them by speaking out,' Suki said. 'And that's not good for the deal.'

'I think you did what you had to do. But please tell me the acquisition is still going ahead,' Claire pleaded. 'My boss is all excited about the big front-page news we're going to get at the conference. He doesn't know what it is... And it's killing him. I keep reminding him I've been sworn to secrecy.' She let a mischievous grin escape. 'Truth be told, I'm enjoying toying with him—'

'Ha!' Suki hooted.

'If I don't follow through with something big,' Claire added. 'I'll be in deep trouble. He's already looking for any excuse to keep me down.'

Before I could ask about that, I heard a slap. The three of us looked towards the rear of the bistro, from where the sound had come. We watched the waitress wave a finger in anger at one of the customers and his arm retreat into his booth.

As the waitress reached our table, Suki asked, 'What was that?'

She rolled her eyes. 'Oh, unwelcome wandering hands.'

My jaw dropped. 'Are you okay?'

She waved her hand. 'Och, I'm fine. Thanks.'

'Shouldn't you report him or something?' Claire asked.

'Oh honey, if I did that every time a man harassed me, I'd never get anything done.' She refreshed the water carafe. 'Anything else?'

'Yes, a medium cappuccino for me please,' said Claire.

'Me too.'

'Me three.'

The waitress walked away, giving the guilty booth a wide berth.

'God, it's relentless, isn't it?' Suki said, shaking her head. 'If we're not being harassed, we're being patronised. You should've heard my managing partner Angus telling me how to do my job when I'm the one who's brought this deal in. He wouldn't know technology if it bit him on the arse.'

'You should hear the horrible sexist remarks Suki gets thrown at her in the office, Claire,' I said.

'Well my boss Darren is also a first prize ass.' Claire pursed her lips. 'Thinks he's this big swinging dick. Doesn't recognise hard work. All he cares about is appearances. He won't give me the sector I want to work on because I don't bloody look the "arty" part.' Claire's face was flushed. She knotted her napkin around her fingers. 'No, all that matters is that his firm looks good. Let's get the German speccy nerd to do Culture. Give Pure Brilliant's clients a supposedly sophisticated person to work with. Never mind I'm more senior, and frankly better at this. To hell with the clients. All that matters is beating Rebel Agency and be the top PR company in

Scotland.' She made a frame with her hands as though that statement should be in lights. Claire seemed to catch Suki's eyebrow, which had been arched for a while. 'Oh my God, Laura, I got onto my high horse and forgot you were a client. I didn't mean it — we do good work.'

'It's cool,' I said. 'I know you do. And I've no need to meet this Darren guy.' I chose not to mention Emily again, not wanting to ruin the growing camaraderie.

'Lucky you.' Claire shuddered. 'Ugh. He summons you into his office, where he sits with his arms behind his head, flashing his muscles in his short-sleeved shirt. Manspreading under the table. He's so vain. Completely obsessed with getting a buff body. Spends a fortune on facials, did you know?' She blew a stream of air out, shaking her head. 'And has the gall to tell women when he doesn't think we've made enough of an effort.' Then she grinned. 'The joke's on him, though. He's got a big bald path growing at the rear, and there is nothing he can do about it.'

'Maybe that will help him look German and sophisticated, too,' I quipped; and loved the rush when the others laughed.

'Maybe next time he gives a speech, you organise for there to be a big mirror as backdrop,' Suki said.

Feeling on a roll, I joked, 'I'll help. I can build a little pulley for you to lower the mirror down behind him while he's talking.'

'That's hilarious,' Claire laughed. What I'd give to embarrass him in public. It would serve him right.'

I smiled. 'Revenge may be wicked, but it's natural.'

'Oo, I like that,' said Suki. 'Where's it from?'

'*Vanity Fair*,' I replied.

'How appropriate,' Suki said.

'The magazine?' asked Claire.

For an instant lost for words, I replied, 'Sorry. No, it's a novel. From the nineteenth century.' I hoped she wouldn't see me as a show off.

'Well wherever it's from, it's bang on,' said Suki. A sly smile grew across her face and she slapped the table. 'Let's do it.'

'What? Hang a mirror behind Darren?' asked Claire.

'No. Well, maybe,' Suki said. 'Or something like it. I mean revenge. Let's grab the bastards where it hurts.' Suki's eyes were ablaze. I wasn't sure where this was going, but it suddenly seemed like a ride I didn't want to miss. 'Come on,' she urged. 'We are each being treated unfairly. My boss is a shit. Your boss is a shit. And your co-founder's cheated you.' I twitched when I heard it put like that. Suki wasn't wrong; and she clearly wasn't done. 'So let's do something about it. The three of us. Together.'

'Like some sort of revenge club?' I searched my mind for a book I was sure I'd read about that.

'Yes! Exactly,' Suki shrieked.

'I love it,' said Claire. 'We find a public way to make Darren a laughing stock. What next? What do we do to your guy?'

I pulled back in my seat. 'Who, Justin? I don't know.'

'Oh, Justin should be easy,' Suki said, nodding to me. 'He's got the ego the size of an elephant. And that makes it a big, easy target.'

Claire triggered her finger pistol. 'Bull's eye.'

Suki slumped onto the bench, her tongue hanging from the side of her mouth, making gurgling sounds that had me in stitches.

'And what about you?' I asked the sprawled-out Suki.

'Angus? I don't know,' she said. 'He's a pompous, patronising git who reigns over a culture of misogyny. It's no surprise the guys who report to him are cocks, too. Do you know, I'm the only woman he's ever hired who isn't support staff? Except for the other partner, Diane. I'm told she *bought* her way in when he needed the cash. It was Diane who forced him to hire me — where else were they going to get a Stanford grad living in Edinburgh?' She steepled her fingers and strobed her fingertips for inspiration. 'Hm... I'm thinking a female revolution.'

'Man the barricades,' fake-shouted Claire, her fist raised.

'I think you mean *woman* the barricades!' I said, daring to raise my fist too.

34.
SUKI

Suki checked her spreadsheet for the third time. At every attempt, her mind wandered off roughly midway between the forecasts for year two and year three. It was going to be a long afternoon.

Robert had walked past her desk earlier, nudging her shoulder with what she hoped was his hip, subtly enough that she couldn't be certain if he'd done it on purpose. She knew she should let it go. But it was unnerving. As she worked, in the corner of her mind, she plotted sweet revenge. Silly revenge, the kind she'd concocted with the girls over lunch.

She smiled at the memory of them falling over on the bistro's benches, laughing loudly enough to turn the heads of other diners and raise a few tuts reminding them of Edinburgh's expected decorum.

It had all been a big joke, of course. A merry, sisterly, evil-slaying fantasy.

At the same time, it gnawed at her.

Why not? What was stopping them? What was wrong with seeking justice?

She glanced at her screen and accepted she would make no progress in this state of mind. After saving the spreadsheet for later, she walked towards the kitchen and pressed the glistening steel espresso machine on. When she opened the fridge, her boiling blood she'd kept at bay started to erupt. Who the fuck helped themselves to her soya milk — again? They didn't even like the soya one. Lazy fuckers.

It figured; they were almost all blokes since Pam had left. Suki was pleased she'd never have to live with a man — she'd probably strangle him. Women were generally more considerate, in her experience.

She was reminded of poor Pam. Thankfully a recent notification from LinkedIn had shown she had found a new job at the Chamber of Commerce. So much for going travelling. It would no doubt be a meeker environment than this one.

From what she could tell, Suki seemed to be the only one to know that Pam's departure hadn't been her choice. Another injustice; that much was clear. You didn't make an employee sign an NDA unless you had something to hide.

Suki hadn't yet congratulated Pam on the new position and contemplated pulling some more information out of her, some ammunition she could stockpile.

She grabbed her mobile and exited the kitchen through the rear door. She reached the smallest patio imaginable, sandwiched between this building and the one next door, whose dripping gutters meant you were always standing in a thin puddle. It was weird, the way these expensive old townhouses didn't have outdoor spaces. The Victorians just made do with the communal garden in the centre of Rutland Square. Nowadays, the small, manicured plot hosted summer drinks receptions by the various professional services firm that had paid a pretty penny for access.

Her feet instantly cold, she dialled.

She was after something that Pam wouldn't want to give, and her negotiation training had taught her that the first step was to build rapport. They talked about Pam's new job, the relief she'd experienced at finding something quickly, particularly since she'd just ordered a new sofa on credit. 'Totally,' Suki replied when Pam said she would have hated to ask her mother for help again at the age of twenty-eight.

Though Suki would have gladly let her tell her the story of her life, like she'd done so often in the office during quiet hours, she sensed an opening.

'Surely your payoff must have given you security for some time?'

'Yes, it did.'

Bingo. Pam never mentioned a payoff before. Only the NDA.

Pam was still prattling on. 'It was stressful, though, because I didn't know when I would find a job again. And I worried when the Chamber asked me for references. In the end, Diane gave me one.'

'Why does Diane put up with it?'

'What?'

Suki realised she'd been musing out loud but grabbed the opportunity. 'Diane. Cleaning their shit up.'

Pam sighed. 'Diane is fiercely ambitious. She's from a different generation. The only way up for them back then was to be one of the boys. And Diane got very, very good at that. That's why she's where she is.'

Suki could almost taste the venom through the phone line. 'I guess you're right. The old boy thing doesn't seem to have changed all that much in finance.' She picked at the chipped paint on the black metal railing, fiery rust staining her nail. 'Will you still not tell me what happened to you? I want to know what stinking, rat-infested ship I'm sailing on.'

'I'm sorry. It's too soon. I wouldn't want them to find out. But it's much the same as with Natalie, who left shortly after you started. Do you remember her?'

'Vaguely.'

'Maybe she'll talk to you. I'll text her your number. I'm making no promises.'

Suki flicked a fleck of dried paint off her skirt. 'Thanks.'

'But if you are looking for rats, I've got a love rat for you,' Pam whispered like they were two old ladies sharing the parish gossip.

Suki's ears pricked up. 'What do you mean, a love rat?'

'Angus has a mistress, has had for years,' Pam said. 'She lives in the Borders. And guess who pays for their jollies, their overnight accommodation at the New Club, when she's in town?'

Blood rushed to Suki's ears. 'The company?'

Pam replied, 'Yup. All goes through the books,'

'Do you think Diane knows?'

'I don't know,' said Pam, her tone chilly. 'Angus always signs off his own expenses. He can do that as a partner — they're only relatively small amounts. It adds up over the course of the year, though. And it's dodgy tax-wise.'

Suki ended the call and stayed on the patio for a while. Deep in thought, she drew figures of eight with the sole of her shoe on the slabs, splashing droplets of gutter water side to side. Was this particular can of worms one she wanted to open? If Angus was capable of this, what else was he doing? What else was he hiding?

She blew out a long stream of air, increasingly disgusted by the culture of this firm, the example set by its lead partner. Her MBA had taught her that culture came from the top. Like apples in a barrel, one corrupted leader meant the rest would become equally rotten.

Madainn was like a stereotype from the 80s, big, entitled egos, the lot of them. But it was the bloody twenty-first century; women shouldn't have to put up with this shit anymore.

When she'd first joined the firm, she'd been excited. It had a female partner. That was so rare. And it had great prestige. The work was exciting, with Edinburgh becoming a hub for super-cool technology companies. She believed she was going to make a difference.

Had she?

As she turned to go inside, a WhatsApp message popped up on her screen. It was in the group she'd formed with Laura and Claire the day before, during the high-spirited inauguration of their revenge club. She'd never expected it to actually be used.

They'd been creative when it came to plotting the downfall of those who had wronged them, but distinctly less original when it came to the name of the club: the Avengers.

The message was from Claire. Underneath an animated image of an evil-looking black cat filing its claws, it read:

Have you got plans tomorrow morning?

Suki replied, with a cartoon of meerkats standing at attention in the desert.

What did you have in mind? I could do with a distraction.

35.
ME

It was earlier than I liked it to be when I reached the front of the Sheraton Hotel on Festival Square the next morning.

Cleaners were spraying away the remnants of the previous night's festivities with industrial-sized water pumps, manoeuvring between the various pop-up structures claiming the large, central space during August.

The white inflatable dome serving as a broadcasting station for BBC Radio Scotland partially blocked the view of the hotel's welcoming water feature, where cigarette butts and take away cups floated in the shallow pool between the large metal mound-shaped fountains.

I climbed the steps to where I expected the hotel's reception to be. Instead I faced the entrance to the restaurant, where guests were eating breakfast in a terrarium of bacon-infused air. Tourists heaped mountains of food on their plates, no doubt to fuel their many miles of walking up and down ancient streets. Early risers, intent on making every hour in this magical city count.

I pulled the baseball cap over my eyes, delighted I'd guessed how to fit in perfectly. My breathing was shallow. I adjusted my bum bag.

At first, I'd dismissed Claire's WhatsApp message as a continuation of our zany, vengeful brainstorming at the bistro. When Suki declared she was in, I didn't want to be the party pooper — not when I finally had a party to join.

Claire asked if either of us had a long-range camera, I'd replied, before having fully thought it through, '*No, but I know someone who does.*'

Still looking for reception, I spotted the lifts ahead, which stood opposite a large staircase going down, a multicoloured crystal chandelier reflecting the ambient lighting. A discreet sign with elegant scroll lettering depicted arrows in all directions, to the many facilities the hotel had to offer. The check-in desks, it turned out, were on the floor below. How confusing; that was the rear entrance to the building.

Would Craig already be here?

I'd been reluctant to call him, but I'd offered his services for Claire's little plan in the heat of the moment, so I had little choice. And when I last left him, he'd said he would help me in any way he could. Incredibly, he didn't ask any questions when I presented the task.

At the bottom of the green-carpeted staircase I looked for instructions on which way to turn. People were coming mostly from the right, which I presumed would be where the bedrooms were. Veering left, I followed a perfumed corridor with well-lit glass displays of luxurious Scottish-themed knickknacks to eventually reach the small, plain reception area — quite a difference from the grandeur and opulence of the rest of the building.

The guests checking out were being catered to with great efficiency by a pair of perfectly coiffed young women in tartan waistcoats.

A teenage brother and sister stood near the exit, giggling and pointing at something. I followed their gaze and saw the pink nose and whiskers of a ferret emerging from underneath the stand holding flyers for local activities.

So much for going unnoticed.

Craig spilt over the frame of the small tub chair. He sat facing the entrance, a black rucksack perched by his feet; a green leash linking him to an orange harness on Scout.

'You brought Scout?' I hunched down to give her a little scratch behind the ears.

A large grin formed inside the stubble on Craig's face. 'I always walk her in the morning. It made sense to bring her along. And I thought you might like to see her again.'

'That's nice. I do.' I got up and wiped white fur from my hand. 'It's just... I was hoping to draw less attention to ourselves.'

'About that... What are we doing here?' Craig asked. 'When you called, you said you needed me to take some shots. I've got the three-hundred-millimetre lens with me, like you asked, and this...' He pulled a baseball cap from his wind breaker's pocket and placed it on his head.

I smiled and straightened my own cap. 'Don't we make a fetching pair.' A flush of heat darted across my stomach at that last word. *Pair.* I quickly stepped back and said, 'Stay here, I'll get the key card.'

Craig's eyes grew wide. 'We're getting a room?'

It felt like every pint of blood in my body rushed to my cheeks. 'No, no. My friend Claire organised a key card for access to the roof terrace. To take the pictures. By the pool. She's an event planner so they know her.' Desperately needing to move away from him before I embarrassed myself further, I said, 'Let me get the pass and I'll explain everything on the way up.'

Craig scooped Scout up. 'I guess I should pack her away. I didn't realise we were staying here when you told me where to meet you.'

'Yes, sorry. That's probably for the best.'

'You didn't tell me to bring trunks either.'

'What?'

'For the pool?'

'Oh.' I giggled.

His broad grin creased the skin around his hazel eyes.

Two minutes later, I motioned for Craig to join me, key in hand. We waited for the lift. An odd movement fleeted across his chest underneath his zipped-up jacket. It took a second for me to register it as Scout.

'The roof terrace is a perfect vantage point to take pictures of someone inside the gym across the street;' I said. 'I wanted us to look like tourists so we wouldn't raise any questions.'

'Do I want to know whose picture I'm taking?' Craig's tone suggested he regretted showing up.

'It's a little joke Claire wants to play on her boss. It's nothing serious or sinister. You see, he's a bit of an ass. Real vain. And she wants to bring him down a peg or two.' I acted as if riding a lift in a hotel with a man you've only met twice to spy on someone else was an everyday occurrence.

I knew it wasn't, but I needed this. It killed me that I couldn't avenge Emily; find the man, or men, that drove her to take her own life. I'd blamed Adam Mooney, but I witnessed the star's contrition first-hand, and Emily had forgiven him... This left me to spend days analysing Twitter data, finding clues, chasing theories, trying to engage the police, only to hit the brick walls of anonymity over and over.

And here was Darren, Emily's boss. If he was as big a dick as Claire made him out to be, it stood to reason Emily must have suffered under him, too.

So yes, I needed this: a swift act of minor revenge on behalf of all women, to make me believe there was such a thing as justice. To distract from this unbearable feeling that I'd failed my best friend — in life, and in death.

The doors pinged open and led onto a plush lounge with a wall of neatly rolled up towels nestled into wooden cubes. We wouldn't need those, nor would we need to access the dressing rooms on either side. Instead, I led the way through a pair of heavy, insulated doors to outside.

A kidney-shaped pool took up almost the entire rooftop patio. We walked to the metal wire barriers to get our bearings.

'There's the gym,' I said. 'What time is it?'

'It's half past eight.' Craig released Scout from inside his jacket, unclipped her lead and let her roam free.

'You see there? On the third floor?' I pointed. 'That's where the weights are. And that woman in the red gym kit, with the black bun in her hair? That's my friend Suki. She's in place. Any minute...'

'Your victim will appear?' Craig completed the sentence, an eyebrow raised.

A feeling of unease stirred in my chest. 'Look, I'm sorry. I shouldn't have dragged you into this. It's nothing to do with you. If you want to leave, feel free.'

Craig silently unpacked his camera. He screwed an impressive looking lens delicately onto the main body. He raised the device to his eye and moved it up and down a few times to train the focus.

'I can't say I'm thrilled at what we're doing. And I certainly don't want to know what your friend will do with the photos, but I'm glad you thought of me.' His disarming smile made my heart skip. 'Besides, you basically accused me of being a stalker last time we met. Who's the stalker now?'

I snorted.

A male figure appeared in the gym window beside the one Suki occupied. He fit Claire's description of Darren. Bang on time, too. Ever since he found Emily in the office gym, he'd moved to this pay-per-play venue on Exchange Crescent.

'That's him. There.'

Craig got into position. 'Keep an eye on the doors, will you? I wouldn't want Scout to escape and freak out all the guests.'

It didn't take long for Darren to get close to Suki up ahead. She could charm the pants off anyone. Plus, according to Claire, she wouldn't need to do anything for him to have a go at a pretty young thing.

I crouched next to Craig, his warm body shielding me from the wind. I strained to see properly inside the weights room at this angle. I had to rely on his skill.

'Here's the thing,' I said. 'We want him clearly flirting with the girl, with the back of his head to us. And if there is any way you can get that reflected in a mirror, that would be superb.'

IT TOOK a while to catch Scout after we were done. Mesmerised by the surface undulations of the swimming pool, she'd darted around it, occasionally placing a paw into the water. Or sniffing it, causing her whiskers to create tiny ripples that reminded me of Atticus.

I was the one to grab her and I gave the furry creature a little nuzzle before passing her over to Craig. He placed her gently against his chest, pulled his jacket's zip as far forward as he could while stroking her fur down careful not to get it caught as he enclosed her. His large hand cupped Scout through the fabric and her wriggling subsided.

We navigated our way out of the hotel, back onto Festival Square.

'Which way are you going?' Craig asked, releasing Scout into the daylight and attaching her leash again.

'Quartermile. To the right.'

'Okay. I'm going left. See you again sometime?'

I didn't know how to respond to his hopeful face. I wanted to say yes, but what reason did I have to visit him? I'd exhausted my photo-related leads. And why would he want to see me again, anyway? I took a few steps in my direction of travel to avoid any awkward goodbyes. 'Thanks for helping out today.'

'No problem. Though next time I'm tempted to offer "any help I can," I'll remember I might get roped into doing dodgy things on a rooftop.' A twinkle of his eye accompanied his wave as he, too, stepped away.

On the way to my office, I pulled out my phone and sent a WhatsApp message to the others.

Mission accomplished.

The link to the photos would follow later when Craig had uploaded the files. He'd reiterated that he didn't want to know how they would be used. He'd only make the folder available for three hours before deleting it, which seemed completely fair.

My first instinct had been to react to his disapproval like I always did, by caving in, apologising. Not this time. I'd made a commitment to my new friends.

And anyway, it was justified. We hadn't started it. We were merely dishing out justice to guilty men.

As if on cue, a notification from my Twitter app filled the screen. Having surrendered to a smart phone that could do everything, I understood how people got addicted; how Emily had been unable to step away from social media even though it was hurting her.

There was only one thing I wanted to see on Twitter: the Inciter. The one I'd worked out was the master agitator of armies of keyboard warriors, Incel losers it proved incredibly easy to excite if you knew how.

His was the only account I followed.

He'd gone quiet recently. The groups of trolls who hounded Emily had dissipated as quickly as they'd come, their broken morality not so warped that they would celebrate their success — since success had meant a woman taking her life.

I hoped they'd been scared and shamed into becoming better people. I was probably being naive. A few stragglers still kicked Emily's corpse; a pathetic act of attention-seeking by someone with an empty life. Why waste my time on them?

The Inciter's newest tweets showed that the attention of the Incel masses had merely been redirected, like squirrel-seeking Labradors. Their collective fury now burned for an alleged miscarriage of justice: a male student falsely accused of assault at a college in the US whose policies were '*unconstitutionally, guilty until proven innocent*'.

On this matter, I would happily give them the benefit of the doubt, but with utter predictability, it was the assaulted girl who became the target of their vitriol. Their macho language was infused with the belligerent verbs and penile similes of gun ads and motorcycle magazines. They pointed at what she'd been wearing. Why was she dancing sexy like that? And she was drunk!

I became transfixed by the exchanges. The militant rats scurried out in support of the male student who, sure, might have gone a little too far, but was that reason enough to ruin his life forever? He was a model student. A venerated athlete. White. Was a lifetime black mark appropriate for a bad decision lasting twenty minutes?

'*The cunt*', they called her. Argued she should have kept quiet. That it hadn't been *that* bad.

You would have thought the Inciter was a US college student himself, from the savageness of his calls to action, his uncanny local knowledge and the intensity with which he stirred up outrage for this particular incident. But his UK spelling gave his foreign status away — not that spelling seemed to be of any importance to any of them. It was like wading through alphabet soup, sometimes.

I skimmed his latest taunts, my revulsion growing with every tweet. How easily they moved on, leaving a trail of ruined lives.

It was harder for me: my friend was dead. And I had no one to blame. The daggers they'd wielded weren't physical, but they might as well have been. I lost Emily. I longed to punish them — someone.

The Inciter was the closest to a single, identifiable culprit, the one with the most blood on his hands. Trying to find him had already drained me of energy — to the point that when Suki discovered I'd used the Network Impact tool on the Twitter data, she told me to let it go.

I couldn't. But I was also getting nowhere.

So I was grateful for my new distraction, a much-needed outlet for my grief and frustration. This crazy little Avengers club that made me feel part of something bigger; righting the many wrongs in the world.

I chuckled, remembering when we chose our group name. Suki had raised her hand and said, '*Can I be the one in the black catsuit?*'

'*1960s Emma Peel or Marvel's Black Widow?*' Claire had asked.

'*Whichever one kicks the most butt.*'

36.
CLAIRE

Claire refreshed the Instagram feed again, shielding her monitor from her colleagues by placing her briefcase on the desk. The gym photo taken that morning was up to thirty-six likes, twelve more than only a few seconds ago.

She couldn't believe what a great job Laura had done. The angle was a little weird, with the image taken from above, but it made it even better than she'd hoped. Not only did Darren's bald patch look bigger than it actually was, he also loomed over Suki like a predator, his giant biceps looking ready to grab her.

Suki had been happy to play honey trap but didn't want to be recognised. Claire had posted a snap where you could see her hot body, but not her face.

Thirty-nine likes.

It was always going to garner attention. Even if it came from a brand-new account, her cunningly selected hash tags would attract the Scottish PR community in a flash. They were all perpetually glued to Instagram, which was quickly surpassing the other social media platforms when it came to corporate public relations.

Forty-three likes, twelve reposts.

They, her industry colleagues, knew better than to comment. A 'like' could always be excused as an unintentional error, caused by a fat thumb. Even reposting could be explained as wanting to share your outrage that such an unflattering photo would have been thrown into the public eye, but to actually comment would be to invite Darren's wrath.

They might not like him, but they feared him.

Even though there was no name in the caption, it was undoubtedly him. Everyone in this small sector would see that. She'd only typed:

Balding PR man thinks he stands a chance with hot chick. Yeah, right. Move over, grandpa. #PR #Scotland

Claire would have loved to sit there refreshing this page all day, basking in the anonymous glory of her mischief, but work beckoned. The audio and video requirements from the Empisoft conference were getting more complicated by the day.

She placed her briefcase on the floor and opened her email. A roar sounded from behind her boss's door.

Claire bit her lip to keep from smirking and looked up from her screen, synchronising startled movements and feigned shock with the three colleagues around her. They must all have seen it — but would they admit to that?

Darren almost pulled the door from its hinges emerging into the open plan office. His fists were balled, and his face contorted into a frightening grimace. 'Does anybody know who did this?'

Murmurs of 'no' and 'what?' filled the room.

He raised his phone up high and pointed with his left index finger. 'This Instagram post. How do we get it down? How do I get the bastard who did this?'

'It's disrespectful,' shouted Otto, brown-nosing as usual.

We all jumped up; troops gathered around their chief, ready for instruction. His angry, hoarse breathing was preventing words coming out.

'I'll get onto IT,' suggested someone.

'That's pretty pointless. IT can't do anything more about this than we can,' said someone else.

Otto stepped to the front. 'While you guys work out how to take this off Instagram, I'll reach out to the PR publications and make sure this goes no further.'

Claire wished she'd thought of that. Even though she was behind this, she had no interest in it spreading too far. It was a little joke, lasting maybe a day; something that would dent Darren's enormous ego just enough that he would possibly look beyond appearances to become a fairer, more reasonable boss.

The more she thought about it, the less it made sense that this would be picked up by those publications — it was hardly news.

Claire went to stand next to Otto. 'I suspect they won't even consider posting an article about an unflattering photo.' She saw Darren's eyebrow twitch. 'And is it even that unflattering?' She spotted Otto about to speak and quickly added, 'I wouldn't worry about it too much. You know as well as I do that these things are a flash in the pan. They blow over within a day. Whoever did this — for whatever reason — would have gotten their kicks already.'

Darren relaxed his shoulders and shook his head. 'That's probably true. It's today's little titbit of entertainment for people who have nothing better to do. You take care of this,' he said, pointing at Otto. 'The rest of you get back to work.'

He retreated to his office, self-consciously stroking his bald patch — something she'd never seen him do before.

'I'd still keep an eye out for anyone with a camera, Darren. In case the culprit isn't quite done with you.' Claire said with a bright-eyed air of false concern.

No harm in stirring things up a little more, was there?

37.
ME

Sally stopped by my side as I returned to my desk from re-filling a glass of water.

'Again?' she asked. 'That's like the third time this morning. What did you do? Eat a box of saltines?'

'Me? No. I just wanted to stretch my legs.'

'You've got ants in your pants, as my mother used to say.' She smiled and walked on.

I sat down, shifting in my chair once more as my bum hit the pad. Did I need to pee now? Christ, what was wrong with me?

Thank goodness Sally didn't think I was hung over. Claire had asked Suki and me out for a drink at Hotel du Vin to celebrate the success of her little revenge plot. She'd been in a great mood. I had only one, small white wine as we celebrated. I wanted to believe that Emily had a good giggle, too — wherever she was.

A cloud passed in front of the sun, casting a shadow across my desk. A shiver ran over my arm. Today's plan had higher stakes.

I distracted myself with work until the clock on the bottom of my screen hit noon. I watched Justin get up from his desk. Nice and punctual. I walked a few steps behind him as he strode towards reception. Would Claire be nervous too? She was the one kidnapping him with the pretext of needing to run him through practice interviews in a radio-style recording studio she was able to borrow from a friend.

I watched Justin skip through Empisoft's main door and have a little word with Suki approaching the building, before jumping into a taxi outside.

'Okay, that's him gone,' said Suki as she joined me. 'Until what time did Claire say she could keep him there?'

'Two thirty,' I said. 'Her friend needs the studio again. Any longer than that, Justin would get bored anyway. It's not like the interviews are for real yet. And Claire can only ask questions unrelated to the acquisition because she's not supposed to know.'

Suki curved her arm across my shoulder. 'Now, I only dropped by to make sure you're okay. You cool to go ahead with this? It's pretty risky. You don't know these guys like Justin does and there are a number of ways this could go. I have only limited experience with your board. I can't be sure which way they'll take it.'

'I know. I heard you.' I swallowed, suppressing the anxious flutters inside. 'And I know that you had some other thoughts, but they would take too long — time we don't have. Some of these board members have been with us for a long time. They've always seemed professional to me. I'd like to think they knew me well enough, having met me a few times, to know that I'm not the type of person to create drama for drama's sake.'

Suki retrieved her arm and patted my back. 'Remember, you're not doing anything wrong. You're only after what's fair. Frankly, if it had been me, I'd be going for Justin's jugular.' She looked at her watch. 'The conference call is scheduled to start in fifteen minutes. There is one director dialling in from a mobile, which isn't ideal. It's good they were willing to convene at such short notice. Of course, they'll expect it will be about the acquisition — not to mention Justin leading the call.'

I shifted my weight from foot to foot. 'Are you coming? I'm going to set up the audio... After I pop to the loo.'

'No, I've got a mountain of work to do in the office. Besides, I told you, I can't be seen to have anything to do with this.' She winced. 'Sorry.'

'That's okay.' I shrugged. 'This is something I need to do for me anyway.'

'Listen. Take it easy. We've gone over what to say. You'll be fine.' Suki retreated, holding both thumbs up. 'Good luck.'

'Thanks.' The lump in my stomach grew as my safety buoy floated away.

A MASS OF black cables snaked across the boardroom table, to feed the telecom- and electricity-starved. I untangled the HDMI from the Ethernet and the charging cables and tucked them neatly into the rectangular recess in the middle of the snazzy, white table. The tidying served as a helpful distraction while time ticked on.

A triangular conference call speaker stood near the head of the table. I would have preferred not to use it, to have the comforting weight of a telephone receiver in my hand, but I needed the room's privacy and the room was not set up for people having meetings on their own.

When the time came, I dialled the number followed by the organiser's PIN Suki had given me. I stated my name and heard my slightly shaky voice played back to me.

The automatic operator announced two new participants, who had voiced their names so quickly I didn't catch them.

'Hello?' I said.

An authoritative male voice spoke. 'Who is this?'

'It's Laura Flett. I'm taking the meeting today. Justin is away.'

'What do you mean?' the man asked. 'Where is he?'

Further protestations were drowned out by the operator announcing another participant, who spoke straight over the others.

'Hi it's Jim. Sorry I'm late. I'm on a train.'

'Hello Jim. This is Laura Flett. Justin isn't here. I suggest we get to business. I know you're all busy and given you're on a train, we might lose you.'

'As the Chairman I find it a little unorthodox for you to sit in, but I'll allow it.' A voice I now knew how to identify said. 'Who's all here?' The names given meant that, minus Justin, they had the full, though faceless, complement of the board. 'Where are we on the acquisition, Laura? I'm assuming this is why we're having the call.'

I wrung my hands together and took a last sneak peek at my script.

'There is a matter of current shareholding that needs to be addressed,' I began. 'It has come to my attention that Justin received growth options at the last funding round. When the acquisition goes through at the anticipated sale price, these will be worth a million pounds.'

Only two of the three directors had been on the board when the share options were granted, the third director having come along after. That one asked, 'Remind me, when was this?'

The Chair intervened, 'And what is the problem, Laura?'

I ran my tongue over my teeth. My mouth was bone dry. 'Firstly, I want to affirm that these growth options were deserved. They pay out only if the company exits at a valuation in excess of ten times what it was at the last round. Achieving that is incredible and well beyond what any of us expected to happen eighteen months ago.' I paused, briefly closing my eyes to collect myself. 'Except Justin wasn't alone in deserving that. And in accepting that reward, he breached an agreement that he and I made when we founded the company. We would always be rewarded fifty-fifty.'

The Chair sputtered, 'I don't remember ever seeing such an agreement'

'It was a verbal agreement, but it predates any subsequent shareholder agreements.' I replied, fully aware of the weakness in my argument. 'When we started out, we had an equal number of ordinary shares and equal pay. You will know that this parity has been maintained until today — except for these growth options. I only learnt about them recently, since they were only ever referred to in board minutes that I do not get to see. Imagine my surprise at finding in the shareholder schedule that was prepared for PeopleForce and lists all the shares and options that I, as the female founder, was not in fact benefiting from equal treatment.'

I had chosen that last line carefully, knowing that in today's corporate governance environment, the merest hint of gender discrimination could open the doors to lawsuits. Suki had warned me not to play this card too strongly, in case they called my bluff. Would they, though? So close to a fabulous exit that would give them each lots of cash? I was counting on them being honourable, or at minimum being greedy.

'As I recall,' one of the directors said, 'these were granted at the time that Justin was closing some big deals with large, blue chip customers. He travelled around the world for months negotiating, suffering a pretty poor lifestyle. He's the one who demanded some sort of extraordinary reward for extraordinary results. I remember there being a threat of resignation.'

Suki had predicted this tactic: them creating the impression of a large contrast between contributions that Justin and I made to the company, to undermine the strength of any formal complaint. And it seemed that the Chair clocked onto what his colleague was doing because he took over with, 'And although we recognise the value that you bring to Empisoft, Ms Flett, Justin is the one who had taken on the vast responsibility of being CEO and the personal corporate governance risks associated with being a board director of this company — a role I believe you rejected?'

He'd called me a formal 'Ms Flett' this time. My chest constricted. But I'd anticipated this line of defence and made my next move.

'I recognise that from a day to day occupation point of view, there is no parity of roles. That has always been the case. The equality of our respective contributions, however, remains. There would be no company at all without my idea. My master's thesis is the foundation of everything we do here. There would be no company at all without my having developed the initial software models. And while Justin was building the company and growing the commercial side, I continued to invent new features without which there would be nothing to sell today.'

'Yes, and —'

'Please let me finish.' I clenched my jaw, expecting a rebuttal — how dare I tell these men to shut up? The line went quiet. Perhaps there was hope. 'The tenfold uplift in valuation did not come from a tenfold uplift in revenues. It wasn't' all Justin's sales. It also reflects the potential of our R&D programme — my programme. And if anything, our corporate finance advisers' current thinking is that it is undervalued.'

The director, who'd kept quiet until then, said, 'This strikes me as something you should have resolved with Justin. I find the way you've called this meeting without him quite inappropriate. And however much I believe in equal pay for equal work, being a solicitor by trade, I know that you would be on shaky ground with a claim.'

I sighed. He'd gone there; litigation.

My decision on that was already made: I would never file a suit. It would put the deal at risk. Justin might have cheated me, but I wasn't about to cheat all our employees out of their hard-earned financial windfall.

It was also too late to threaten to resign, like Justin had done, because that would need to be declared to the acquirers. Even though PeopleForce would have tens of super-talented data scientists in California who could do my job, the fact that half of Empisoft's new technology sat inside the head of a founder who might resign could easily spook them away.

I had only one card left. 'I disagree with my claim for equality being on shaky ground. If anything...' I couldn't believe I was about to say this. It felt so big headed. So *masculine*. Suki had pressed onto me I'd just be doing what any man would do; bluster. 'If anything, I am the most important person in this company.'

'How so?' he snarled.

'Are you familiar yet with our newest Network Impact model?'

'Yes, I saw it listed in the product roadmap. It looks very interesting, this ability to identify the so-called heroes and villains in a company on the basis of their influence on others. It's good work.'

I bit my lip and went for it. 'I ran the data on Empisoft... The hero here is me.'

There was a moment of silence.

'That may be the case, Ms Flett.' My heart sank: Ms Flett again. 'But that model has not been validated. Either way, I think it's time to let it lie, don't you? You stand to make a double-digit million-pound return for a few years of your life. This seems like fair recompense. Surely it's not worth rocking the boat for a measly million more?'

I wanted to scream, 'That's not the point. That's not the frigging point.' I composed myself. The last thing I needed was to be accused of being a shrieking woman.

'I could ask you the same thing, Mr Chair. Why not do the honourable thing? It's only a few growth options. They would only dilute the other shareholders by a measly one percent.'

This was language that Suki coached me on. She'd explained that the value of the company remained the same no matter how many shares were handed out. Like the size of a pie remained the same no matter how many slices you cut it into. If one person's slice got bigger, everybody else's slice would shrink a little. In finance terms, they would be 'diluted'.

But it seemed their pie slices were too attractive. They didn't cave.

'It's too late, Laura,' said the other director gently, perhaps trying to play good cop. 'I'm sure that I speak on behalf of all of us when I say that it would only be right and proper to reward you in some way. Perhaps we can give you a pay rise? But we are on the final stretch with the PeopleForce acquisition and the share structures have already been distributed at the highest level in their management. We can't change them at this stage. And say what? That we made a mistake in the numbers? They might start to wonder where else we've made mistakes. That risks prolonging the due diligence even more, them wanting to go through everything with a fine-tooth comb again. Surely you don't want that any more than we do?'

'That's it? Justin threatened to resign and gets a reward, whereas I never complained and get nothing?' I asked.

'Maybe you should have paid more attention at the time,' said the Chair.

My heart sank. My battle was lost.

At least Claire got what she wanted. And hopefully Suki would fare as well.

38.
SUKI

'Good night, Suki,' said the Aussie temp from reception ending his usual round of turning off unnecessary lights. He loosened his tie and collected a few abandoned cups. 'Is it going to be a late one?'

'No, it should be fine, thanks. Is that everyone?' She'd seen a number of her colleagues come and go during the day, but ever since she started to look at the place through a new lens, she'd distanced herself.

It helped that most of them were in London half the time, given that's where the clients and the work tended to be. She was delighted the tech scene in Scotland was strong enough that she didn't have to be a 'Willie.' She smiled. It was Pam who'd first introduced her to the expression: Work In London, Live In Edinburgh. Suki reckoned that, being single, she wasn't in a position to judge; but she was still surprised at this ever-increasing breed of Monday-morning, latte-sipping, trolley-hauling, blue-suited airport dwellers in financial services who chose to be apart from their family rather than sacrifice the wife and kids' standard of living.

'Only you and Diane left,' the temp said as he left.

Perfect.

Suki slid her stockinged feet into the shoes she'd kicked off for comfort earlier and wriggled her toes to pump-prime the blood circulation. She took a deep breath, the dry cardboard air of a not-yet-paperless office filling her lungs.

Lying awake in bed the night before, she'd rehearsed the conversation ten different ways. She was hoping to appeal to Diane's professionalism and sense of fair play.

Sadly, that hadn't worked out too well for Laura. Poor Laura. Too trusting, wanting to believe logic and decency would win the day. Look where that got her.

Turning her mind back to her own needs, Suki wondered where Diane's loyalties would lie. She suspected it would probably all boil down to ego again, ambition. Why did that have to cloud everything in business?

Diane's office was next to Angus's at the end of the corridor. Suki figured his was slightly larger to reflect his status as managing partner; but Diane had the benefit of longer stretches of natural light.

Suki knocked on the door and entered when summoned.

'Hello, Suki. What can I do for you? I was about to pack up.' Diane stood by her cabinet, placing manila folders neatly into its drawers. Somehow, her shoulder-padded power suit had survived the day without a single wrinkle and her bob flicked into a perfect curl at her chin.

'I was hoping to have a chat,' Suki said.

'Is it about PeopleForce?'

'No, it's more to do with the firm.'

Diane stopped filing and searched Suki's face. 'Oh?'

'May I?' Suki gestured towards the two armchairs that surrounded a coffee table littered with tombstones. She cast her eye over a few of these engraved crystal trophies, checking which of the firm's successful conclusions of a merger, acquisition or substantial investment they represented.

'Sure.' Diane pointed at her desk. 'Will I need to take notes?'

'I don't think so. I wanted to have a word... Woman to woman.'

As they sat, Diane asked, 'What's this all about? Have you got a complaint?'

'More of an observation... and a question.'

'Shoot,' Diane said. She tucked her hair behind her ear, which Suki recognised as a no doubt well-practised subtle signal to convey to clients she was listening.

Suki gathered her own hair with a rapid scoop and pulled it forward over one shoulder, her neck exposed to Diane, the two women sitting bare ear to bare ear. 'I'm wondering what your view is on the firm from a gender equality point of view.' She detected a small twitch in Diane's eyebrow. 'When you hired me, I assumed that, with a female partner, this would be a good place to work. You're such an amazing role model. The deals you've done...' Suki gestured towards the crystal tombstones.

Diane frowned. 'You're leading the Empisoft acquisition — our biggest project at the moment. I don't understand what more you want.'

'This isn't about status or responsibility,' Suki said. 'It's about the culture. I find the firm... backward. You know, boys being boys. Inappropriate jokes. Sexist, homophobic undertones. Angus's patronising attitude and bullying ways. I would have thought this would be something you cared about.'

'I see. Well, what can I say?' Diane shrugged. 'Welcome the world of finance. The young ones will grow out of it and dinosaurs like Angus will retire soon enough. Trust me, it used to be a lot worse when I started out.'

Did she really just dismiss it all out of hand? Suki sat up straight. 'That doesn't make it right.'

'No, it doesn't. I'm remarking on the journey that we women have already undertaken. I may have reached senior partner, but it's through hard graft and putting up with a lot of crap. There were no female role models at all in my day. There was no feminist movement — not even laws that guaranteed equal pay or fair treatment. You wanted to reach the top? You had to work like the men and play like the men.' Without any sense of irony, she reached for the whisky and poured them both a drink. 'The less you looked and sounded like a woman, the better you did. You either shut up and uncrossed your legs to get ahead or made knob jokes with the rest of them.'

The whisky burned in Suki's throat.

'So no, we're not fully there yet,' Diane continued. 'We can't rock the boat too quickly. We're making such great progress. Slowly but surely. Look at you! And to be honest, I can't say I've noticed it at Madainn all that much.'

Suki nearly spat her drink out. 'Well, you wouldn't, would you? This is not the kind of behaviour that is targeted at the boss. Or at one's mother...'

Diana lost all the pink from her cheeks. 'What are you accusing Robert of? What has he done to you?'

Had Suki hit a working mother nerve? Criticise a woman at work, fine, but criticise her mothering at your peril.

'God, Diane. I've not been raped or anything,' Suki said. 'It didn't even bother me that much at first. Like you said, it's endemic to finance, what's to be expected. But come on, you must know the culture in here is toxic. And that's something that either comes from the top or is *condoned* by the top — or in this case, both.' Suki breathed deeply while the accusation hung in the air.

Diane rubbed the rim of her glass with her thumb and forefinger.

'I know about the payoffs,' Suki said. 'About Pam, and before. There are hardly any women left — how can you let Angus get away with this?'

For an instant, Diane looked confused. She quickly collected herself. 'What would you have me do?'

'You said so yourself, he's a dinosaur. And he's a bad example. You've managed to keep his payoff secret — to an extent. But it is bound to come out. If you deal with him firmly, the others will be shaken enough to fall into line.'

Diane listened with a cocked head and squeezed eyes that suggested her brain was thinking it though.

Suki reached for Diane's arm. 'Angus won't change just because we ask him to. You have to make him change... or maybe even leave?'

Diane's lips curled at the sides and a fire shone in her eyes. 'Let's explore this a little further — hypothetically, of course. If I were interested in your suggestion, what did you have in mind?'

'Angus has a mistress. Hypothetically, we could hit him with that.'

Diane burst out laughing.

Suki's cheeks tingled.

'My dear girl, you want to blackmail Angus about his mistress? Everybody knows about his mistress — even his wife knows about his mistress.' Diane drowned the chuckles with some more booze. She turned serious. 'It's also a personal matter. One that really doesn't affect me. If we want to do this, we need to use something better.'

We.

Suki had her. A partner in crime — or in this case in justice.

'But it does affect you,' Suki said. 'As I understand it, his extramarital activities are billed to the firm,' said Suki.

'Yes, well... I'm not in favour of inviting an examination of our books.'

Damn. Back to square one.

Diane drummed her fingers on her knee and gave Suki a sideways glance. 'I do know another way that we could bring him down. I'd need your help.'

Suki's smile stretched as wide as it could. 'I'm in.'

'Good,' said Diane. 'Because once the girls are in charge, we'll all be better off, won't we?'

39.
ME

No matter how much I cleared my inbox every day, it would fill up again overnight as the USA woke up. Today was no different: my inbox was teeming with emails from salespeople eager to give me a demo of their latest technology solution. Their tactics were more brazen the higher the value of a contract with Empisoft might be to them.

On the edge of my desk lay a cheap phone one guy had sent to me with a note asking me to turn it on and he'd call, any time day or night. It was impossible for him to know if or when I would comply, and I imagined this desperate chap dialling the number every hour on the hour in the faint bonus-fuelled hope that I would pick up. I felt some kinship with him today; it was as futile an exercise as my attempt to reason with the board had been.

Mid-morning, Claire summoned Suki and me via WhatsApp to A New Leaf at noon. I asked what was so urgent. She wouldn't say.

I thought of possible reasons for having the Avengers regroup. One scenario that *wouldn't* happen was Claire somehow discovering a clever solution to the Justin problem I had failed to resolve. Even though our fun brainstorming sessions had shown her to have a rapid, wicked mind, Claire's knowledge of finance or technology wouldn't stretch that far.

Perhaps, like with Darren, the trick was to play with Justin's ego. Lord knows it was big enough. And it wasn't an act anymore, like it had been when we'd started Empisoft; two snot-nosed young graduates trying to convince investors and big, serious potential customers that they knew what they were doing. A bit like the emails in front of me. To this day, I could still feel the blushes I'd been unable to keep at bay when presenting. Justin had done drama at school and was able to better contain his nerves, so it made sense to make him take care of that side.

I remembered how we'd practised his pitches over and over until they came so easily that he eventually exuded a natural confidence. It worked, and the business grew. As did his public profile, which he loved. He was now well-known across the technology scene, gathering geeky — and female — admirers. I smirked. Little Scotland's answer to Elon Musk.

I replied to Claire's message with a thumbs-up.

What could she have in mind?

The whole thing was terribly distracting, and I struggled to focus on the newest due diligence requests from PeopleForce that Suki had sheepishly shared that morning. Until then, Suki had believed we were on the home stretch.

Where was she, anyway? She was due to come and help.

I adjusted the headings in one of my databases. The other side's team hadn't been able to make sense of what I sent across before. It was tedious, albeit necessary work.

As Suki never showed, I left for the bistro alone at the required time.

I wished we'd chosen somewhere else for our team base. The crowds were getting tedious, as was the crap on the way. By the end of the festival each year, the colourful celebration of all things cultural grew into a messy, flyer-strewn, poster-plastered extravaganza of bad taste. And the giant, inflatable purple cow-shaped venue that occupied the best part of Teviot Place was the worst culprit.

Thankfully, it was still quite early for lunch, and the tourists were only starting to show their faces, after late nights of shouty comedy.

There were a few empty tables in the restaurant. Suki was sitting in their usual booth, tapping away at her phone.

'Hi. I was expecting you in the office,' I said.

'Yes, sorry. It's all getting a little hectic. PeopleForce are seriously starting to put the pressure on, and for some reason are asking for all sorts of new information. They're not even hiding the fact that they're talking to your competitor anymore. It's a worry. I'm hoping it's just posturing.' She put her phone down and ran her fingers through her hair to keep it out of her coffee. 'How are you? Heard any more from Claire?'

'No. She should be here any minute.' I grabbed the menu.

Suki waved her hand in the air. A new waitress stood by the display that held the various pre-made salads to take away.

As our orders were being taken, Claire stormed in. She unwrapped her oversized knit scarf from around her neck and dumped it next to me together with a shopping bag. She shooed Suki to make room, sat and barked at the innocent waitress who'd asked if she wanted a drink. 'I won't be staying.'

'Bloody hell, Claire. What's up with you?' Suki asked.

'It's all gone to pot. And it's all your fault,' she said, jutting her chin out at me.

'What did I do?' My throat constricted. I'd never been good with being yelled at — not that it had ever happened much outside of gym class.

Claire's eyes were ablaze. 'Why did you send the picture of the trespasser at Adam Mooney's party to his people?'

'What? That was ages ago,' I replied.

'What are you talking about?' Suki asked.

'Miss Genius here seems to have given Adam Mooney's publicist a photo from the opening party for his play that shows there was a trespasser hiding away, taking pictures of all the guests.'

'I'm confused,' Suki said. 'What is this photo, Laura?'

'It's nothing. I was trying to find who had released the photo of Emily with Adam Mooney that got onto the Internet and led to all the personal abuse. And the official photographer, Craig, found there had been a trespasser. We had no way to identify him. I gave it to the police, who were completely unhelpful, saying this was a private security matter. Then I sent it to Adam's people, thinking maybe they could do something with it. Also, I thought the guy might be stalking Adam and they could keep an eye out. What does this have to do with anything?'

Claire fumed. 'That private security at the event — which we've learnt was completely ineffective — was hired by *my* agency. Remember? We organised it. And that stupid movie star's publicist has been blabbing to everyone about how we couldn't keep their star safe. Pure Brilliant now look like fucking idiots.' The waitress came with the drinks and Claire contained her fury until she'd gone. 'And right after our joke on Darren. None of the PR publications or social media groups would have done anything, because it isn't exactly industry news. Except now it is. Both the intruder image and the embarrassing photo of Darren are shown in an article taking the piss out of us. A PR agency that can't even contain its own publicity.'

'Ah,' Suki said.

I clutched my sparking water close to my chest; the ice cubes clinked against glass as my breath quivered. 'I'm sorry, Claire. I never connected the dots. How was I supposed to know? God, I feel terrible.'

'I don't care how you feel,' Claire said. 'Darren is in a stinking rage. Plus, I got a call this morning from my smart watch client —

the one who sponsored the event — complaining how embarrassing this was for them, and that they were minded to go elsewhere.' Slim pools of angry tears formed along her lash line. 'Don't you see? If I lose them, I'm going to be tufted back to doing handbags and fucking charity gigs. So thanks a lot.'

'Come on.' Suki pushed down Claire's accusatory finger. 'Calm down. You can't really blame Laura for this. How was she supposed to know the photo of the trespasser would get a life of its own? You're also not completely blameless in this: *you* asked Laura to take that photo of your boss.'

'I'm sorry,' I said. I hadn't moved an inch since the attack began. 'It's Emily... I've been trying to find someone to blame for her death. That's all I cared about; all I could see. Even helping you out with Darren, I partly did for Emily.'

Claire's incredulous eyes couldn't have gotten any bigger. 'What? Why? What's he got to do with Emily's death?' She searched Suki for support, as if to say, 'are you hearing this?' but Suki handily stuffed her face with taco. 'Look. I know she was your best friend. And I liked her too. The abuse she suffered was completely uncalled for, but bloody hell, what was she thinking, making a big stink? She just had a bad date.'

Suki gasped. A small piece of cabbage flew into her windpipe, triggering a coughing fit.

'How... How can you say that?' I asked, checking on Suki with a sideways glance.

'For fucks' sake, she was in PR. She should have known better than to write about it. Plenty of women believe that it wasn't that big of a deal what happened with Adam Mooney and that she should've kept quiet.'

Suki recovered. 'Yes, but I didn't think that included us.'

'There is no "us".' Claire formed a circle with her finger. 'Whatever we were doing here is over. I'm out.' She slid to the end of the bench, jumped up and grabbed her stuff. 'Goodbye.'

After taking two steps towards the door, she turned around again, straightened up, and shook her hair into place. 'I would be grateful if this didn't become a problem for our professional relationship, Laura. Pure Brilliant values Empisoft's business tremendously and I'll remain one hundred percent focused on making your conference a success.' She spun on her heels and left.

'Wow. Are you okay?' Suki asked.

I pressed my cool fingers to my temples. 'Not really.'

'Don't let it get to you. She's hot-headed. I've seen her lambast someone before.' Suki rolled her eyes. 'And she complains about her boss being a bully. She'll get over it.'

I put on a little fake smile. I rubbed my napkin between my fingers, not sure whether the tears building up behind my eyes would force their way out or not. This all served me right for believing I'd made new friends. You didn't make friends that easily. God, I missed Emily.

I'd always be better off on my own. No one to hurt me.

Suki snapped her fingers in front of my face. 'Hello?'

'I'm fine. I'll be fine.'

'Sod her, Laura. We didn't need her anyway. I haven't even told you about my chat with Diane.' Suki leaned over and snatched the napkin from my hand. 'Don't mope. Our trio is down to two — big deal. Do you have any idea how many times the Avengers have reformed? That's never stopped them from their mission.'

I tilted my head.

'Okay, you got me,' she said. 'I have no idea what their mission is. Something to do with five stones?' She grinned broadly. 'Come on. Cheer up. Onwards and upwards.' She grabbed my wrist across the table and forced me to lift my glass while saying with a high-pitched voice, 'Onwards and upwards.'

It was hard not to smile.

40.
ME

'Did you think I wouldn't find out?' Justin's voice made my heart flip. I'd been so engrossed working on my data model since lunchtime that I hadn't sensed his presence next to my desk.

Curious heads popped up from nearby monitors. Justin tossed his head in the direction of the meeting rooms, signalling this conversation was better had in private.

It was a silent march past reception and into the boardroom, whose frosty glass matched the atmosphere between us.

He sat at the head of the table, leaning back with his hands behind his head and his legs wide apart. An unreasonably relaxed pose that made me want to kick his exposed nuts.

'What's up?' I asked, crossing my arms.

He hunched forward and laid his palms flat onto the table. 'What you did was ballsy. I didn't think you had it in you. What were you hoping to achieve with the board? Did you really think they wouldn't be on the phone to me within seconds?'

I shrugged. 'It was worth a shot. You made it perfectly clear to me, after Suki called you out on having the growth options, that I should leave it alone. I figured you weren't going to share, or champion me, and I took matters into my own hands.' I sat in the seat opposite, shaking my head with pursed lips. 'So much for fifty-fifty. Or don't you remember that? Our promise. Our pinkie-promise in your digs late at night when we'd finished the first draft of the business plan and had finally gotten the demo to work for the investor showcase.'

'Listen to you. A pinkie-promise. We're not kids, Laura. This isn't a game.' He held his arms out wide, as if to embrace the whole office. His blue Empisoft-logoed polo shirt stretched across his chest. 'I put everything into this business, working day and night, travelling, endless schmoozing. While you swanned in late morning, did your bit, and buggered off home again to be with your books and feed the cat.'

'Don't bring that up as an excuse,' I spat. 'You've always said the hours don't matter, it's the output that does. The output has always been there and it's my R&D programme that has kept customers loyal and the competitors at bay.'

Justin crossed his arms with a deep sigh. 'Fine. Even if that's true. I'm sorry you're feeling unappreciated or undervalued, or whatever. Why is it important to you all of a sudden? We're going to be filthy rich. This is what I have worked my tail off for. It's too bloody late to change anything. And I'm not going to let you cause huge problems all because of some romantic sense of fairness or entitlement.'

I leaned into the table. 'Why should this cause problems? It's just the truth. I have been as important as you in the growth and success of this company, and people needed to be aware of that.'

'Well, you've achieved that... but it comes with strings. And you're not going to like them.'

'What do you mean, strings?'

Justin nudged towards me. 'The board were pissed. But they also believed you. Problem is, they now have an obligation to list you as a Key Man and that is what I'd been trying to avoid. To protect you.'

'I don't understand.'

He tugged at his collar and sat back. 'When I negotiated my growth options, it was because I was frustrated that the investors would get such a big return for all of our hard work if the company did as well as I expected it to. In the grand scheme of things, they'd only put in some money they could stand to lose; and proceeded to give us a hard time for the first year and a half when things weren't going that well yet. We did all the hard work.' He rose and started pacing around the room. 'And I had a vision. I knew we could grow this company well beyond what these investors considered success, to be one of the truly great technology companies to come out of Edinburgh. And I was right. Look at us. But at the time, me claiming I could increase the valuation by tenfold was bold and crazy-sounding. They granted me the options, believing they'd never be worth anything.' Justin crouched next to me and looked up with a friendly face. 'And I did think of getting them for you, too. Of course I did. Yes, we had a deal. Fifty-fifty. But my vision also included selling this company quickly, making our millions and riding off into the sunset — or into a library, in your case,' he said, smiling. 'And you wouldn't have been able to do that if I'd explained to them how incredibly important you are. They just saw you as a clever girl, a hard worker, and because you'd opted not to be a director, they didn't give you much attention. If I had made the case for growth options for you on the basis that so much of Empisoft relies on you, they would have made you a Key Man. Like me.'

I pushed my chair back a bit and shook my head in confusion. My ponytail swung against my shoulders. 'Stop. What is this Key Man thing you keep mentioning? So what? Why is this a bad thing? You got extra options out of it.'

He rose, his knees creaking, and perched on the side of the table. 'A Key Man — or woman — is someone who is critical to the operation of a business. Companies take out insurance for them. You know, if you get hit by a bus, at least the company get some cash to ride out the impact. That's not why it matters here. It matters because in the case of an acquisition — which you need to remember is what I was planning for all along, a big fat exit — contracts will stipulate that the Key Men will need to stay with the acquiring company for a set period of time, usually two years. So you see, I needed to downplay your role. I couldn't ask for growth options for you because if it all went to plan, I wanted to give you the ability to cash in straight away and go live your life. To give you freedom.'

'By you getting paid more?' I gave him a defiant look, quickly tempered by a guilty twinge for challenging him on this again. He seemed genuine and caring, gazing gently down at me. Had he really meant well all along?

He shrugged. 'I figured that by the time we were looking at a hundred-million-dollar exit, the added cash from the growth options wouldn't matter anymore. What's a measly million at that point in exchange for two years of your life?'

'You should have told me. This wasn't your decision to make. Besides, I don't mind working. I love this job. I have no idea what I would be doing with all that money anyway.'

'Well that's just as well,' he said. 'Because you'll have to wait two years to get your hands on it.'

'What do you mean? I thought you said I only had to work for two years.'

He bit his lip and grimaced. 'No, it's a lot more complicated than that, and I'm afraid you've shot yourself in the foot. I tried to shield you from all the extra obligations and complications that I have, as CEO. But you've blindly gone around making your point about how instrumental you've been, how you're the only one who knows how the new projects work. Fact is, because of this, you're not going to get your money any time soon.'

226

'Why not? I own like a third of the company. Aren't PeopleForce buying all the shares?'

'Yes, but Key Men are expected to sign warranties. That's basically promising everything we told them is true. A guarantee that there will be no skeletons in the closet; that we've traded like we say we did, and we own the intellectual property we say we do.'

This was all too much. All these new financial constructs I wasn't used to. I knew what the words meant, just not how they all fit together. There was a reason I'd tried to stay away from the business side. It seemed weird — how could they keep hold of my money?

I rose to my feet to meet his eye line. 'I haven't lied. I don't see the problem.'

'*You* don't lie. The problem is that some people do lie. Companies acquiring others find issues all the time. Months, years later. I know of a founder being sued for actual fraud seven years after his company got acquired. It's a nightmare. Like every company in their position does, PeopleForce have demanded a way to recoup some of the money, to cover their ass in case they find something wrong later. There are special clauses in the contracts for that. For any Key Man, which you now are, the proceeds of the sale of your shares — your millions — will not be paid out to you at the time the sale goes through.' Seeing my blank face, he added, 'The money will be held in a separate bank account, that nobody can touch until certain criteria are met. To give them a way to claw it back. You're going to have to work for PeopleForce for two years, and you'll only start to get the money for the share of the business you've sold after twelve months, then another bit six months later.'

'You mean you're not getting your share of the business paid out for two whole years... and neither am I?'

'I'm sorry, Laura. I was aware that would be the case from the start. I did my homework early on. And I was willing to be in that position — because someone had to be. This company is my life. I signed up for this. You've always valued your home time and I didn't want to see you tied down if we were successful. Yet here you are.' His dark eyes suddenly glowed with scorn. 'But I don't feel sorry for you. You and your great big need to kick up a self-important fuss. Forcing the board to make last-minute adjustments to the contracts. Angus at Madainn is going apeshit because PeopleForce are getting seriously fed up with us and are threatening to call the whole thing off.'

My heart pounded in my throat. I took a step back. I'd never seen Justin so mad. Had I really messed the whole thing up? If the deal fell through, would it all be my fault? Imagine having to be the one to tell our staff I was the reason they didn't get a huge bonus; a bonus big enough to pay off mortgages for some.

He barked, 'Where are we on the due diligence documentation?' I flinched as his angry words hit me. 'Because we can't afford any more delays. No more skulking on Twitter. You've not been focused on what matters: getting this deal over the line. No more surprises, Laura. I'll *never* forgive you if you screw this up.'

As he turned to leave, he said, 'I absolutely want to have it announced at the conference. Get on with it.'

So that was it.

My head buzzed. Nearly four years of close partnership, friendship even, reduced to a fight about cash. Cash I wasn't even going to get my hands on — or cared about.

This reminded me of another relationship gone awry, one I could maybe still fix.

'About the conference, Justin,' I said as he held the door open. 'Claire from Pure Brilliant knows about the acquisition.' Justin frowned. 'Don't ask why. Long story,' I said. 'She's been managing a real and a fake schedule for weeks and it would make her life a hundred times easier if she could talk freely to Marketing about it.

Can you make that happen? I promise I'll dive straight back into the due diligence.'

He nodded. 'Anything else?'

But he didn't wait to hear me say 'no' and slammed the door.

41.
ME

After the embarrassing 'privacy incident' weeks before, Sally had joked I should hang a sock on the stationery room's door handle whenever I was in there reading. But the last thing I wanted to think about was another discarded item of clothing in my sacred space.

Who has sex at work, anyway?

Book in hand, I entered the tiny room. The photocopier was churning out a large batch and I waited for the counter to reach zero. I was careful to keep the papers in order as I placed them on the floor outside in the corridor. Someone would be coming for them soon and I couldn't bear the thought of being interrupted.

This was my space. I'd even asked for an internal lock on the door. Refused. Apparently, that represented a health and safety hazard.

It had been a while since I'd sought sanctuary, hardly making the time to read at all lately. Whenever I tried, the words were only words. They no longer drew me deep inside a setting, with its sights and smells and sounds, or incited skipping heartbeats and quickened breaths alongside the characters. I'd thought at first perhaps Emily's death had caused me to shut off, but as I suffered through my emotional turmoil — with this whole new cast of people; the ups, the downs, the confusion and the misunderstandings — I reckoned it was because my own world was too full already.

Reading brought me peace and I was desperate for it, for the soothing familiarity of its universal stories, for the predictability of characters' life journeys. How much simpler than real life was it to be swept away by a thriller's ticking clock and broken hero beating the villain just in time; epic battles between two tribes with the most unexpected warrior being the one to see the truth and vanquish evil; by happily-ever-afters for the local girl and the mysterious visitor in small seaside villages?

I settled into my usual nook and read back a few pages to remind myself of where I'd left off.

It was evening at the concentration camp and the mother wrapped herself around her infant, her emaciated body providing what comfort she could against the freezing temperature. The guards' shouts echoed between the sick bay's stone walls.

But this all felt wrong.

My ponytail was caught between my shoulder and the photocopier, tugging at my scalp. The book felt heavy, stretching the tendons in my forearms. The copier's warmth made me itchy and its humming overpowered the click-clacks of the saviour-nurses' heels. Only the officer's bellowed orders made it through to my consciousness.

They sounded like Justin; an angry Justin I wasn't used to. An angry Justin I didn't know was justified or not, who would put all the blame on me if the deal went south. Rightly. An angry Justin who swore he'd had my best interest at heart when keeping me in the shadows, uninformed, under rewarded. I wanted to believe him, yet my gut told me something was off.

Who was I kidding?

Why would I have an instinct for people? One thing I'd learnt of late is that they weren't the predictable flawed-but-ultimately-good or one-dimensionally evil imaginary beings I was used to. Those I'd chosen to spend my time with since I was little because there was beauty, heroism, courage, friendship, love in their stories. And comfort. Shy, sheltered and self-conscious as I'd been, it was a joy to be anyone I wanted to be inside a book.

But not one of the people that had recently unsettled my world — Suki, Claire, Craig even — were predictable in any way. The spontaneous closeness, the mixed messages, unreasonable opinions, hidden motives. The sudden and unearned loyalty. Suki defending me in front of Claire.

I dropped my head in my hands. Claire's rage and Justin's fury reverberated, dark swirls of resentment accusing me of making a mess of things, of being a bad friend. To them. To Emily.

A WhatsApp notification buzzed in my pocket. A message from Suki:

We shouldn't speak for a while. Sorry. Shit hit the fan with PeopleForce because of the last-minute change. Justin has convinced Angus I'm to blame.

Conscience-infected tears stung in my eyes. Everything was my fault. Poor Suki.

I scrolled back through our messages, an animation-laden rally of plans, complaints and exaggerations that had made me snort on more than one occasion. Would I lose this, too?

A shiny, red motorcycle standing against a desert sunset drew my attention. It was the one Suki said Justin would buy when the deal went through. Suki had sent a joke along with it.

What's the most dangerous part of a motorcycle? The nut that connects the seat to the handlebar!

From where I was sitting, Justin was no nut. He'd done his research, been in control, had a singular vision all this time of where the company could end up, and done everything to come out a winner. His growth options would pay out as soon as the deal was signed, a cash windfall to keep him in toys while being tied-in to PeopleForce for another two years and had to wait for the big bucks. The real fruit of his labour.

Of *our* labour.

And here I was. Sulking in a closet, facing the same two-year wait, with no upfront reward. Whether I'd been thoroughly duped by a man I'd trusted for years or had royally messed up Justin's well-intentioned plan, I wasn't sure. One thing was clear: there was no way I could engineer growth options for myself anymore, with the acquisition hanging on a thin thread.

What a loser. I seemed to have a knack for steering straight into dead ends, with pig-headed conviction. All that effort for nothing.

I gasped. It was worse than nothing... Mum.

How would she take it? Biting my lip, I cast my eyes to the heavens and speed-dialled Mum's number. It was four o'clock. She wouldn't be at the restaurant yet.

'Hi, darling,' she said as soon as she picked up. 'I'm getting changed for work. Oliver and I have come from the florist. There was too much choice! I'm running a little late now. More importantly, how are you?'

How was I? Even with my mastery of words, I couldn't even begin to assemble letters resembling the state I was in. Despondent? Bereft? Guilty? Definitely guilty.

'Mum, I've got something to tell you. I've made a mistake.' A small sob escaped from my lips. 'I'll fix it. I promise.'

'What is it, sweetheart? What's wrong?'

'It's about your wedding. The money I thought I'd have will take longer to come. I won't get my hands on it for another year or longer. I'll figure something out. I'll get you the deposit for the hotel. Don't worry.'

I winced while only a small crackle darted between us on the line. When I could no longer stand the silence and opened my mouth wanting the shame and disapproval over with, Mum said, 'Well, I guess we'll have to change our plans a little. Get the community hall after all. I'm glad you've told me now.'

'No, Mum. I've got some savings. I'll dip into them.' I had no idea what weddings costs, but worst care, Justin could give me a loan. It was the least he could do. Although with our relationship strained, even that might be hard to pull off. 'It may not be enough so I may need a bit of time. But I said I was going get you a dream wedding and that's what I'm going to do. I want it to be perfect for you.'

Mum signed. 'It will be perfect, darling, because you will be here. Our friends. Because Oliver and I love each other. Don't you see? Nothing else matters. I don't want your money. Happiness doesn't come from expensive flowers. Happiness is the people you surround yourself with. It will be fine... Are you crying?'

I sniffed and wiped my nose with my sleeve. 'I'm okay.'

'Don't feel bad, Laura, sweetheart. I'm proud of you. I love you. You're a good daughter.'

But at this point, I didn't think I was a good anything.

42.

CLAIRE

Claire took a second chocolate biscuit from the plate in front of her. They were the cheap kind, which was fair enough as her client was only small and not yet turning a profit with their new digital advertising platform.

A loud bang against the window startled her. It was a polystyrene chips box, thrown against the building by a gust of wind.

God, she hated coming to Leith. It was only two miles from Edinburgh's city centre but took an age to get to by car or bus. Incessant roadworks in preparation for the new tram had obstructed the main road for years, and somehow morphed into a new set of perpetual detours long after the city's mismanagement of the project meant the trams would never actually reach Leith.

If it wasn't for her clients and some of the nicer, hipper restaurants increasingly clustered there, she'd happily avoid the former crime and prostitute-riddled waterfront area altogether.

It was her third visit this week to the converted old sugar refinery, which offered small companies a modern, affordable alternative to the cramped and pricey commercial accommodation in town.

She'd been twice to her other client, one floor down, a medical imaging company that had been a shining light of innovation before it was acquired by a large Japanese firm. The R&D still happened in

Edinburgh, but with all other functions performed elsewhere, it would never grow to provide the jobs the country sorely needed. She figured the same was likely to happen to Empisoft after they were sold next week.

Emily had gushed about the medical software's latest features, when she was still taking care of them. How you could see deep inside a patient's lung and navigate through each blood vessel as if in a little capsule riding through the body.

Hadn't there been a film about people lost inside a body? Claire vaguely recalled reading about a possible remake by a top director. That would be much so more fun to do the PR for. But here she was, stuck in techno-land.

'Claire, did you get that?' a male voice asked.

She looked up from the paper clip she'd been twisting in her hands to find the whole room looking at her. 'Of course. Though I'd like to get a copy of the presentation if I could please?'

There was no way she could admit her mind had wandered off when the team had specifically organised this update for her, to help her prepare for a magazine article she'd secured.

'No problem. Whatever you need,' said the eternally enthusiastic founder.

How did he do it? Entrepreneurs were often unusually chirpy and optimistic. They kinda had to be. But it was all the more remarkable in this guy's case. She had to raise her head to return his smile, since he stood strapped to a metal frame holding him upright. Apparently, it provided relief from sitting too long in his wheelchair.

Claire had no doubt their artificial intelligence-driven product was first class. She also knew the magazine wouldn't have given her as big a feature if it hadn't been for the additional intriguing angle of the spinal stroke the founder suffered the year before.

So yeah, her job might suck, but things could be a lot worse.

On the screen was an advert they'd placed for a luxury jacket, an example of the micro-targeting they could do. It was gorgeous, a soft, blue leather trench with oval buttons made of green glass. Claire recalled seeing it on an up-and-coming actress on the red carpet at the Edinburgh Film Festival.

Another client she would not get to serve. She mentally sneered at thieving Otto.

Having only listened to the presentation with half an ear, she checked the words on the screen: *CTR, CPM, ROI.* She recognised them as measures of advertising effectiveness, but what the hell was a genetic algorithm? Or a data refinery?

Claire's head hurt thinking about it.

Laura would know. She was super good at explaining complicated data science things in simple terms.

A small knot formed in her stomach. She hadn't spoken to Laura since their blow-up at the bistro. It had been extremely unprofessional of her to tell Laura off. Darren would tear Claire's head off if he knew. Empisoft was their biggest and sexiest client.

Laura had kept it between them, a kindness that gnawed at Claire's conscience. She'd grown to realise she'd been too quick to blame Laura for last week's public humiliation of Pure Brilliant. How was Laura supposed to know the photo of the trespasser would cause problems?

But whenever such guilty feelings reared their ugly little head, Claire reminded herself Laura wasn't totally blameless. She had no business going to Adam Mooney's publicist directly. That was an introduction Claire had made, through her network — and what a thrill she'd had knowing her network extended directly to Adam Mooney. It was *her* connection and it was simply not done, in her world, to bypass the introducer like that.

Then again, how could she expect Laura to know the world of PR? Besides, Claire couldn't ignore her own role in her agency's disaster.

She'd only meant to dent Darren's ego a bit, bring him back to Earth through their little photographic taunt. And sweet Laura had helped her. Even though there wasn't anything in it for her — other than some weird thoughts about avenging Emily which made no sense to Claire at all.

Darren might be a complete dick, but he hadn't mistreated Emily. Not like what he did to Claire: making her juggle multiple briefs with no recognition whatsoever; unfairly denying her longed-for promotion to Culture.

Though, admittedly, to call all that 'mistreatment' might be a bit of a stretch. And his punishment was maybe, just maybe, not entirely deserved.

Claire took another sip of water. The company founder announced the last slide, a welcome diversion from the nagging thought that was running through her brain: the possibility that she'd been an unjustifiably vicious cow to Darren. And to Laura.

43.

SUKI

A new pack of soya milk stood on the top shelf of the fridge, towards the left, where she usually kept hers. Plenty of dairy there, too. The temp from reception walked past and smiled. Had he done this? Suki picked up her milk, feeling guilty she couldn't remember his name. Who knew he'd stay so long? It would be too awkward to ask now.

As she waited for the machine to squirt out her espresso, she was struck by a gust of wind from the door to the patio. August was coming to an end. The weather had turned from changeable — bouncing between mild-but-wet and sunny-but-chilly — to the more static grey misery of autumn.

'Do you mind closing that door? It's fucking freezing in here,' she snapped at the junior associate vaping outside.

She crossed her arms across her blouse to cover her nipples' reaction to the cold before some eagle-eyed Neanderthal spotted it.

At her desk, there wasn't anywhere to put the coffee. Sheets of paper lay scattered across her work surface, in what might have looked like a total mess, but in fact benefited from subtle order; legal documents on one side, financials on the other.

She sat down and got to work. It was crunch time. If she didn't get the revisions to PeopleForce by tonight, they'd lose another day because of time zones, and that made the difference between signing prior to the conference or not.

Angus had lectured her in the morning that failure to close this deal in time for the big event was not an option. She'd had to swallow her pride. Jerk.

All she needed was a little patience. He'd get his comeuppance soon enough, when she and Diane put their plan into action. What mattered most at this moment was getting the acquisition over the line, whatever it took. And it was taking all her waking hours — many robbed from the night — and all her concentration.

Yet that was why she'd come here. This was exactly why she'd picked this line of work: the thrill of the deal, the loud ticking of the clock, the myriad obstacles to jump over, the financial puzzle. Not to mention the size of the prize, the giant bonus that awaited her when Justin and Laura signed their baby away.

It still grated that Justin was getting more than the woman who'd contributed as much, if not more. She shook her head thinking how Laura's clumsy attempt at getting what she deserved had backfired.

She'd warned Laura that straight-up asking for things almost never got you what you wanted. You had to be *smart*. To scheme. And Suki had asked for some time to work out a smarter plan. But Laura, sweet Laura, naively thought the world was as logical as her mind, as the software code she wrote. If there was an error, you'd naturally fix it.

At least Laura wouldn't need to work with the asshole who betrayed her anymore. Justin's new job description and his cushy new remuneration package lay atop Suki's keyboard, fully approved. Global Director of Digital Labs.

Good riddance. Shame she couldn't tell Laura yet.

A wry grin lifted the corners of her mouth. It was quite a technical role and, from what she's seen, he wasn't up to the job. PeopleForce would see straight through him once he got Stateside.

She put the document aside and shifted her focus to the amended Key Man provisions. They'd all been fine at first glance; but as Laura had become entangled in this, she wanted to doubly make sure.

Such a nice girl, Suki sighed. And they'd been having good fun. There was something about Laura that made her want to protect her. Suki was surrounded by sharks all the time. Hell, she liked to believe she was one herself, so she recognised a defenceless flounder when she saw one.

PeopleForce had been shaken by the late addition of another Key Man. Their nervousness had infected Angus and Diane, who'd hovered around Suki earlier wanting to make sure everything was on track. She scratched at the paper with a blue pen, doing her damnedest to address everyone's concerns. There was no way she'd let PeopleForce choose to buy Empisoft's competitor at this stage in the game. And by all accounts, this threat was real.

Fuck. What if it all went wrong?

Justin had pointed the finger at her as the troublemaker. Was it because she'd not responded to his charm? Angus had happily believed him, of course. Who would challenge the big client? All this meant she needed to crack on, lay low, jump when told to jump, grin and generally be a good girl. Ugh.

There were three pages of new clauses left for her to review in the whole contract. Problem was, they featured a complicated cross-Atlantic tax-avoidance structure she wasn't familiar with. But she knew who was. Double ugh.

She leaned back in her chair and waved one arm in the air.

'Robert? Hey. Can you give me a hand, please?' she shouted.

Four desks away, Robert sprang up. After an initial look of confusion, he strutted over, demonstrably adjusting his tie in front of the others.

'Need my help, do you?' he said. 'Stanford not teach you everything you need to know after all?'

Suki resisted the urge to roll her eyes. 'Have a look at this, please. It looks like the scheme we set up for the shipping company last year. There are a few differences, though, and I can't work out who stands to benefit from that.'

'Sure, anything to help a lovely lady.' He pulled a seat over, placing it within an inch of hers. His breath smelled of bacon roll with a hint of residual alcohol. They partied hard, the finance boys.

He stretched across her to take control of the mouse, his elbow unashamedly brushing against her breast. Did men really think women didn't know about 'elbow tit'? Did they really think we hadn't figured out the lurid game they played in bars to see who could notch up the most supposedly accidental boobie-wobbles in a night? But we knew. Suki had also learnt from experience that calling them out on it usually ended badly, with either mock-outraged accusations of imagining things or, worse, being told you should be grateful for the attention.

Suki thought of all the poor women who had to put up with this shit. Those who dared to complain and ended up taking payoffs rather than fight, knowing the men would always have the upper hand; those who suffered in silence because they didn't have the luxury of a good education and a choice of jobs, like she did, or because their self-worth had been eroded through years of under-appreciation.

The temptation to stomp on his feet was strong. Instead, she got up and stood a generous distance to his side while he read.

Accommodating.

Silent.

Boiling.

Soothed by the knowledge that soon, real soon, she and Diane would strike.

44.
ME

I arrived at the weekly IT Operations meeting six minutes late and apologised. It was unusual for me to attend, so it had slipped my mind. Most of my work was early stage, irrelevant for the purposes of the main systems in the company. That is, until I caused a whole sequenced reboot because my Network Impact code had gone rogue.

Because Justin and I were both joining, Grant had booked a room and even ordered coffees rather than hold the meeting informally around his desk, as was usually the case.

Grant stood by the screen, squinting. His presentation was only partially readable due to the angle of the sun, prompting his teammate to fiddle around with the blinds.

Justin typed on his phone, looking exasperated.

I sat far away from him. I'd limited our interactions to the minimum required, still raw from my defeat, still torn about his role, his intentions, throughout this whole thing. Still unsure we could ever rebuild our relationship, or if I wanted to.

Watching him out of the corner of my eye, and feeling the tension rise across my shoulders, I dreaded the moment we'd have to make peace. We'd have to work together for another two years after the acquisition.

Grant explained it had taken considerable forensic work by his team to establish what had happened and he took the room through the security protocol settings that had failed to raise the alarm.

'Can we skip to your recommendation?' asked Justin. 'I have somewhere to be.'

'Yes, of course. Let me jump to slide nine,' Grant replied, seeming already frazzled by his delayed start.

I sipped at my water. Grant had been gracious in not assigning the blame of the incident to me too openly and stood explaining the new protocols he had designed for everyone to follow.

Justin snorted at his mobile and tip-tapped away with his fingers, his opinions punctuated by the occasional shake of his head and the odd tsk.

'How do you spell "insolence"?' he asked.

'I-N-S-O-L-E-N-C-E,' I offered automatically, wondering who had bruised his ego this time.

'Ah, so it is with an "E" instead of an "A". I always get that wrong.'

I thought it a strange word to get wrong. It seemed obvious to me. There was only one person I'd ever seen write it with an "A".

My heartbeat quickened and the room grew dark. I clutched the table for support. Could it be? There was only one way to find out.

I sprung from my seat. 'This all looks awesome, Grant. Well done. I'm sorry again you had to go through all this. At least we know it won't happen again. But I'm sorry, I need to go. You'll send me the instructions later, won't you?'

Without waiting for an answer, I ran out the door.

THE TWO occupants of the last-choice salsa room looked at me like startled owls as I yanked open the door. How could everywhere be full? Bloody open plan offices.

I drummed my fingers on the laptop clutched to my chest. Where could I go? The stationary closet wouldn't do. Too cramped.

Retracing my steps, I double-checked there were indeed partial heads visible through the small glazed rectangles in the doors of every single meeting room.

Once at reception, I said to Liv, 'I'm going out. I won't be long,' 'Sure thing, Laura. See you later.'

The wind propelled me towards the central square of the Quartermile. The cold air on my neck overpowered the stress-induced flush that coursed through my veins. The clash of temperatures hurt.

Through windows, I spotted an empty table in the nearest café.

The barista was slow. I danced on the spot, like a child needing the loo.

With my Earl Grey finally in hand, I plonked onto the wooden bench and woke my computer. Come on.

The WiFi needed a password. I checked all four sides of the promotional pyramid on the table and scanned the walls. A small blackboard invited coffee-lovers to sign up to their newsletter. Underneath, the password.

I accessed Twitter and searched for Justin's account. He was an avid tweeter, averaging what I guessed was twenty tweets a day. Mostly about the company; mixing musings on industry news and events with an occasional glimpse into his private life.

A quick mental calculation told me I'd only need about seven months' worth. That wouldn't take long.

I entered the parameters in my scraper and let it loose on Twitter. I'd have to be patient.

The tea was soon gone. I twirled my ponytail around my finger.

Twelve minutes later, the scraper had captured all 4213 of Justin's tweets from the selected period into a small database. I saved it onto my desktop.

I opened the giant database that held Emily's Twitter abuse and extracted the account data I needed to confirm my hunch. My heart thumped at a furious pace. I navigated to a collection of models for Natural Language Processing I used frequently. I chose the one tailored for casual speech. It was one of many that formed the basis of Empisoft's sophisticated product.

My hands trembled as I set up the model to run on the two small databases I'd just created and pressed *Enter*.

Within seconds, the results began populating my screen. My eyes followed each line as it appeared. I knew from practice that the information I wanted would fall roughly two thirds of the way down

There.

A 91% match.

@JustinG and @chosenone2.

Both Twitter accounts used the same language to such an extent that they could only belong to the same person. The same words, the same grammar, the same quirks in their turn of phrase. The same misspelling: *insolance*.

I let out a great big sob and thrust my head into my hands, dizzy with a confusing mixture of shock, anger... and relief. To think I'd given up after all those days and nights exploring mazes, hitting so many dead ends. But here he was; the man who'd stirred the sexist Incel army into a frenzy, pushing, motivating and provoking their vile attacks on Emily from all corners of the Globe.

And it was Justin.

Justin was the Inciter.

Justin caused Emily's death.

45.
CLAIRE

In the toilets, Claire primped her hair and ran a thick pencil over her eyebrows. She fixed the collar of her white blouse, selected for the occasion. She took a mindful breath. You deserve this.

Her one page of notes lay on the marbled surface. A neat bulleted list of irrefutable evidence. When Darren confirmed she could have a word with HR about that pay rise she'd asked for, she'd done her research. She admired her reflection in the mirror. She had the memory of an elephant and never left a fact or detail unchecked. It's why she was great at running events.

She glanced over the figures one more time. Her friends across the PR community hadn't been shy about sharing their remuneration packages. They might all have snazzy titles like 'PR Specialist' and 'Account Executive', but the sector was notorious for underpaying. She'd fallen for it too, at first, like all the other bright-eyed and bushy-tailed juniors the agencies convinced were trading money for a life of glamour, and that greater reward would follow. But that was a long time ago.

She took her sheet back to her desk. It wasn't quite time yet. Unfortunately, her peers' roles were too varied to determine a clear, tight range of the salary she should expect; their client portfolios spanned the spectrum from tiny family businesses to global brands. It also made it difficult to check if there was any systemic gender pay gap, which must suit the bosses just fine.

She'd pilfered websites like Glassdoor where people could post their salary anonymously. It was depressing. Up here in Scotland you never got anywhere near the London dosh.

At ten o'clock she knocked on HR's door.

'Ah, Claire. Good.' Linda's papers and folders lay scattered on her desk like plaster from a collapsed ceiling.

How could she find anything?

'Is it okay to move this pile?' Claire asked pointing to the overflowing chair.

'Yes, sure. Put it by the cabinet.'

Easier said than done. Claire left it on the floor, conscious she was not supposed to see some of the private documents peeking out at her.

'First of all... Congratulations.' Linda's hands strobed together in a tiny gesture of applause. 'How's it going?'

Be positive.

'Very well. I've got Empisoft's conference in a few days and it's going to be a belter.'

'Good. And are you managing with the content? I certainly don't understand half of what our clients do.'

'Absolutely. I'm getting completely stuck in,' said Claire, projecting a confidence that almost convinced herself.

'That's great. A hidden talent, because I would have thought you'd be more suited to Culture. And that's where Emily thought you should go.'

'Emily?' Claire thought her ears has deceived her. It had been a while since she'd heard that name in the office. Her colleagues tended to pussyfoot around what happened, glossing over the event, and by extension, Emily's existence. Although many had stopped going to the gym and nobody had moved to her desk yet.

Linda nodded. 'Emily had caught wind of Jacob's plan to move to London and came to give her thoughts on how we should reorganise briefs when he was gone.'

Claire straightened her shoulders. 'And she said I couldn't handle Technology?'

'Quite the opposite,' replied Linda. 'She had only good things to say. Thought you were wasted on Charity. Told me you were passionate about the arts, film, TV, and knew everything that was going on.'

'She did?'

'Don't sound so surprised. She was a big fan.'

Claire blinked. She and Emily had jousted for position. Was she wrong about their rivalry? It made no sense. Had Emily's throwaway *You can do better than that, Claire'* comments been meant as encouragement all along?

'So what happened?' Claire asked. 'I mean, not that I'm not happy with Technology, but I'd like to know why Otto got Culture.'

Linda grimaced. 'After the thing with Adam Mooney kicked off, Darren didn't value Emily's opinion anymore.'

'He *was* cross, wasn't he?'

A stony smile spread across Linda's face. 'Anyway,' she said, rubbing her hands together. 'It's all fallen into place, and we are here to talk about your pay rise.' She looked around the desk, searching for a document.

Get in there.

Claire leaned forward. 'Before you tell me your thoughts, Linda. I wanted to share some of the figures I've seen for similar types of roles. I think it's important we recognise market rates.'

Linda smiled and nodded. 'You've done your homework.'

'I think it's important to know your worth.' Claire handed her research over. When Linda extended her arm to receive it, her elbow bumped a heap of paper that flooded the floor.

'Oh dear,' Linda said, keeping hold of the next, tottering heap.

Claire sprang out of her chair. 'Let me.' She crouched down and swept the various documents together, their corners jutting out at clumsy angles. She spotted a big, bold title *Termination Letter.* Unable to contain her curiosity, Claire peaked at the name of the addressee. Her stomach churned. *Emily Nairn.*

She climbed to her feet, her heart beating against the stack of papers she held by her chest. 'Was Darren going to fire Emily? For what happened?'

It would have been easy to miss Linda's gulp, but there it was. 'You know I can't comment, Claire.'

'Did Emily know?'

'Again, I can't comment.'

CLAIRE SHOULD'VE been happy. She'd negotiated a tidy package for herself. But she couldn't help thinking Linda hadn't put up much of a fight and wondered if she'd caved a little too easily to make up for Claire discovering the truth about Emily's dismissal — to buy her silence.

Instead of a sweet rush, Claire tasted bitterness as she closed Linda's door behind her.

A hubbub rose from the far end of the office, where colleagues stood huddled around a series of posters for the launch of a publisher's new book.

Had any of them known?

She walked to Emily's empty desk. Claire had collected the various gadgets relating to their technology clients, out of necessity. It seemed that others had gradually plundered the pens and pencils, the paper clips and the stapler without any qualms. An abandoned whiteboard eraser rested on the corner, ready to delete her altogether.

Surely, you couldn't fire someone on a whim? She'd been off sick. Well, Claire supposed 'sick' was the closest thing you could call it: Emily just stopped coming. And it was true that the company's reputation had suffered once the Internet trolls had worked out who Emily was. They took down the website. They even came to the door shouting abuse. Claire suspected Darren had been most upset that Pure Brilliant's name was mentioned whenever someone wrote about her sexual assault story. It was definitely not true what they say; that any publicity is good publicity.

Still... What nonsense reason could they have used? Gross misconduct? A PR man, of all people, should have known it would pass. Why sack Emily, when she was such an asset? And, as Claire had just learnt, such a team player. A champion.

Claire returned to the toilet. She ran her wrists under the cold tap and bent down to take a sip. She wiped the water from her chin and caught sight of her pale reflection. She pinched her cheeks and rubbed her lips with her finger.

Let it go.

But she couldn't.

With her colleagues still distracted, she collected her things and put on her coat.

Outside, she turned to the more private side of the building, where security had left Darren to recover that fateful day. She squeezed her eyes shut and held her forehead. After a deep breath, she secured her hair behind her ear and took out her phone. Laura's number was among the recent dials.

'Hey, it's Claire. Have you got a moment?'

'Is it urgent?' Laura's tone couldn't have been colder.

'Look, I'm probably not your favourite person at the moment, but I think you want hear this.'

'Okay. What is it? Be quick.'

'Are you sitting down?'

'Jesus, Claire. Spit it out. Is it the conference?'

'Sorry. No. It's... You were right. I know you've been frustrated trying to figure out why Emily would kill herself. Needing someone to blame. And we all know it was a whole bunch of things, all coming together, and...' Claire balled her fist. 'I gave you a hard time for saying Darren had anything to do with it. But you were right. I'm sorry.'

'What are you saying? What did he do?' Laura asked.

'It wouldn't have been enough in and of itself, but it might have been what tipped her over the edge. Darren sacked Emily... I promise I didn't know.'

Laura gasped. 'Oh my God.'

'It makes sense, doesn't it?' Claire said. 'Why else would she have gone through all that trouble? Coming into the gym that morning...' Claire pressed her hand against her churning stomach. 'She knew he would be in next. He's regular as clockwork. She must have wanted to punish him.'

Claire heard Laura's laboured breaths, and feet running. Where was she going?

'Laura? Are you okay?'

A muffled roar replied. 'I can't believe it. That bastard.'

'I'm shocked too. To think I was starting to regret our little trick on Darren because it had spiralled, but—'

'We didn't give him nearly what he deserved,' Laura spat.

Claire took a second to think. 'We still can.'

46.
ME

That afternoon, I paced in Empisoft's reception area, waiting for Suki to show up. The marketing team were busying around me, inspecting full-size banners for the conference that had just been delivered. Justin's canvas face rose from a metallic strip on the ground and towered over me as it was hooked into the top of the frame.

'Everything okay, Laura?' Liv asked.

'It will be.' I hoped that was true.

Suki's silhouette approached across the street, from the direction of Tollcross. She must have walked from her office. I willed her to speed up. Suki reached the glazed entrance, her head cocked in a puzzled expression. I was practically jumping up and down.

'Hey—'

'Come,' I said. I took her by the hand and dragged her to the meeting room I'd reserved to go over the absolute last due diligence matters.

Suki tottered on her heels. 'Steady. I can't go that fast.'

I activated the frosted wall and threw Suki into a chair.

'What's going on?' she asked.

'I've been waiting all day to tell you. You're not going to believe it.' I continued to pace flapping my arms to shake my hands loose, to release the energy that had built up inside. 'They're all bastards. They're all guilty.'

'What are you taking about?'

'Emily.'

Suki looked down and let out a deep sigh.

Did she not care?

I grabbed both her armrests. 'Justin. Darren. They're both responsible for Emily's death. It's not these random, anonymous trolls. It's them. It's people we know. It's people *she* knew.'

Suki frowned. 'I don't understand. Justin and Darren sent the dildos?'

I shook my head. 'Do you remember me telling you about the Inciter? The Twitter account. Network Impact identified the main agitator behind the torrent of abuse she got? The one who egged people on to do all these horrible things online — and in her home.'

'Yes, I remember.'

'It's Justin. Justin is the Inciter.'

Suki's jaw dropped. 'How did you—'

'He's the one behind all this venom that came at her from these horrible strangers. Unrelenting. Attacking, attacking, attacking. And she already couldn't handle it. Then to top it all off, she got fired by her boss.'

'No way.' Suki's hands flew to her mouth. 'How do you know?'

'Claire found out. She called me. And she apologised for acting like I was nuts when I thought Darren had mistreated Emily. Turns out I'm right. And I'm a hundred percent certain I'm right about Justin. And I have *had it*.' I slammed on the table.

Suki looked at me, aghast. 'It's really gotten to you, hasn't it?'

'Can you blame me? We know them. They're both here, acting like nothing ever happened. Justin pretending the growth options were to protect me, and me almost believing him. Not now. Not now I know he did this. He's got to pay. They both do.'

Suki's eyes were as wide as can be. She'd never seen me angry before. And in truth, I didn't recognise myself. But with the adrenaline coursing through me, and questions that had troubled me for so long finally answered, it felt right. Right, and almost good.

'Claire is thinking how we might get back at Darren,' I said. 'This is no longer about being unhappy with her boss. This is about Emily. She's in. Are you?'

'I didn't know Emily.' Suki raised her shoulders and grimaced.

'Come on.' I placed my hand on hers. 'What happened to kicking butt, Suki? Each one of us, including Emily, has been victimised in some way. All for being a woman. That's not okay. We need to fix it. I know you're doing something with Diane to change your firm. That's great. Happy to help if you need me. But let's take care of these two bastards: teach them a lesson that being a dick is not okay.' A tiny smirk formed in the corner of Suki's mouth, giving me confidence to go on. 'I know this Avengers club was a way for us to vent, to get some petty revenge, have a laugh. I'm not laughing now. We are onto something. We can do something about all these injustices. And we're stronger together. Women on the barricades.'

'How long have you been rehearsing that speech?' Suki chortled; but her laughter was short-lived. She released her hand from under mine and squeezed my fingers while she looked at me intently. 'This can't become some woman versus man revenge thing. It's not all men. They're not my personal cup of tea, but there are plenty of good guys.'

'I know there are.' I felt a faint flush as I thought of one good guy in particular. 'It's just them. I promise. Darren and Justin — and your Angus. We want to grab them where it hurts.'

Suki blew out a long breath. 'You'll need to show me how you figured out Justin was behind this. And we absolutely cannot have it impact the acquisition in any way. On that basis, I'm in.'

I punched the air. 'Great. Let's get some work done first and arrange a time to make a plan with Claire. Maybe I can even find you that black, skin-tight cat suit.'

47.
ME

Suki left me with only three more things to do and the PeopleForce team would have everything they needed. Hallelujah.

Headphones on, with white noise playing, I got through her task in half the time I'd expected. My fingers danced over clattering keys. I was on fire; riding the buzz from having a new purpose.

A hand waved in the space between my head and the screen. I looked up and my heart leapt. Justin. He stood, with a giant grin, next to a young woman in a red pencil skirt.

I freed my ears.

'This is the illustrious Laura Flett, head of R&D, working at her magic.'

'Hello,' I said.

'Hi,' she replied, with a wide crimson smile.

Justin beamed. 'Jessica here — can I call you Jess? — is writing an article on yours truly for *Look Here* magazine. They're running a feature on "eligible" entrepreneurs, would you believe.' He placed his hands on his chest with quite obviously false humility. 'She wanted to meet you too. Seems you've got a bit of a fan club.'

'Really?' I got to my feet.

'Jessica,' she said holding out her hand, a twitch in her cheek partly obscured by her wavy, brown hair.

'Nice to meet you, *Jessica*,' I said as I shook her hand and looked Justin in the eye. I turned my attention back to her, tilting my head. 'A fan club?'

Jess nodded. 'My little sister is studying computing at Uni, and you are totally her role model. She's going to freak when she finds out I met you. Would you mind joining us for the interview? I know it's only about Justin... this time.' She chuckled. 'But it would be great to hear about when you guys started out, and how you've maintained such a good relationship ever since.'

I was barely able to contain my laughter. This woman's timing could not have been worse.

'I'm sure Laura would be delighted to join us, Jess—ica. Come, we're in room three.' Justin led the way.

As he held the door open for us both, he whispered in my ear. 'Don't talk about the acquisition.'

'I'm not an imbecile,' I said.

Seated around the table, I answered Jessica's inane questions. Did he have any bad habits? Was he ever grumpy? Because, apparently, he came over as 'terribly chirpy.'

Yes. No. Yes. No.

Whatever.

I could tell from the woman's face that she regretted inviting me in. There was a distinct chill in the air that made her eyes dart between Justin and me.

'Has he changed much since you've become successful?' she asked.

That one threw me. Where to begin?

A picture of a younger Justin popped into my head. Gelled-back hair and a pale complexion in keeping with his indoor lifestyle, moving only between lectures and a computer screen.

I examined the man in front of me. He'd become handsome. That wasn't something I'd necessarily noticed, but the steady stream of dates in the last two years was hard to miss. He'd sort of grown into his face, his rounded chin now a chiselled jaw, the small lines around his eyes conveying maturity. His square shoulders and lean body that of a man at his peak. He'd traded the gaming for outdoor runs.

He'd told reporters before that he loved running up and down Arthur's Seat because the world-conquering view from the top of Edinburgh's dormant volcano inspired his best business ideas. I knew better. It was because he'd been a little pudgy at Uni. He'd been teased for it by the Business students he often trailed to pick up snippets of advice on venture capital. He'd felt cursed by his weight. And even though he'd attempted to hide it, I could always tell when he tried his luck with a girl and it hadn't worked. He'd brood for days.

His physique had since changed, and so had his luck. And once the acquisition released his millions, he'd have even more women flocking to him. I didn't like the way that happened, women throwing themselves at rich men. It happened the other way, too, of course, only less often. And could I really blame them? A lot of these girls didn't have many opportunities.

My mind flashed through the many nights with him in my digs, working out our plan of attack, arguing about the features of Empisoft 0.1, eating oily fish and chips. We were a team. We were a team for a long time. What happened?

I smiled at the interviewer and quipped, 'He wears a better type of shirt.'

After the two had a good giggle, I asked, 'Anything else?'

Jessica patted her notebook. 'I think I've got everything I need. Thanks a lot.' Turning to Justin, she said, 'I'll be in touch about the photo shoot, okay?'

Justin reached the door first and held it open. The woman was halfway out. I'd wanted to wait with confronting him until I'd formed a plan with the others but having him alone proved too much of a temptation. 'Jessica, do you mind making your own way out? Justin and I need to talk. Sorry. I know it's a bit rude—'

'That's okay.' She gave a mournful wave no doubt regretting not getting a proper goodbye from this hot, eligible businessman.

'What was that all about?' Justin asked. 'You know the drill. We've done this a dozen times before,' he said.

'Oh, I'm sorry. Did I not big you up enough?'

'Don't be like that. What's gotten into you? You're like a different person.'

'*I'm* a different person? Are you kidding me? Mr Chosen One. Strike that. Mr Chosen One number 2.'

'What?'

'Your Twitter handle. @chosenone2.'

A deep frown furrowed his brow. 'How? Why —'

'Why do you do it?'

'Why do I do what? I still don't know what Twitter's got to do with anything,' he said, wide-eyed.

'You have an anonymous account. It's horrible.'

'Oh that.' He chuckled. 'That's not for real. You know me.' He rested his bum on the conference table. 'It's how I wind down. It's a game... of strategy and influence. I like to see how far I can go.'

'Telling others to ruin people's lives?'

'I wouldn't put it that way.'

I poked my finger in his chest. 'You're an egomaniac.'

He swatted my hand away. 'I'm just toying with a bunch of losers. It's an experiment. All these worked up highly flammable dudes itching for a fight. I like to send them off scurrying with their pitchforks. And they have no idea who I am. They think I'm one of them: sad, pathetic, unable to get laid. Idiots,' he snorted.

I winced. 'That's not *fun*. You destroy people, Justin. Women. It's criminal.'

'Now hold on there.' He raised both hands in defence. 'Given that you've been snooping through my Twitter account — and I don't even want to know how you found out that was me — you'll also know that I never say anything that could be considered harassment. Or make any *direct* threats.'

My mouth hung open. It sounded as though he'd consulted a lawyer. How insane would that be? Dear solicitor, please can you explain where the line is, because I'd like to commit many atrocities online, just not crimes. Didn't he know? Nobody knew where the line was. Even the police said it was too hard to tell. There was a pool of obvious black on one side — calls for rape and physical assault — and a pool of white on the other. Everything else in between was a foaming, turbulent ocean of grey.

'You did worse,' I said. 'You incited others to make threats, to hurl abuse. You stirred them up until they could only see one way of thinking. They were your puppets.' I counted the insults on my fingers. 'The woman is wrong. She's a heartless, manipulative slut. Go get her. Emily is a cunt and deserves to die.'

Justin flinched. 'Emily?'

I dropped my hands. My shoulders slumped. Angry tears flooded out. I hated that; it made me look weak. I wasn't weak. These were streams of pure rage. I wiped my cheek with the palm of my hand and sniffed. 'You're a monster. She was my friend.'

'I'm sorry,' Justin said, his head bowed.

Was this an admission?

He stroked the surface of the table. 'I didn't know who the Adam Mooney accuser was when I started. It was just some girl. When I saw she was Emily — when the photo came out — I stopped. I was horrified. You have to believe me. But the damage was done. It was like a frenzy of ravenous rats.'

'You could have stopped them,' I said. 'People listened to you. That's how I found @chosenone2. I ran Network Impact on the

Twitter abuse. You came out as the biggest inciter. You had influence.'

Justin stiffened. 'Network Impact singled me out? I mean, I knew what I was doing was working. I could see it in their reactions... I never thought I mattered so much.' He reached for my shoulder. 'I never meant to harm Emily.'

I shook him off me. 'No, you thought it was perfectly fine to harm some woman you didn't know. Why? Because they used to reject you? Was your ego bruised?' I gasped at a sudden realisation. 'You asked Emily out once, and she said no. Is that why?'

His face turned a light grey. 'No, I told you. I didn't do anything once I knew they targeted Emily.'

'You should say "we" targeted her. *You* made this happen.' My jaw was sore from clenching my teeth.

'That's not fair.' He stood, his full frame facing me 'Yes, it was mean, I admit. But it wasn't real life. These were people thousands of miles away, screaming into the ether. Screaming things nobody is forced to read. Emily could have stepped away from it all. She didn't, and I'm sorry this affected her so incredibly badly.' He rubbed his chin and sighed. 'It was supposed to stay online. It was a game. I was testing the subliminal command stuff I'd developed years ago. You remember?'

A flicker of recognition. That war game back at Uni. Was he still working on that? I shook my head. 'I don't care why you did this. Your intention is irrelevant. All I know is you are guilty.'

His eyes bored into me. 'You can't pin this on me. I accept I let it get a little out of hand, but there's nothing anyone can do about it now.'

I trembled, my fists white with balled-up fury. 'There's plenty I can do, Justin. You sit tight and see,' I hissed and walked out the door.

His excuses rattled in my head. Would Emily still be alive if only she'd stopped looking? My heart sank thinking how I'd failed to protect her. I should've stayed on top of her more...

I shook my head. No. I wasn't to blame.

Nor was Emily.

He was.

48.
SUKI

At her desk, Suki pasted a link into the secure folder containing the latest version of the Empisoft due diligence into an email to the lawyers. They'd better be quick; it needed doing that day. She re-read her note to make sure it conveyed the necessary level of urgency. Lawyers were always slow. No matter how much you tried to project manage them into starting things early, they always ended up being the bottleneck to any deal. You'd think they'd learn.

The instructions were simple, and it shouldn't take long. All they needed to do was double-check everything was inside before she could pass the link to the PeopleForce team.

She rubbed her eyes and stretched her arms to the ceiling. She burped. Who cares? Everyone else was gone for the night. Her desk was practically clear, everything stacked in a single pile of documents to shred when the deal went through.

Her coffee would be cold. She shook her stainless-steel water bottle to feel its weight. Only a dribble left. She licked her lips. Parched.

In the kitchen, she filled her bottle from the tap and searched through the cupboards. 'Ha,' she said, finding leftover biscuits she'd missed the other nights she'd skipped dinner lately.

Not long to go. The deal would be over the line within days. They'd have the obligatory blowout celebration and she'd take a few days off to recover. Sleep. Shop!

Her mobile rang in the distance. Who could it be at this hour? Knowing the lawyers would also be working late, she ran to her desk.

A mobile number she didn't recognise.

'Hello?'

'Hello, Suki?'

'Yes. Who is this?'

'Natalie. I left Madainn around the time you started. Pam asked me to call you. I hope it's not too late?'

'No,' said Suki, sitting down. 'I'm glad you called.'

It had been a while since her former colleague Pam had suggested Natalie might be willing to speak about why she left the firm so suddenly. She'd forgotten all about it. Having her on the line, she felt a tingle of excitement. Would she get more dirt on Angus?

Suki uttered the polite platitudes that were expected, enquiring about Natalie's current situation, making positive sounds about the new job she'd secured. Once she figured she'd put Natalie sufficiently at ease, she asked the big question. 'When Angus negotiated your payoff, what was it for? What did he say?'

'It wasn't Angus. It was Diane.'

It felt as though the floor dropped an inch. 'Huh? Are you sure?'

'Yes of course I'm sure,' Natalie said tersely. 'I don't know if you've ever been bullied, Suki, or sexually harassed, but that's not something you forget easily. And it's not every day you get paid a five-figure sum to bugger off and keep quiet.'

It wasn't what Suki had expected, but, thinking about it, if you wanted to handle things sensitively and not inflame matters in a no doubt already gender-charged situation, it made sense to send in the female partner. Have her clean up after him.

'I'm sorry,' Suki said. 'I guess I'm disappointed that Diane was willing to cover up for Angus like that.' Suki scratched her head. 'I know this might be hard to talk about. I'm grateful you called. Could you give me an indication of what he did to you? I don't need any details.'

Natalie sighed. 'Why do you keep talking about Angus? I don't know what you think went on. I was harassed by Robert.' Suki's cheeks tingled as Natalie continued, 'I went to see Diane to complain. I have kids. They're younger than hers, but I thought that if I went to her, mother to mother, she'd be horrified, like I would be, and do something about it. Turns out, instead of keeping her son in check, she gave me a big cheque.'

The room swirled around Suki. 'You're telling me Angus had nothing to do with it?'

'No. Well...'

'Well what?'

'He'll have known what happened because Diane doesn't have the authority to approve that size of payment. It takes both of them,' Natalie said. 'He must have just done what she told him to.'

Suki bit her lip. 'Do you think?'

'I don't know. Aside from being an old-fashioned, pompous sexist who doesn't seem to see what's happening in front of his nose because he's always self-importantly in his office, he's probably not to blame. I guess he didn't want his firm besmirched.'

The cogs in Suki's mind whirred. 'Maybe Diane's got something on him.'

'What?'

'Never mind,' Suki said. 'I'm sorry you had to go through that, Natalie. Thanks a lot for the call. One more thing.' Suki braced herself. With one answer everything could be tipped upside down. 'Did the same thing happen to Pam? Was Diane covering up for her son?'

The line went silent for a few seconds. 'Don't tell her I told you, but yes.'

Suki sunk deep into her chair and massaged her forehead with her fingers. How could she have gotten it so wrong? It was Diane... She'd played her.

That bitch. That duplicitous, complicit bitch.

49.
ME

I stood outside Madainn the next morning, leaned against the black wrought iron fence around Rutland Square Gardens. I rubbed my arms and wished I'd worn another layer. The air smelled of rain-washed stone.

People in suits streamed into the various workplaces on the square; the lawyers, the fund managers, recruitment agents.

I saw Suki emerge from the alley, confident strides on impossibly high heels. 'Suki!'

She gave a startled look and a little wave before coming over. 'What are you doing here?'

'I didn't want to meet at Empisoft,' I said. 'The staff are getting too curious about who you are and why you're always there.'

'Well, the secret will soon be out. I got all the stuff over to the lawyers last night. I'm super confident we'll be able to make the announcement at the conference on Thursday.' She eyed her office door. 'I'd ask you inside, but I'm afraid you'd have Angus and Diane fawning all over you. You're their little cash cow. Let's go to Pret.'

She led me through a small alley to Shandwick Place, with its wall-to-wall choice of coffee shops. A step behind, I smiled: she'd remembered I liked the Pret tea the best.

Standing at the counter, Suki asked. 'Have you had breakfast? It's a bit early for you, isn't it?'

'I'll have a croissant and an Earl Grey, thanks. I've been awake half the night, confusing Atticus by getting up and getting back into bed. I figured I might as well get up and find you before you got too busy.'

The noise of the espresso machines and people around us ordering their morning takeaways made it pointless to say more.

Eventually, we settled on wooden stools around a high, square table.

'Why couldn't you sleep?' she asked.

'I've been wracking my brain about ways to punish Justin. I feel stupid. I warned him I was going to do something to him, but I can't think of anything — other than sabotaging the acquisition.' Suki gave me a warning look. I waved my hand. 'Don't worry. I won't do that. That's the problem. It would hurt Justin the most, but it would also hurt you and all the staff who own shares, the shareholders...'

'And you.'

'And me.' I shrugged. 'Though that's a sacrifice I'm willing to make.'

'Sorry. Can't help. I haven't given it much thought yet. Been struggling with my own vendetta.'

'Angus?'

'No, would you believe.' She came close, as if imparting a secret. 'Diane.'

'What?' I jerked back.

'I'll tell you later. Let's stick with you.' She chewed on her pastry and rinsed her mouth with coffee. 'We can't let other people suffer. The deal needs to go through. On the plus side, that gives us a bit more time. Perhaps we can come up with something after the conference?'

'I guess,' I said, shoulders slumped. 'Is there really no way to take away his growth options? That's the only money he's going to see straight away.'

'Not without reducing the valuation of the company,' she replied. 'And that means hurting others again.'

A young man in a suit sat down at the table next to us with a drink and a muffin. He was joined by a heavily made-up girl wearing a black-suited uniform and a Debenhams name tag. I couldn't hear what he was saying, but whatever it was, the girl was lapping it up, smiling and playing with her hair.

'How about something with a woman?' I offered. 'Maybe get him dumped or cheated on?'

Suki patted her lips with her fingers. 'I thought he only ever went on dates. Has he had a proper girlfriend?'

'No.' I shook my head. 'Besides, who would we find to help?' I picked at my croissant and sucked on a buttery flake.

'If you want to dent his ego, though, I've got an idea. We expose him.' A vicious grin spread across Suki's face. 'Think about it. That Chosen One Twitter account he's been using. He's a fraud. He's got an army of awful Incel followers that think he's one of them.' She moved her cup aside to paint a picture with her fingers. 'How do you think they would respond if they found out that they've been manipulated by a good-looking, successful millionaire who can get all the girls he wants?'

My eyes widened. 'They'd turn on him.'

'Yup. Like a pack of wolves. And he'd have nowhere to hide because — and this is the beautiful irony of it — he's got such a public profile. Everybody knows who Justin Travers is. And if they don't, it takes only two minutes to find out.'

My stomach churned. 'We can't do that.'

'He doesn't need to know it was you.'

'No, that's not it,' I said. 'I *would* want him to know it was me. God, I'd love him to know I ended up with the upper hand. But we just can't do *that*. We can't use Twitter. We need something precise, targeted, and that we can control. Look at how quickly Darren's stupid photo got a life of its own. Look at what it did to Emily... If we went ahead with this, knowing the damage these Incel guys could do, doesn't that make us as evil as all of them?'

Suki flicked the crumbs off the table. 'I guess. It did have a certain beauty to it though, don't you think?'

'Yeah. Maybe I can still fantasise about it a little bit,' I grinned.

Suki sighed. 'How will we make sure Justin doesn't just get to cash in and start his glorious new life in California?'

'California?'

'Oh, you've not been told yet? PeopleForce have kept that close to their chest. When they announce the takeover at the conference, they will announce that Justin is their new Global Director of Digital Labs. You should hear him. He's so fucking excited about it. He's even placed his order for that ridiculously expensive motorcycle.'

'He's leaving?' I hated him, but he was also Justin.

'Yes, good riddance. You'll be reporting to a nice guy in San Francisco — I looked him up to make sure, what with the hoo-hah they've had lately. The good news is they seem to be bending over to make things right. I suspect they'll leave you alone to get on with your R&D.' Suki searched my face. 'Aren't you pleased?'

'It's a shock... all this change.'

'It's good change.' Suki placed her hand on mine. 'So... How can we sabotage his motorcycle?'

I pulled a face. 'Don't even joke about that.'

'How about we cancel his order without him knowing?' She bubbled with all the ideas that had evaded me overnight. Hitting his ego, his wallet, his career.

None felt right. They were either too terrible or not terrible enough.

50.
SUKI

The temp jumped up from the front desk when Suki stepped through the door, his white shirt rolled at the sleeve. 'Sandy Evans has been trying to reach you. He's called three times. Said he tried your mobile but you weren't picking up.' He offered her a yellow post-it. She didn't need it.

Suki fished the phone from her bag's side pocket. She kept it there precisely so that she would always hear it. She checked the screen; the volume was muted. How did that happen?

'I'll take care of it,' she said. 'Thanks, erm...' She flashed him a smile, wincing inside, hoping he hadn't noticed the omission. She rushed to her desk. Please God, let there be nothing wrong.

She dialled Sandy's number. He picked up straight away.

'Sorry, so sorry, Sandy. It's Suki. What's up?'

'I've had one of my associates trawl through the files again this morning,' he said. 'And he's noticed there's an IP assignation missing.'

A spiky jolt rushed up her spine. 'Which one?'

'The original one. The document where Laura Flett signed the ownership of her master's project to Empisoft.'

Suki's mind whirred. She'd never seen it, yet it must have existed. Nobody invested in a technology company without making sure it owned the intellectual property it said it did. It didn't matter whether it was a patent, trademark or copyright or who in the company had originally made the invention. It all got assigned to the company.

She mentally flicked through the library of folders she'd painstakingly pulled together over the last few weeks. There was definitely a zip file that contained what they called the 'bible', all the documentation from that first investment, with Empisoft fresh out of the University. She remembered receiving it from the company in an email but realised she'd never checked what was inside. Why would she? That had all gone through two sets of lawyers years ago.

'That's strange,' she said. 'How could there not be one in the bible?'

The lawyer cleared his throat. 'I can't comment. My firm wasn't acting for Empisoft then. We'll need to disclose it to PeopleForce unless we get Laura Flett to sign a new one and backdate it... Shall I draw one up?'

'Let me have a word with her, find out what happened with her thesis,' Suki replied. 'And if one's really needed, I'll get her to sign it.'

Suki sat at her desk, resting her chin on her clasped hands. Surely there must have been a reason for there not to be one? She played through different scenarios she'd come across in her short career; and that she'd heard of at Stanford, where she'd been surrounded by students starting up new businesses.

Angus's voice boomed from behind her. 'Suki? Can you come give me an update on Empisoft, please?' His hands were in his pockets. His elbow pointed to his office.

'Yes, of course.'

She followed him down the corridor, taking in his shape; his expensive shoes, the slightly moist wisps of grey hair at the nape of his neck. This man who'd approved payoffs to victims of harassment at his firm. Who hadn't challenged his partner on her son's behaviour. Why? Did he not care?

'Are we on track?' he asked, remaining standing near the door.

Good. He hadn't invited her to sit; this was going to be a quick one. 'Yes,' she said.

He rubbed his hands. 'Excellent.'

'There seems to be one last-minute missing piece of paper. The original assignation of Laura Flett's master's thesis. It's nothing to worry about because she can sign a backdated one if needed.'

Angus scratched behind his ear. 'You're friendly with the girl. Take care of it. Don't let her open up that growth option conversation again, though. There's no time for that.'

She turned towards the door just as it opened widely, smacking her in the forehead. She stumbled backward and held out her hands to soften the blow as she hit the floor. Pain shot through her coccyx, wrist, elbow.

Robert stormed in. 'Angus, the crane company wants to know when their compliance—'

Angus lurched toward Suki. 'Good God, man. Look what you've done.'

'Oh, sorry, Sooks. Didn't see you there,' said Robert. 'I'll come back later.' He disappeared as quickly as he'd come.

Angus took Suki's forearm while she hoisted her skirt a little and pushed herself up feeling about as gracious as a newborn fucking giraffe. She stroked her throbbing wrist. Angus shook his head. Her ears pricked up as she heard him grumble, 'Nothing but trouble, that one.'

When she'd checked her blouse, skirt and hair were again equally straight, she picked up the business cards that had fallen from her pocket and said, 'I'll go take care of the assignation.'

'Are you all right?'

For a second, he looked genuinely concerned, but Suki wasn't about to let that take her off course. 'I will be,' she replied, as she felt the weight of the cards in her hand — in more ways than one.

SUKI'S NAILS click-clacked on her desk as she drummed her fingers. Laura's phone rang out. It wasn't unusual for her to leave it lying around so Suki waited a few minutes and tried again.

Background music and chatter engulfed Laura's 'Hello.'

'Where are you?' Suki asked.

'Clr Md me go shPing.'

'What?'

'Mm SHOPPING t Claire f CLOTHES... mm... Wt... Quiet.'

Suki sighed and rubbed her phone ear.

'Is this better?' Laura asked, crystal clear.

'Yes. Did I hear you say you were clothes shopping with Claire?'

'She made me. We're in Jenners getting a new outfit for the conference. She says the black-shirt, blue-jean technology entrepreneur look is *so* 2000s.'

Suki smiled, imagining Laura trying to shoo Claire off her. 'Don't let her convince you to get your eyebrows done.' They laughed together. 'Speaking of which, tell Claire we're still on for 6PM at my parents' place. But I need to see *you* urgently.'

'Something I need to worry about?'

'No,' Suki replied, bubbles of excitement rising in her throat. 'If I'm right, it's quite the opposite. But before I'm sure, I need to ask you some questions.'

51.
ME

The black-and-white bags of Jenners department store weighed down my arms as I strode from one end of Princes Street to the other. My blow-dried hair bounced around my head. I made myself small to weave through the people waiting at the bus stops, hoping they wouldn't notice I was wearing four kinds of perfume.

I stretched my neck and yawned. All those stairs to confounding mezzanine floors and balconies in the store had taken their toll; all that trying on; all that arguing that no, I wouldn't be caught dead in mustard-coloured culottes no matter how much Claire thought they were spectacular.

We'd had a good laugh, though, at this forced induction into a timeless girlie ritual. Claire was so enthusiastic about my make-over that I couldn't help giving in more than I'd planned. But was all this primping necessary? Couldn't we just *be*?

Emily had never tried to change me.

I shifted two bags into the other hand to give my left shoulder some relief. I crossed the road to walk alongside Princes Street Gardens to avoid the blaring bagpipe music coming out of tourist shops selling half-priced cashmere, stuffed Loch Ness monsters, and other tartan tat.

A Saltire and a Union Flag flapped in unison above the entrance to the Waldorf Astoria. I still couldn't get used to its new name; The Caledonian having been re-branded after a massive refurbishment some years before. Like other locals, I'd probably always referred to the hotel as 'The Caley.'

I slipped through the revolving doors. Suki had suggested it as a good place to meet. It was private and less than a hundred metres from her office.

It was also stunning. Curved beech desks, each with a pair of elegant table lamps, formed a ring around a Greek-patterned circle shaped inside the marble floor tiles. Overhead hung the largest lighting creation I'd ever set eyes on; ochre orbs dangling among the twinkling lights. I subtly brushed down my jeans as I walked past the staff greeting me with a silent nod.

I stepped into Peacock Alley, the opulent bar just off the lobby, to the right. It smelled of coffee beans and freshly baked scones. I sank into one of the wide cream armchairs with burnt-orange trim and a uniformed waiter appeared almost instantly with a glass of water. A juniper berry and a sprig of mint floated inside. I could get used to this. And in only two years, I could choose to come here every single day if I wanted — even get a room, for kicks.

Suki appeared through the archway. I waved and nearly flung a small sculpture to the ground.

She eyed the bags. 'Success?'

'Yes, I think so. I ended up spending a little more than planned,' I said sheepishly.

'I think you have every reason to treat yourself. And I look forward to seeing the whole new you at the conference tomorrow,' Suki said.

I stroked my sleek, loose hair. The waiter took our orders. Suki crossed her legs. Her elegant shoes belonged here more than I did.

'I need to talk to you about Empisoft's intellectual property,' she said. 'Incredibly, some paperwork from when you first started out has gone missing.'

'That's years ago.'

'It's important. Do you remember signing any documents that gave ownership of what you'd created to Empisoft?'

I lifted my eyes to the ceiling and sucked in my cheeks. 'Yes. I remember, because I had to burn the software we were assigning onto something silly like five different discs and my CD-ROM drive was unreliable. The discs were coupled to an assignation for the software that Justin and I both signed.'

'I've seen that document. But did you sign away your thesis?' Suki asked.

'My master's thesis? No. Why would I?'

Suki took a sip of her coffee. 'The software you rightly signed away was based on your thesis, right? So the basic IP sits in the thesis. Unless you've specifically assigned that, you still own it.'

I twirled a coaster between my fingers to jog my memory. 'The lawyer said that because I'd handed my thesis into my supervisor at the University without marking it with *Confidential*, it was considered in the public domain and so it didn't count as protectable IP anymore.'

Suki's eyes lit up.

A lump formed in my stomach. Had I done something wrong? 'There was a whole argument about it and that delayed the investment,' I said. 'That's why I remember. In the end, all the investors cared about was the software, since that was ready and gave the company a big first-mover advantage. I was told you couldn't patent my research anyway.'

I watched Suki expectantly. A giant grin lifted her cheeks. Relief washed over me.

'Ha!' Suki slapped her knee and bounced in her armchair.

'What is it?'

'They made a mistake. Back then, they made a mistake. I don't know where you got your shitty lawyer from.' She chuckled. 'Patents have nothing to do with this, that bit is correct, but it seems he got muddled up between a PhD thesis — which gets published by the University unless you specifically instruct them not to for commercial reasons — and the master's thesis which, frankly, nobody cares about except you, for your grade, and doesn't go anywhere.'

I nodded, still unsure what the point of this was. 'My adviser moved to Cambridge shortly after I got my grade. I suspect my thesis was tossed out with the rest of the papers he didn't need.'

'Now, before I get too excited,' Suki said. 'One more question. In any of the upgrades you've developed at Empisoft, did you use the discoveries and algorithms in your master's thesis?'

'Yes, but I'm an employee. Doesn't Empisoft own all the IP I've created while working for them?'

'Yes, but if you used your thesis... you've again based the work on something *they do not own.*'

'That doesn't sound good. Why are you so excited?'

Suki drew lines with her finger between the two cups and the vase on the table to explain. 'Because, my dear, due to this mistake, you actually still own a lot of the IP that sits at the core of the products Empisoft sells its clients. IP that PeopleForce think they're going to own. Your current lawyers, at the last minute, have figured out this assignation is missing. And they want you to sign a new one.'

'Fine.'

'Ha! You're not seeing it. This acquisition rests on you signing this document. Suddenly, you hold all the cards.' Suki leaned back in her chair, her arms outstretched. 'Here's the crux: do you sign this paper and let Justin walk all over you and get away scot-free, or do you play your hand?'

My pulse pounded in my ears. I'd finally understood. 'What did you have in mind?'

Suki searched for her phone 'I want to set up a meeting with PeopleForce the minute it's morning for them. You, me and them. Don't worry, I won't screw up the acquisition. I promise. It's a long shot, but given their recent problems, I think it's going to work.'

52.
ME

I pressed the bronze-plated doorbell of Madainn Finance, its ding-dong exactly like I'd expect an old-world bell to sound. A clean-shaven twenty-something man opened the door with a welcoming smile and motioned me onto the yellow carpet.

'I'm Laura Flett.'

'I'm Doug. Suki is expecting you in the boardroom,' he said. I noticed an Aussie accent. Long nails on his right hand suggested he played guitar. Was he here for the festival?

He pointed up the long corridor as if I was supposed to know where to go.

'It's my first time here,' I said.

'Oh, apologies. Let me take you.'

We walked past two offices. Sunlight streamed through the sash windows onto the rows of unoccupied desks. It was eerily quiet. Where was everyone?

A bit further up, he opened a thick mahogany door into a space furnished as though it was still a Victorian dining room. Brick red wallpaper lined the walls; twin-masted boats sailed inside thick golden frames.

Suki stood with her back to me.

'Thanks, Doug,' I said.

Suki spun round, her face beaming. 'Yes, thanks, Doug.'

I walked to her side. She fiddled with various cables. 'I'm setting up the video conference. We've got four minutes before PeopleForce come on.'

I picked up the square control panel from the sideboard. 'Anything I can do?'

'No, we're good to go. Can you sit in that chair, please?' She tweaked the camera to focus on me and the empty chair beside me. I hated seeing myself on screen.

'You think we actually have a shot?' I asked.

She crossed her fingers. 'I'd wanted to try this angle before, when we were looking for fairness in the growth options. I wasn't sure it would work. Having the IP assignation as a back-up is great. I'd rather not use it because I don't want them to think this is a shakedown.'

'Fair enough. I'll let you do the speaking.'

Suki held up two plastic bottles. 'Water?

'Please.'

The screen popped to life. I twisted the cap off my drink.

'Here goes nothing,' whispered Suki.

Two forty-something men sat on the other side of the world, their walls modern and colourful. Both had similar short haircuts, similar tans and similar polo shirts. One was a little older than the other. The only thing Scotland and Silicon Valley had in common right now was the branded water we drank.

One of the men was mouthing to someone out of sight and an icon on the screen confirmed their microphone was still muted. Soon they both smiled at the screen and their voices came through, 'Hi.'

Suki wrote their names and job titles on a notepad for my benefit, in the order they were sitting. I looked at the paper. It took a moment to digest that here I was, speaking to an actual director and vice-president of *the* Peoplesoft.

She started with, 'Thank you so much for taking this call at such short notice. It's nice to finally see you both in person after all the email to and fros.'

'No problem,' he said. 'Our CEO is already in the air. He waited until the last minute to make sure everything was in order and it wouldn't be a wasted trip.' I felt Suki bristle at my side.

After mutual introductions and a few weather-related observations, Suki went straight to business. 'It's been a lot of work and I am delighted that we will be completing — and celebrating — the acquisition tomorrow. But given your staff's walkout last week, it's important to have complete transparency with regards to gender equality at Empisoft.'

The men's tans faded instantly.

Hardly surprising. It had been all over the news that PeopleForce suffered an unprecedented walkout by their employees at HQ when word got out that not one, but two senior executives had left with multi-million-dollar packages following sexual misconduct allegations against them. The protest had spread to their offices all over the world, to condemn claims of sexual harassment, gender inequality and systemic racism at the company. They were working round the clock to repair the damage to their reputation.

The VP, in the red shirt, cleared his throat while the other guy glugged down half a bottle of water. The no doubt air-conditioned room would prevent their sweat from showing, but there was no hiding their discomfort.

Suki had explained to me that part of the reason they'd ultimately picked Empisoft over its competitor — and it had been a tight race up to the end — was because Empisoft gave them a stronger PR opportunity at a sensitive time: a female co-founder and a forty percent female data science team, set in a cute country that everybody liked, where men wore skirts and women led government.

'There is no mention of any issues in the disclosures,' said the younger man, stony-faced.

'Indeed.' Suki replied. 'We are here primarily to rectify your possible impression of the management team. Particularly, since you're about to appoint Justin Travers as Global Director of Digital Labs.'

Both men leaned forward.

'You see,' Suki said. 'The brains behind Empisoft is this woman here. And whilst Justin might be the face, we've established through in-house analysis that Laura is in fact the number one influence behind its ongoing success.'

The director, in the blue shirt, scratched the base of his neck 'Not that we are challenging this in any way, but what analysis are you referring to?'

'It's the Network Impact tool. A small R&D project in the pipeline,' Suki replied.

Blue shirt said, 'Isn't that experimental? My understanding is that this hadn't even been tested properly.' He raised his palm in defence, the Californian political correctness coming out again. 'Not that we are in any way suggesting we don't believe you.'

'The information you received about the R&D roadmap shows it as being at concept stage,' Suki said. 'However, things have moved on extremely rapidly in the last week. Laura, would you care to explain what happened?'

Suki scribbled on the notebook.

Lean in. This is your moment.

I beamed my largest smile to California. 'While I was playing around with the Network Impact tool on an unrelated database scraped from Twitter, it accidentally ran on Empisoft's internal communications.' The VP's frown unnerved me and I quickly added, 'It was a minor failure in a security protocol, which I can assure you has been —'

He interrupted by raising his hand. 'You ran your tool on Twitter data? Did it work?'

'Well yes,' I said, my nerves on edge. 'The point is Network Impact worked full stop. If you remember, its purpose is to find the hidden—"

'The hidden heroes and villains when it comes to influencing groups,' he said. 'Yes we know. We've been very interested in this concept, which we thought hadn't been proven yet. Are you telling me that a) it works and b) it works on Twitter?'

'We'd certainly want to run some more tests. And —' Suki elbowed me. I got the message. 'Yes. Yes it does.'

'Give us a minute.' The Californians muted their microphone. Suki and I looked at each other and muted our own.

'What do you think is going on?' I asked.

'I think we might have hit on a goldmine without realising it,' Suki raised a mischievous smile. 'Let's see how this plays out.'

We watched as the men nodded at each other.

The director reached forward to press the button to restart the conversation. 'Okay. We're interested. Very interested. The Network Impact tool add-on for our client companies is neat, but the real value of what you've got is in the ability to run it on social media. This is a whole new ballgame. Marketing companies will do almost anything to identify true influencers. It could transform the way brands choose where to spend their advertising dollars.'

After a second's hesitation, Suki sat up extra straight. 'You see why Ms Flett is more important than you had initially anticipated. Not only is she the most important influencer of Empisoft's performance, she's a technical visionary able to take the company in valuable, new directions.'

I wanted to hide. Casting my eyes down. Suki's hands were pressed against the table, her knuckles white. She was improvising. Bluffing?

The VP squeezed his eyes into small slits. 'What are you looking for?'

Suki put on an innocent voice. 'You see, the gender issue we wanted to raise was that Laura has been cheated by her trusted co-founder out of some growth options. Nobody wants to delay the deal due to a historical injustice — or, God forbid, stop it from going ahead. The thing is, Laura might not be terribly motivated to develop this any further. And half of it is in your head, isn't it, Laura?' Her eyes instructed me to go with it. Stand firm. 'All she wants is what she rightfully deserves, and should get from a company like yourselves, committed to stamp out gender discrimination: equality with her co-founder. Is that something we can agree to?'

I remained straight-faced. Suki had these two men sputtering in agreement, almost competing to confirm their complete and unrestrained alignment with the feminist agenda.

Suki took notes as she began listing demands. 'We'll forget about the inequality of the past and focus on the now. Seems fair to me.' She theatrically drew a line — across nothing. 'All we're asking for is the equivalent of the moving expenses you agreed to pay Justin, in cash, as a *golden hello*. From recollection, this is fifty thousand dollars.'

'Done,' the VP said.

I gasped. I hadn't expected this. It would more than pay for Mum's wedding.

Suki squeezed my knee under the table. 'And clearly a small uplift in valuation is in order, now that you now understand the full extent of the opportunity of what Laura has created... Three million dollars.'

I couldn't believe Suki's audacity.

. PeopleForce were paying one hundred million dollars for the company already. What was she playing at? I worried the allure of money had distracted her from our goal.

'Just a minute.' The men muted their side again. If only I'd learnt to lip read.

Their head jerking morphed into small nods and Suki cursed under her breath, 'Fuck. Should have asked for more.'

The VP said, 'Done. We'd be happy to have the lawyers quickly make that change. It's not an amount of money we need CEO approval for. Just as well, as he's out of reach. Before we agree to this, we need some assurances.' He twirled his pen. 'First, we need Ms Flett to agree to fully document what's in her head. Since she is staying with us for what?' He looked over at his colleague who raised two fingers. 'Two years. We trust that she will be motivated to lead the development of this new product.'

Suki jumped in. 'And she'll expect an increase in remuneration commensurate with the role.' She flashed a smile. 'The same salary you've agreed to pay Justin.'

The blue-shirted director, who was probably on a similar salary, grumbled.

His superior shushed him. 'Done. Lastly, we need absolute certainty that the IP for this sits within the company. Because you made it sound like modifying the Network Impact to run on Twitter was a little side project, Laura.'

A side project? How could they call my quest for justice for Emily a 'side project'?

'Funny you should say that,' Suki said before I could comment. 'Turns out there was a missing IP assignation from the time of the company's inception. But I'm proud to say we caught it on our side while making sure everything was perfect for you. We wouldn't have wanted you to be the victim of a historical oversight. And

Laura will gladly sign a backdated document which would also cover the Twitter work.'

'Good. Then it's all sorted.' The VP looked at his own notes. 'Fifty thousand dollars sign-on bonus for Ms Flett. A valuation of one hundred *and three* million dollars for tomorrow's acquisition. And you will provide us with the IP assignation today.'

I nodded and Suki said 'Perfect.'

'Expensive call,' the VP quipped.

'Ha! Funny you should say that also, because there's one more thing we want — but this will actually save you money.'

While my stomach did somersaults, they agreed to that request, too.

53.
ME

'It's down this little street,' I said as I guided Claire to the Fragrant Orchid for dinner. The chippy on the right was doing a roaring trade, a swarm of men in tracksuits pressed inside, backs against the window wet with oily condensation.

We reached the lotus-lanterned restaurant. 'It's so cute,' Claire said.

Suki's mother welcomed me with arms thrown wide, even if I would never be the daughter-in-law she longed for. She cast an approving eye over Claire and led us to the best window-side table for dinner. The drinks swiftly followed.

'Cheers!' We clinked our Siam Marys together.

'I hope Suki won't be long. I'm starving,' said Claire, eyeing the colourful menu.

'She must be tying up some loose strings in the office after our video call with PeopleForce,' I said. 'You should have been there, Claire. Suki saw an opportunity and went straight for it. A master negotiator. I could tell she was nervous, but she exuded nothing but confidence to the other side. We got everything we were going for and more — and never even had to use our trump card. She made it all sound like we were doing *them* a favour.'

'Do tell.' Claire rested her chin on her clasped hands.

Towards the end of my update, Suki showed up. She collapsed onto her chair and waved at her mum, who came over to give her a drink and a kiss. Such a close family. I thought of my own mum. Thanks to the golden hello Suki negotiated, I could look my mother in the face again; give her the wedding I promised.

'I hear you kicked butt, Miss Aksornpan,' Claire said. 'Remind me to hire you to negotiate whenever I want to buy a flat.'

'Oh my God, that was the best.' Suki glowed. 'I'm still buzzing. And then, once I'd finished updating the documents for tomorrow, I went to tidy up my cups in the kitchen and I overheard Diane and Angus squabbling. Argh, that woman.' Suki bit into the shrimp that hung from the side of her cocktail and chewed with fire in her eyes. 'Anyway, as I was on a high, I thought "Fuck it" and cornered Angus. That's why I was late. Guess what?'

'What?' Claire and I asked at the same time.

Suki shimmied her shoulders and rotated her fists around each other in a disco dance. 'Heads are gonna roll.'

When she told us what they'd agreed, I couldn't have admired her more.

'Miaow,' Claire joked, holding out claws.

'It's only fair.' Suki winked.

Forever attentive, Suki's mum brought two fresh cocktails. Bless, she probably thought she was being discreet in signalling to Suki that Claire was quite nice-looking. Suki waved her away.

I thought my stomach would pop as we were presented with enough food to feed a small army. But we needed the ammo while the three of us plotted the culmination of all our efforts. Justice at last. Claire took notes; she was so organised. There wasn't much left for me to do. I sank back, imbued with a little too much alcohol and a perfect dose of righteous satisfaction.

The dessert was a glistening lychee sorbet that melted on the tongue in a prickle of ecstasy. Suki insisted I should suck on the mint leaf first, to make it tingle more.

Claire licked her spoon, eyes downcast.

'What's wrong, Claire?' I asked.

She smiled faintly. 'Nothing.'

'Come on. Spill,' Suki said.

'I'm thrilled at all this, I am... I just feel we've forgotten someone. Darren.'

Saliva flooded my mouth at the sound of his name.

'Good shout,' said Suki. 'We're not finished. Let's think. What is it that he treasures most?'

'I'd thought of something before, but I couldn't do it — until now, until your chat with PeopleForce. But it may be a big ask from you, Laura.'

'I'm in,' I said.

'I haven't even told you —'

I squeezed a shoulder on each of my two friends. 'That's okay. I'm still in.'

54.
CLAIRE, NOW

Claire arrives at the conference centre at 8AM. She spreads her arms and breathes the large venue in.

Today's the big day.

Everything has built up to now.

The floor shines and the scent of lemon fills the air. Doors won't open for registration until nine thirty, but Claire always makes a point of showing speakers where they will address their audience in advance and giving them a last run through of the sequence of events. Can't leave anything to chance.

The florist rushes around lancing last-minute willow twigs to bring more volume to the rose and dahlia arrangements. Quite right; they cost enough.

Justin enters at the far end of the hall. He looks small. Neat, though; pressed chinos and what looks like a brand-new white shirt. Fake tan?

Claire's smile lifts her cheeks so high her lashes meet.

Showtime.

She walks towards him. 'How was breakfast?' she asks, knowing he'd been due to meet PeopleForce's CEO.

'It was good,' Justin replied. 'I mean, it was awesome to meet him. He's such a hero of mine.' He shrugs. 'He seemed a little disinterested, considering what's going to happen later.'

'He only arrived last night. He's probably still jet-lagged.' Claire pats his back. 'I'm speaking to him later and I'm sure everything will be perfect. I even got you two beautiful silver ballpoint pens to sign the documents with. To keep.'

'That's a nice touch, Claire. Thank you.'

She leads him to the small breakout rooms where he, Laura, and some other industry experts will have their sessions, and keeps the best for last: the auditorium for the keynote speaker events. The raised stage features a giant screen emblazoned with the Empisoft logo, fronted by theatre-style seating for four hundred people.

He seems to take the scale of it all in. 'This is going to be a great day.'

Claire smirks behind his back. Is it?

'Is the signing ceremony here?' he asks.

'No, this room isn't suitable for the press. We've moved the "Conference Close" session on the agenda from here to the main bar. There will be canapés and drinks. Even though the delegates don't know there will be an announcement, they are certain to stick around for that. And it will give the press a better opportunity for celebratory-looking photos and interviews.'

'Can I have a look?' he asks.

'Sure. I think they'll still be setting up the cocktail tables.'

Claire escorts him up the stairs. The bar stands on the side of the building with floor-to-ceiling windows overlooking the surrounding offices. The caterers are knotting large red and green ribbons around the tablecloths on the elbow-high tables dotted around the room. Claire thinks of the box she left at the entrance; the Empisoft goodies she still needs to scatter around.

'What have you told the press, in the end?' Justin asks.

'I've had to pull out all the stops,' she replies. 'Call in some favours. You don't normally get the national papers to come without them knowing why. They know there will be an announcement and I've promised them something big. PeopleForce's CEO will need to lay low until the end.'

Justin points to the five golden chairs set up in a semicircle at the rear of the small stage erected for the occasion. 'There's a band?'

'Yes. Let me run you through the proceedings.' Justin follows Claire to the side of the stage. 'First, people will gather here for drinks, and a jazz quintet will play softly. Then, your Chairman takes the stage and thanks the conference delegates for coming. He introduces PeopleForce's CEO — our surprise guest.' Justin's face lights up. Claire savours his excitement. 'There will be a thin, transparent lectern set up already with the silver pens and documents.' She ushers Justin onto the stage. 'You step onto the stage directly behind him and stand on his left side, here. He makes the announcement of the acquisition.'

'And the delegates go wild.' Justin gives a mock cheer.

'Yes, they probably will.'

Justin steps across the stage, practising his placing. He looks out onto where the people will stand. Claire gives him a moment. This is huge for him. The crowning glory of years of work.

She almost feels bad.

Almost.

Claire walks to his side. 'You give your few lines saying how thrilled you are about the acquisition, and that Empisoft gets to continue operating under its own brand, yada-yada. The CEO announces your new role. Congratulations, by the way. California, eh? That's so cool.'

Justin puffs up his chest and rubs his hands. 'It's going to be the best thing ever.'

Claire raises her index finger like a schoolteacher. 'Now, it's critical that you leave the stage when he motions for you to leave.

Okay? We don't have much time to keep everyone's attention. When he extends his left arm to the side, you go. Okay?'

'Yes, yes.'

Claire's cheeks tingle. She's worried she belaboured that point a little too much. 'Throughout this all,' she says, 'the photographers will be taking pictures. Make sure you stay close. And as soon as it's all over, you and he will be taken to a side room for interviews.' She points to the curtain through which the VIPs enter and leave the wings. 'Got it? Any questions before you go get ready to open the conference?'

'No. It's all great. Only seven hours to go to change my life. I think it won't truly hit me until later.' He brings both hands to his head.

In hers, Claire warns him to brace for impact.

55.
SUKI

Angus draws the heavy velvet curtain behind his desk partway across the window. 'Better?'

Suki un-scrunches her face. 'Yes, much better. Thanks.' Her right cheek still feels warm from where the morning sun hit it. She flaps her white blouse at the open collar to let in some air. She feels the moisture build under her arms — but that's not from the sun.

The door opens. There are no office sounds; they'd agreed to meet extra early.

Diane enters, carrying her tea in a porcelain cup. Suki long ago noticed that Diane never offers drinks in a meeting and had put it down to Diane taking a subtle feminist stance. So often it was the woman doing the catering, 'being Mother', that it became the default, which could skew the power dynamic in the group. Suki had adopted the practice herself, and it had served her well, but watching Diane ignore her and Angus's empty hands while gleefully sipping from her cup, she realises her previously inspiring role model might just be equal to the 'old boys' in another way: selfish.

Diane gives Suki a knowing look. Suki acknowledges it with a nod.

Diane lowers herself in the armchair next to her, facing Angus. 'Well, guys. We're going to have some celebrating to do tonight.' Diane raises her cup. 'Suki's done an excellent job; don't you agree?'

Angus leans forward and says, 'Yes, great job.' He opens his mouth.

Diane speaks instead. 'And apparently PeopleForce's CEO was so impressed with Suki, and her technological insight, that he is retaining us to keep them informed of any exciting new companies in Scotland they could be interested in.'

'He is? That's excellent.' Angus rubs his hands. 'That will certainly help with the monthly fees. And there may well be more acquisitions to follow. Excellent work, young lady.'

'Thank you.' Suki lets the 'young lady' slider. She waits for Diane to strike. Her wet blouse itches at her armpits. It's one thing to play hardball on behalf of your client; it's quite another to shake things up for yourself.

Diane clears her throat and smooths her dark grey skirt. 'I think it's important to capitalise on this. The technology sector is where it's all at. Our manufacturing clients are in decline. Other sectors are stagnant. This can help us propel Madainn to the forefront of corporate finance in Scotland again — don't you think?'

Angus nods, looking slightly puzzled at Diane telling him what he surely already knows.

Diane purrs like a Jaguar engine. 'Here's the thing. If we're going to be the pre-eminent corporate finance boutique for the technology sector, and maybe attract more companies like PeopleForce to give us a watching brief on the sector, I think we need to be projecting a fresh, modern brand. Hipper. More diverse.'

Suki inhales deeply.

Diane delivers the lines they'd agreed upon perfectly. 'I'm convinced — and Suki is too — that this is the right time for a renewal, a change in leadership.' Diane lets that hang a few seconds, no doubt expecting Angus to sputter, to object.

But Angus grins.

Suki's heart is racing.

Here we go.

'Funny you should say that, Diane,' Angus says. 'Because Suki and I are thinking the same thing. It's time for *you* to go.'

Diane's head flips between Angus and Suki.

Suki struggles to maintain a neutral face as she squeals inside. She shrugs demonstratively. The two dinosaurs can fight it out. She's keeping her powder dry.

Angus rises from his seat. 'You see, Diane, I do not believe that condoning sexual harassment fits with — what did you call it? — a fresh, modern brand.' He's pacing, as if speaking to a wider audience. 'In fact, we don't think it's very *hip* to be covering up for your pathetic son's disgusting habits.' His eyes grow cold. 'It's time you retired.'

Diane pushes herself up. They stand squared off against each other, only a foot apart. She's lifted to his eyeline by her heels.

She purses her lips, then spits, 'You're making a big mistake.' She looks down at Suki, nostrils flaring. 'You both are.' She presses her index finger against Angus's chest 'Don't you pretend you're such a pillar of morality... adulterer. And I thought we had an understanding... Or would you like me to share your dirty dealings with the wider world?'

How predictable. When Diane plotted her coup with Suki, she shared some of the accounting skulduggery that Angus had been involved in as a director of a trust. It was dirt she'd had on him for years. Last night, Angus had confessed to Suki that he was tired of Diane holding that over his head, forcing him to go along with the payoffs to the women Robert had pestered.

They were both despicable people. Privileged, old school, believing they had all the power. On that, they were wrong. Suki had just allowed them to treat her like a pawn in their games, while she figured out who was worse, who deserved to be booted out.

She knew the firm wouldn't survive if they both went, and she couldn't do that to her colleagues. One would stay standing today.

Suki feels she has the power. And still, she waits. And watches.

'Listen, Diane,' Angus snarls. 'I think it would be in your own interest to leave voluntarily, on good terms. You see, Suki's tremendous achievements in this firm have opened my eyes to the value of a diverse work force. I've become a staunch supporter of the MeToo and TimesUp movement.' His tone is a little too sarcastic for Suki's taste, but she'll deal with that later; he's on a roll. 'And I believe that in this climate, the press would be very hungry for a story of an older, *complicit* woman. One who put the interests of her badly-behaved son above the interests of her sisters. Bring in a couple of poor victims who've been bribed into silence, and you've got yourself a cracking story. And a son whose career prospects are utterly shattered.'

Diane's mouth opens and closes like a fish. 'You wouldn't.'

'I would,' he says, calmly.

'But Angus, you signed off on these payments too. Plus, I've still got the trust files on you.' Diane's voice wobbles like the last, defiant pin on a bowling alley.

'Indeed,' he said. 'And doesn't the story get so much better when the despicable, conniving woman has also blackmailed her partner to cover it all up? I bet they'd find that much more interesting than "financier fiddles with accounts". Who hasn't seen that a hundred times before?'

They've both still not moved. They hiss at each other within a breath's distance, oblivious to Suki's presence. She watches the exchange with her heart thumping in her chest. Witnessing her strategy fall into place.

One more push.

Angus shuffles a few steps to the side. He raises his open palms in a gesture of offering. 'It doesn't have to be this way. You can leave and maintain your dignity. You can keep your reputation intact, if you leave. Both you and Robert need to leave.'

Ashen-faced, shoulders slumped, Diane surrenders. 'Agreed.'

'Good. I'm glad we've sorted this out.' Angus moves towards his desk. Smug, self-satisfied. It makes Suki sick that he got this victory — for now.

'I want to be the one to fire Robert.' Suki's voice startles the other two. Their heads turn towards her. She fixes her gaze on Diane. 'If you want both of you to leave here smelling of roses, I am the one firing your son. Unless you'd like to do it yourself? You'd be more than welcome to.'

Diane's jaw falls. 'No.'

Of course not. What mother would?

Suki extends her arm towards the door. 'You can go. I still have some business with the firm's *one and only partner.*'

A perplexed-looking Angus falters midway through sitting down. Did he really think that was it, just because it had all gone to plan?

Diane slams the door.

Angus shakes his head and gives Suki a cynical look. 'I know what's coming.' He drops into his chair, elbows on the table, his fingers steepled. 'I bet you want me to make you partner. After all, you've now got the dirt on me, too.' He blasts a whiff of air from his nose. 'You're all the same.'

Suki rises and shifts her bum from the chair to the corner of his desk. The word *insolence* springs to mind. She smiles.

'Ah, Angus, that's where you're wrong. I have no interest in blackmailing you with what I've learnt. And that's my problem with you.' She runs her hand through her hair. 'Women are not all the same. Women are not all "girls." There's as much difference between women as there is between men. And women are as competent as men are — if not more. Think what I've achieved with PeopleForce.'

Of course, he hasn't even heard the latest.

She continues, 'Women are not subordinate. We are *equal*. And attitudes like yours have got to stop. Here's what is going to happen...'

Suki raises three fingers.

Not one.

Three.

Angus strokes his neck nervously.

'I really have no interest in blackmailing you.' She watches him, imagining his internal fight: could he trust her? Only she knew she was telling the truth. 'First, the easy one,' she says. 'We're going to change the tone in this organisation. No more talk of "girls", no more tolerance of sexual innuendo — by anyone. You will lead by example, and discipline where needed. You'll need to take a course on systemic bias.'

Angus follows her lips, nodding. Probably has no idea what she means. She sees his jaw stiffen. He'll be wondering what number two is.

'Second, initiate a progressive recruitment policy. No more old boys' network. No more nepotism. I have shown you what women can do. Now get more of them, openly and fairly.'

His features relax.

Oh, I'm not done.

Suki tells him about number three.

'You can't be serious,' he sputters.

'I am. This is what it will take for you to keep leading this firm, for your unsavoury financial dealings to remain buried. It's a steep price to pay, but you'll pay it.'

Angus's spirited objections fall on Suki's deaf ears. He looks defeated. 'I'm worried that when I tell Diane, she'll explode and who knows what she'll do. It's like kicking her after she's down. It's just not gentlemanly.'

'Ha! Have her announce it, then. I'm sure she'll be delighted with the boost to her reputation. Consider it a farewell gift.'

Angus wipes his brow with his handkerchief. 'Are we done?'

Her mind jumps back to the start of their conversation. He opened a door; and she wasn't one to leave such a door ajar. 'I said I had no intention to use your secrets against you to force your hand in making me partner. And that's true. I promise you that they're erased from my mind.' Suki sweeps her fingers across her forehead and whistles. 'But let's be clear: I do want to make partner. And you're in a bit of a pickle because legally, the firm can only be a partnership if there is more than one. Diane will soon be gone. You need to pick someone, and I want that someone to be me. And believe it or not, I want it on merit. No special treatment. Nothing sinister. Purely on performance.'

Angus frowns. 'And what? You think the Empisoft acquisition ticks that box?'

'Oh, no. That was me merely doing a good job. It's time for you to see what a *great* job looks like.' Suki smiles. 'I bet I can squeeze another three million dollars from PeopleForce — on top of the hundred million valuation — by the time the acquisition is announced this afternoon. And if I succeed, I'll have proven myself worthy of your blessing.' She curtsies for effect.

Angus guffaws. 'You, my young lady, have a giant pair of balls.'

'Now what did I tell you about the language around here?'

He crosses his arms. 'You're on. It's too late, anyway. You'll never manage that.'

Except she already has.

SUKI CLOSES THE door to Angus's office behind her, her throbbing heartbeat punching holes into her breaths. She checks the corridor is empty and does a little dance on the balls of her feet. The front door slams shut in the distance; she retracts her outstretched arms. Was that Diane leaving?

She struts toward her office, mentally playing out the further victories today will bring. She spots Robert walking to their office from the front of the building, head down, texting on his phone.

'Ah, the man of the hour,' Suki says.

He stands up straight; looks her up and down. He grins, his swelling ego pushing his chest out. 'I certainly am. What is it I can do for you sweet Suki?'

'You can pack your bags.'

He tilts his head 'Eh?'

Suki rubs her hands together. 'Pack your bags. You're fired.'

He steps forward and turns into their open office. 'Piss off.'

Suki follows him in. 'I'm not joking.' She points behind her. 'I've just been in with Angus. Ask him.'

Robert's eyes narrow. 'You're full of shit, Suki.' He swivels back toward the door. 'I'm going to see—'

'Mama?' Suki smirks. 'Here's the thing, Angus also fired Diane. Actually, Angus *and I* fired Diane — and you. Together. And now you can go.'

He steps to within a hair of her, looming menacingly, his hot breath in her face. 'You bitch. I don't know what you've done, but I will k—'

Doug appears in the doorframe, behind him. 'Everything alright here?'

Suki holds up her hand. 'I got this, Doug.' He nods and leaves. She slowly kicks off her heels; loses five inches. She lifts her head, her chin reaching no further than his chest. She squints and says, 'Go on. You were going to...?'

He searches her face. 'You're nuts.'

'Try me.'

He steps back. His lip curls into a snarl. 'This isn't over.'

'I think it is,' Suki says. She hooks her fingers into her shoes and flips them over her shoulder. She pushes past him to leave.

'I'll make you pay for this, you cunt,' he yells behind her.

She throws him a backward wave. 'Stay mad, sweetheart.'

56.
THE NEW ME

Hot ears.

That's the only thing I'm achieving with the hair dryer this morning. I curse the hairdresser who was adamant it would be a cinch to learn how to recreate my new, sleek and flicked style for my conference appearance. I grumble, blowing the hair from across my nose and out of my mouth.

Not so.

I briefly consider pulling it all into my usual ponytail, but don't want to disappoint Claire. How am I meant to roll my locks over the round brush at the back of my head without dislocating a shoulder? I try again, gaining some control over the flow of scorching air. I sniff, the smell of burning not quite at the level to have me worry.

After a little while, I run my hand through my hair. It's dry-ish. I check in the mirror. It isn't sticking outwards. I shrug. It will have to do.

Atticus peeks around the door post, no doubt checking the big bad noise is truly gone. He hops onto my bed.

'No, you terrible furball. Not on my new blouse.' I dread to think what his claws would do to silk. And he sheds.

I'd protested when Claire declared this emerald-green blouse with a super-thin golden stripe the winner. It's so colourful. I remember how Claire insisted it complemented my eyes and was perfect, and that was that. Plus, she'd said, the stripe was small enough that it wouldn't impact any photos or videos that would be taken.

Who knew patterned clothes were a no-no for TV? I'd only ever worn black.

I sit on the bed and adjust my greying bra. No way would I have let Claire drag me to the lingerie department.

Atticus climbs onto my lap and purrs. His claws dig rhythmically into my thighs. I lift him up gently. Red dots freckle the skin on my leg. I stroke the soft down behind his ear.

'This is it. It's finally happening.' My nail snags onto Atticus's worn leather collar. 'Maybe I should get you a new one of these.' I bring him to my face and rub my nose to his. 'Would you like some bling? A diamond encrusted choker, perhaps?' He pulls away, scowling. 'Quite right. Let's not let the money change us.'

My new, navy, wide-legged trousers hang on the back of the chair. I slip them on, over my bare legs. Tights are a step too far. Maybe in time. The tiny golden belt doesn't do much to keep my blouse in place. What's the point of it?

My phone rings.

The caller display says *Mum*.

'I wanted to wish you good luck for today, my darling. How are you feeling?'

'I'm great, Mum. A little nervous. I think I'll lay off the tea today. Not sure my bladder could handle it, with all the stress.'

Mum lets out a sweet-sounding sigh. 'I'm so proud of you. Did you say you might be on the news tonight?'

'It's not guaranteed. Claire is hopeful.'

'Who's Claire?'

'Oh, she's the PR... She's a friend.'

'That's nice, sweetheart.'

'Yes, it is,' I say, smiling.

'Well, I guess I'd better let you go, Miss Important.'

I snort. 'Thanks for calling, Mum. I love you.'

'I love you, too.'

I turn the mobile to face me, to find the red square with which to hang up, but remember there was one more thing. 'Did Cringletie House agree to upgrade you the premium wedding package?'

'They did. Thank you. Oliver and I can't wait to see you again soon.'

A warm glow fills my chest. Thank God for Suki's negotiation skills. I button up the blouse and shimmy my hair like I was taught.

A quick glance in the mirror.

Weird. But nice.

Time to go.

The blue ballerina pumps are by the door, next to my bag. I check its content to make sure I haven't forgotten anything. In the red folder, I find the presentation I'd printed out so I can stand with my back to the screen and look out into the audience. I flick the pages. I almost know it by heart.

Next to it is the blue folder. Claire secretly shared the PeopleForce CEO's speech with me. Turns out he isn't a spontaneous speaker, and they have to load it onto a tele-prompter. Imagine that. For such a senior guy. I skim the three pages again. It's like holding a stick of dynamite. The surprise acquisition, Justin, everything.

It will blow people away.

And I love it all.

Ready to go, I walk over to my bookcase and gaze at the framed photos. I sigh. I've come a long way from the little wellie-wearing, pig-tailed girl in front of Peebles library. I would trade it all in to have Emily by my side again. I kiss two fingers and press them onto my dear friend's wee face, adding to the multiple fingerprints I've not had a chance to clean.

Convinced I'll never lose the feeling I failed her, I at least take solace in the possibility others might be saved.

My mind jumps back to the PeopleForce meeting. They'd showed such excitement about the application of my Network Impact tool for brands and marketing agencies, that I'd suggested another possible market for it. One I only came up with because of Emily's death: law enforcement and anti-terrorism. I'd explained the models could identify covert agitators with minimal effort. No more need for humans to try to work out who was who. Hours and days of wasted time. Lives at risk. They could possibly even find the elusive Russian influence on politics.

I still couldn't believe the beauty of it. They'd be able to simply run my programme on a selection of Twitter data, and job done. Inciters identified with statistically significant certainty. Enough to convince judges to hand out court orders for Twitter to hand over the account's identity or whereabouts.

I snicker, remembering Suki jumping up and down after the meeting. *'Oh my God, Laura. You couldn't have told me all of this before? What else have you got up your sleeve? We could have milked them dry! Millions left on the table.'*

My silk blouse slithers luxuriously over my arm as I hang my bag over my shoulder. I look down at the suede shoes I'm worried wont' survive a drop of rain.

Suki should know by now the money is not important to me. Butterflies stir in my stomach. Not money; but by the end of the meeting, when the Californians were embarrassingly gushing over my 'innovative intellect', I did ask for one more thing.

I grab my keys and step out the door.

On the landing, I check my watch. There's no time for a detour to St Leonard's, but soon. Soon I'll go back to that objectionable policeman, DI Reddy, with his excuses and his limited resources, and I'll give him the news. I picture his face when I tell him that once the law enforcement version of the software is developed, PeopleForce will license it to Police Scotland for free.

Forever.

So that nobody needs to die like Emily again.

57.
SUKI

It's warm in the auditorium. An oppressive amalgamation of coffee breath and body odour hangs in the air. Suki winces, thinking about the four hundred people that have marinated here through six keynote presentations.

Suki stands by the door, breathing in the occasional whiff of freshness as people pop in and out.

The speaker is wrapping up.

It's been a super interesting day. She's grateful for Claire remembering to set aside a ticket for her, despite it being sold out. She wouldn't have missed it for the world — and not just to witness things kick off later. If she's going to be the partner responsible for building up the technology practice within the firm, she needs to keep abreast of developments in the sector. All the opportunities arising from the use of artificial intelligence. She might even pick up a client or two.

Claire steps through the door. She holds a clipboard and looks surprisingly sprightly for someone who's run around all day, making sure everything goes to plan. Suki catches her eye and Claire joins her.

'Hey,' Suki says. 'I think he's nearly finished. You've done an excellent job. A great line-up of speakers. And it all seems to have run smoothly.'

'Thanks. I made an extra effort for things to be perfect. Can't have Rebel Agency regret hiring me,' Claire says.

'I doubt they would.' Suki waves her hands up and down Claire's fabulousness.

'Yeah. You're right,' Claire snorts. 'I suspect I can do no wrong after handing them Empisoft as a client. They've been wanting to do their PR for ages. They practically chewed my hand off when I offered it to them. And all I asked for in return was getting to own Culture. Which is a tiny part of what they do.' She takes a deep breath. 'I can't thank Laura enough. She really came through for me.'

Suki nods. When Claire shared her idea to get back at Darren at the restaurant, Laura hadn't hesitated; had agreed even before she knew what she'd be expected to do. Because they were a team, she'd said.

It was such a straightforward plan, with nothing sinister about it, that Suki wonders why Claire ever bothered with the ridiculous Bald-Patch-Gate. Laura said it would be a fairly easy task to instruct Marketing to appoint new PR agency for Empisoft. It was technically Justin's call, but Justin no longer cares. And why would he? He's focused on his new, big, important role in California. Bless him.

'How did Darren take it?' Suki asks.

Claire laughs loudly. 'How long have you got? I stole his sexiest client and left him in the lurch staff-wise by resigning. He called me every name under the sun. I thought him calling me an "ungrateful cow" was particularly ironic.'

Suki chuckles. 'Any regrets?'

'None.'

Applause floods the room and the lights come on. The speaker remains on stage. A trickle of attendees climb the stairs to meet him.

'Where is Laura, anyway?' Suki asks.

Claire checks her watch. 'She'll be having her photos taken with some of the other speakers. I hired that guy Craig to do them. You know, the one who took your photo with Darren in the gym. I felt I owed him something.' She shrugs. 'He seemed delighted.'

An usher opens both the doors and locks them in place to let the audience out. Claire nearly gets carried away in the crowd.

'I've got to go take care of some people. See you for a drink later,' she shouts.

Suki lifts her thumb and smiles.

It's time for the fun part.

SUKI IS AMONG the first to enter the bar. The countertop is lined with trays holding champagne glasses. A small jazz band kicks off in the corner of the stage.

She grabs a drink and positions herself at a cocktail table towards the front of the room, which gives her a great vantage point for the closing session, and for checking out the people who walk in.

She fondles the small pocket on the side of her blue, tailored suit jacket that she'd had to have sewn in behind the misleading flap of fabric. What was it about designers denying women pockets? She takes a few business cards out for ready access, recognising a few faces of up-and-coming entrepreneurs in the technology scene.

A flutter of nerves skitters across her stomach as she spots Diane, taking a glass from a waiter walking past. She looks tired and utterly fed up. When Diane sees Suki, hostility drips from every pore. Suki smiles broadly and raises her champagne in a mocking toast. The death stare she receives back feels extra rewarding.

Suki scans the room. Who else is around? A few investors she's worked with. Some people from Scottish Enterprise — they're everywhere. Just like the lawyers and accountants, perpetually on the prowl for business.

Suki does a double take of the woman who walks in wearing a green silk blouse and navy trousers. She arches an eyebrow. Laura scrubs up well. Suki watches Laura speak to a chunky man in an ill-fitting jacket, who could have made more of an effort with the razor blade. He holds a large camera in his hand and points it around, seemingly explaining its functions.

Laura twirls her hair. She laughs. She places her hand on his shoulder, lets it sit there for a second and walks away.

Suki doesn't know whether to be happy or horrified when she sees him take a sneaky picture of Laura from behind.

She waves in Laura's direction.

58.
ME

I'm on a high. What a day. And there's Suki waving.

I snake my way through the different groupings enjoying their drinks. Not something we've ever served at the conference before, but Claire said it was necessary to encourage the kind of celebration she would want captured on camera once the acquisition announcement is made.

'You look nice,' Suki says, looking me up and down.

I stroke the wrinkles from my trousers. 'Thank you.'

'How did your breakout session go? Sorry I missed it. It was full by the time I arrived.'

'It went well. I was a little nervous. But not as nervous as I am now.'

A waiter walks past. Suki fishes a glass from his tray. 'Here, you'll need this.' She winks.

A young man with a delegate pass around his neck approaches. 'Laura? I just wanted to say how much I enjoyed your presentation. I'm working on random forest models, too. Maybe we can grab a coffee sometime?'

'Sure. Um. Call the office, okay?'

'Who was that?' Suki asks after he correctly gets the message to leave.

'Oh, I met him at a student entrepreneurship competition. He's planning to start a business. Something to do with education. I can't remember. I was just helping out. A favour to the Uni.'

Suki nudges me. 'You're too kind. They'll take advantage. Anyway, please introduce me next time. He could be a future client.'

'Sorry, of course. Would you like me to send you both an email introduction?'

'That would be great. You know, this is going to get a lot worse. Once you have your money, all the little entrepreneurs will come scuttling out of the walls like cockroaches to see if you're willing to invest in their dream.'

I shrug. 'I don't mind helping them along. Not sure about the money side, though. Maybe you can teach me about that sometime?'

'No probs,' she says. 'Could you introduce me to the PhysioMedics founder after the closing speeches? I hear they're going gangbusters.'

My heart jumps. I don't want to let her down, but all the same... I have somewhere to be. 'Maybe I can send an email introduction for that, too?'

I see a question flash across Suki's face. I turn away and say, 'Look, there's Claire on stage.'

Claire is obviously trying to be discreet in placing the lectern onto the centre of the stage. The AV man joins her and attaches the tele-prompter, a nifty, high-tech rectangle of glass that will let the speaker read while the audience can still see his face. I've never seen one before. Claire pats her side pockets. For a moment, she looks distressed. She runs offstage and promptly returns holding two silver pens.

My heart swells; I'm so proud of her. Every detail has been taken care of all day.

The band completes a song with a series of accentuated chords that leaves no doubt their gig is over. Some people clap.

Suki grabs my arm. 'This is it.'

I wish I'd peed.

Empisoft's Chairman steps onto the raised platform, and his mere presence silences the room. He unfolds a square of paper and places it in front of him. The glasses he keeps on the top of his head drop in front of his eyes.

Suki nods his way. 'He'll be out of a job. You won't need a Chair when Empisoft becomes a subsidiary of PeopleForce.'

That hadn't occurred to me before now. My last interaction with him was far from pleasant. This makes up for it.

'But I bet the old boys' network will have him in a cushy non-executive director job in no time again,' Suki adds disdainfully.

A cluster of standing folk line the front of the stage. Large video cameras roll into place on metal frames. Suki and I pull our table a few inches to the side to see better.

His speech is predictably boring, peppered with the requisite compliments to the guest speakers, and thank-yous to the organisers. After several inane observations on the state of the industry, he clears his throat.

My stomach contracts.

He looks intently at the crowd over the top of his glasses. 'And now we have a wonderful surprise in store for you. I have the distinct honour in welcoming Dr Steve Steele, chief executive of PeopleForce.'

There's an enormous joint intake of breath. The room buzzes and voices mutter when the CEO bounds onto the stage with an enthusiastic double-armed cheer. The Chair shakes his hand and leaves.

Various people turn to Laura in admiration. A frantic press scuttles into even better position.

Suki is chewing her lips.

'Thank you very much. Hello Edinburgh,' the CEO starts. 'I'm super excited to be here. I have only ever been to this country once before, and that was to visit the Isle of Skye, where my grandmother was born. It gives me tremendous pleasure to experience Bonnie Scotland again.'

Suki rolls her eyes.

'You may be wondering why I'm here.' The audience laughs. He smiles. 'Okay, I *know* you're wondering why I'm here. As a surprise, like this. Well, we thought it would be fun to reward those people who are closest to Empisoft — you — by letting you witness the signing of a historic agreement. Shh... Quiet down. It gets better.' He flashes a wide row of California-white teeth. 'My friends, right at this moment, an announcement is making its way to the Nasdaq stock exchange. But you are officially the first to hear that we will pay one hundred and three million dollars for the privilege of bringing Empisoft into the PeopleForce family.'

The room erupts in a cacophony of shock.

The CEO moves his hands up and down to calm them. 'Yes, I would have preferred a round one hundred million, too. But what can I say? They drive a hard bargain.' He smiles and the audience laughs. 'And here he is, the man of the hour, Justin Travers.'

Justin joins him in a single, show-off, leap. He brings the papers. Both men hold their pens up high before placing their signatures on the two sets of documents. They hold hands and raise them up, giving the photographers their money shot.

Justin adjusts the microphone. 'Hello,' he says to cheers and shouts from those assembled. 'I'll keep this brief. I'm sure you have many questions and they will be answered in due course. For now, I just wanted to say how thrilled I am that PeopleForce have recognised the tremendous efforts by our staff here in Edinburgh in creating something spectacular. You know me as a bullish entrepreneur, but today exceeds even my aspirations from when I started the company all those years ago with Laura Flett.' He looks out over the audience. 'Laura, where are you?'

I wish the floor would swallow me whole. Suki turns to me clapping, joining all the others. Those hundreds of faces smiling at me, waiting for a reaction. I pull the corners of my lips up meekly and wave, turning three hundred sixty degrees for everybody to get an excruciating good look.

My knees wobble as I see a woman with long blonde hair turn around, almost in slow-motion. Emily? Reality hits and I bring my hand back. If only she could be here now.

Justin says a few more things that get drowned out by lingering applause. PeopleForce's CEO steps to his side again and takes hold of the mike. The room falls silent. I feel sick.

'As a founder myself,' he says, 'who sold his start-up to PeopleForce over six years ago, I can completely relate to what Justin is going through right now. It's an amazing feeling.' The two men nod at each other in mutual recognition. 'And I have to admit, that I am quite jealous of Justin today. Because, unlike me, he has decided to step away from the business, take time off and pursue his personal passions.'

Justin's eyes grow wide and his jaw falls. His head darts between the man who has unexpectedly just fired him, publicly, and the nearly thousand eyes cast upon him.

I squeeze Suki's hand. We both press our lips firmly shut to prevent an unacceptable reaction. Under the table, we stomp our feet to let the pent-up energy out somewhere.

A brouhaha of admiration and incredulity fills the void left by Justin's shock. The CEO extends his left arm to invite Justin to leave the stage. He doesn't move.

I see Claire, in the wing, waving him over, looking picnicked. Eventually, she succeeds and he follows her like a zombie through the green curtain.

'Thank you, Justin,' Dr Steele says, clapping. He puts on an exaggerated frown. 'Lucky bastard.' He takes a deep breath, looks over his shoulder, and continues. 'Now I can imagine that some of you may be concerned about the impact of the acquisition on this wondrous city. And I can reassure you that we at PeopleForce consider this a first step in a strong alliance with Scotland, which has grown to be a terrific hub of talent and enterprise.'

I think that, under any other circumstances, the audience would suffer from applause fatigue by now, but they're still going.

Claire skips over to us, a full glass in hand.

'How's Justin?' Suki asks.

'I think he's literally in shock.' Before I can ask more details, Claire turns to look at the stage and says, 'He's almost done.'

The CEO wraps up. 'PeopleForce have committed to maintain the R&D centre for Empisoft here, and we're projecting to increase head count as we expand our product range further in close collaboration with colleagues in California. But I'm delighted to say that PeopleForce's commitment to Edinburgh is not restricted to product development. It extends to embracing you into our corporate social responsibility activities, to the benefit of all your residents. I'd like to invite Diane Campbell of Madainn Finance to join me for another exciting announcement.'

The cameras shuffle around to change angles. The reporters are by now sitting down scribbling in notebooks that are no doubt filling up more pages than they could have expected.

Suki holds her breath. We know what's coming: our last nail.

Dr Steele and Diane stand side by side, a row of smiles. He speaks, 'They often say it takes a village to raise a child. I can assure you, it also takes a village to make an acquisition go through. It has been my personal pleasure to get to know Diane over the last few weeks. She's Empisoft's corporate finance adviser. A formidable woman.'

I whisper to Suki, 'They've met?'

Suki shakes her head. 'No. He's just saying that. Look at her smile. It's fake as hell.' She chuckles.

'And Diane and I share a passion,' Steele continues. 'To celebrate confident women in the workplace. To make sure that any employee, anywhere, regardless of their gender, their sexual orientation or their religion, can flourish at work.' He clears his throat and looks down at the press. 'Now you are well aware that we, ourselves, have recently failed in this. It is therefore all the more important that we step up and lead by example. PeopleForce launched the Upright Fund across three cities in the US two months ago. For those who do not know, this is a ten-million-dollar not-for-profit initiative that will give free legal advice to people in work who believe that they have suffered discrimination or harassment in the workplace.' He breathes in. 'Today we announce the Edinburgh chapter of Upright, and we are honoured that Diane has agreed to be its Chairperson. And not only that... Diane?' He makes space for her.

She leans in; her thick, gold chain rattles against the microphone. A professional-looking smile precedes the announcement we've been waiting for. 'I'm extremely grateful to Dr Steele for asking me to lead this fantastic initiative. And in recognition of Madainn's commitment to uphold these same values, my partner Angus McLeod and I are donating the bonuses we've earned from the Empisoft and PeopleForce transaction to further fund Upright's work here in Edinburgh.'

The whoops and hollers are higher pitched than before: women celebrating this act of sisterhood.

Claire shakes her head in disbelief. 'Two million dollars, was it, Suki? Oh, that must hurt.'

'One point eight million to be precise — I wasn't about to forego my share,' Suki says, grinning widely.

It seems reasonable to me. After all, she made it happen.

Dr Steele gets the last word in before the press invades the stage. 'Thank you very much. Stick around and celebrate with us.'

As if on cue, a waiter passes by our table. I grab three glasses and divvy them around. This is it. Mission completed.

'Here's to the Avengers,' Claire toasts. We clink glasses together.

A male voice says, 'Hold it right there.' Craig rotates the lens while we maintain our glasses up and our teeth out. 'That's great, thank you.' Craig drops the camera, for it to hang around his neck again. He looks around. People near us are dispersing. The VIPs are being ushered offstage.

My heartbeat quickens as he walks towards me. I give him a warning look. Will he understand? I haven't told the others yet.

'Are you ready to go?' he asks.

I wince. My head darts between Suki and Claire's surprised looks. I feel the blood rush to my face. I give my friends an apologetic — but excited — look and step towards him.

'Yes, I'm ready.'

59.
I, SUKI

Claire and I watch Laura run off with her sneaky new beau.

'I'll be damned,' I say.

Turning to face me, Claire blinks a few times. 'Well, I didn't see that coming. Did you?'

'Nope.'

Claire takes another sip of champagne. 'I wonder when that happened.'

'Beats me. She's a dark horse, our Laura,' I say, taking a sip of my own.

I nudge Claire. She nearly drops her glass. 'Is that Andrew Bevan from the Scotsman over there?' I nod at a chap in red corduroy trousers.

'Yes. Man, he was hard to convince to come. Too senior,' she says, in a mocking tone. 'I couldn't tell him about the acquisition yet, but I promised I'd make it worth his while. He can't complain now! Why do you ask?'

I slip my hand into the small side pocket of my jacket and pull out a USB device. A mischievous grin spreads across my face. 'I am going to give him just enough information for him to work out Justin's double life on Twitter. As commander of Incel scum that attack innocent women like Emily.'

Claire's hand shoots to her mouth. 'You can't. Oh my God. Can you imagine the damage?' Her eyes widen. 'Bloody hell, Suki. It would spread everywhere.' She drops her hand. 'Wait. Didn't Laura say you shouldn't ages ago? Justin would be branded for life.' She shakes her head. 'No, Laura said no.'

I twirl the USB stick between my fingers in front of her nose. 'Come on. We can't let this whole thing end Laura's way. She's much too nice — particularly when it comes to Justin. I mean, yes, he might have lost his dream job in a very public and embarrassing stunt, but boo-hoo. He's still walking away with millions.'

Claire checks who's around and leans in. 'Are you truly going to do this?' she whispers. 'It'll be carnage. The Incel trolls will eat him alive.'

I turn my eyes upward, searching my conscience. I come up empty, and wink. 'I don't care.'

She struggles to suppress a smile, a cheeky glint in her eye. 'You're wicked.'

I shrug. 'He started it.'

Time's up

ACKNOWLEGDEMENTS

I can be a stubborn old cow.

My first novel, 'In Servitude', didn't fit neatly into a genre and even though everything I read about the publishing industry said you must conform to genre to be successful, I chose once again not to listen: I had a story to tell.

I'm immensely grateful to the team at Red Dog Press for taking the risk of adopting my genre-fluid baby and introducing it to the world; celebrating the beauty of all its facets; joining me in defiantly declaring it crime fiction in recognition of the insidious harm of everyday sexism.

If you think I'm stubborn, though, you should meet my editor Sara Cox. She never let up. Never let me get away with 'good enough'. In your hands is the product of an incredible investment of time and emotion from her, for which I cannot give enough thanks.

I am indebted to my author friends for being willing to read, share tips, laughter and commiseration any time day or night: Jonathan Whitelaw, CS Duffy, Alison Belsham, Rob Parker, SE Smart.

This book has benefited from the enormous support of blogger and reader friends, who enthused about the story and provided suggestions from the very first draft. Thank you to Donna, Jessica, Jo, Laura, Martijn, Naomi, Rachel, Sarah, Sascha, Shalini.

A stickler for accuracy, I'm grateful for friends who sanity-checked the plot with specialist knowledge: Sandy McKinnon for IP; Linda Woods for data science; Cat McLean for partnerships.

Many characters were named with you in mind – though never the baddies!

Thank you to my mother Lyda and the many valiant others battling for equality and freedom from sexual harassment so that my Delphie, and all our daughters, can shine unencumbered. I'm blessed with three generations of good men who lead by example: my father Floor, husband Grant and son Marcus.

Lastly, thank you in advance to male allies for paying attention and calling out behaviour that is not okay, as we jointly make meaningful change — soon.

ABOUT THE AUTHOR

Heleen Kist has been fondled, patronised and ordered to smile by random men. So she wrote 'Stay Mad, Sweetheart', a feminist tale of revenge.

Whilst her professional knowledge of technology start-ups fed the novel's setting, its theme of harassment and workplace discrimination required no research: it is familiar to all women.

Heleen was chosen as an up and coming new author at Bloody Scotland 2018. Her first novel, 'In Servitude' won the silver medal for Best European Fiction at the Independent Publishers Book Awards in the USA and was shortlisted for The Selfies awarded at London Book Fair.

A Dutch strategy consultant living in Glasgow and married to a Scotsman, she's raising their son to be a good man and their daughter to kick ass.

You can follow Heleen Kist on Twitter @hkist, or sign up to her newsletter at heleenkist.com to keep up to date with her news.

ALSO BY HELEEN KIST
IN SERVITUDE

When Grace's beloved sister Glory dies in a car crash, her life spirals out of control. She discovers Glory was indebted to a local crime lord and laundering money through her cafe. What's worse, Grace is now forced to take over.

Defying her anxiety, Grace will stop at nothing to save herself and those Glory left behind from the clutches of Glasgow's underworld. But her plans unravel when more family secrets emerge and Grace is driven to question everything she believed about her sister – even her death.

IN SERVITUDE is a gripping roller coaster of family, crime and betrayal. Perfect for lovers of page-turning suspense.

QUESTIONS FOR BOOK CLUBS

The three central women in the story wanted those who'd done wrong to pay a price. But did the punishments fit the crimes?

What is your view on how the friendship dynamics change between Laura, Claire and Suki as the story progresses?

In your opinion, who is most to blame for Emily's decision to end her life?

What instances of 'getting carried away' did you encounter in the book? Why does this happen?

There were multiple examples of sexism throughout the book. Which ones would you shrug off?

What responsibility do victims of harassment or discrimination bear in reporting it?

Did you feel this was a 'women versus men' story? Why or why not?

Printed in Great Britain
by Amazon

34468107R00199